UP

"Let us go then, you and I,
When the evening is spread out against the sky
Like a patient etherised upon a table;"[1]

- T.S.Eliot -

---

[1] The Love Song of J. Alfred Prufrock (1917);
   published by Faber & Faber Ltd. Used by permission.

Onwards and Upwards Publishers,
Berkeley House,
11 Nightingale Crescent,
West Horsley,
Surrey,
KT24 6PD

www.onwardsandupwards.org

Author's note:

With thanks to my friend, fellow minister and former colleague, Rev. Heather Leake Date, Consultant Pharmacist, for ensuring that I did not employ lethal choices or doses of medication in an otherwise fictional foray into healthcare environs.

ISBN: 978-1-910197-05-9

Printed in the UK

For Vicky and Sarah

1

It began here, in a backstreet, at dusk.

A colourless, grey spring day was heading towards that dusk, flinching at the swirls of cold, misty rain that gathered around the streetlamps. Somewhere in the distance, out over an invisible sea, a clattering tumble of thunder drifted slowly towards the promenade, shooting tiny shards of lightning ahead of it into the side streets. It was time to hurry home.

Visiting time was over. No one rang a bell to announce the fact these days. No one strutted up and down the ward like Florence Nightingale. Everyone could see the clock. Why state the obvious? They had exhausted all the small talk. Why spin it out any longer? Why not just go home? People were waiting to get on with other things. Goodbye, glad you're looking so well, see you soon. And the relatives drifted away from the bedsides and stood in the doorways for one last smile and wave, and then they were gone, heading off along the corridors and down the stairs, following all the luminous exit signs until they discovered the late-duty porter guarding the front door and waiting to smile and nod them into the drear black night.

Sometimes they passed people heading the other way. Night staff, nurses, pushing their way through the two doors with a look of deep gloom, managing to bring the damp air in with them, before they wandered off down the corridors, switching off the lights as they went.

At last everyone had gone or arrived, and the front door was closed and locked like a prison gate; and the porter, swinging a bunch of keys like a jailor, settled into the tiny switchboard overlooking the street and began to flick through a newspaper. Nine o'clock and the beginning of a very long night.

The tiny hospital occupied a street corner. It had what the architects call a small footprint. It stretched between the ends of two narrow terraced streets like a bookend, and it boasted a short, sharp frontage on the main road which was half hidden by trees and missed altogether if you blinked when the bus went by. It contained just six wards and a grand total of sixty-four patients, when all its beds were filled. And there was a complex labyrinth of corridors and passageways and narrow little staircases to explore, and any number of nooks and crannies to get lost in. The building was five storeys high and two centuries old, and, like any other place where so many people had lived and worked and died, it had gathered together a great many intense moments and long, lingering histories of human concern. It was a place of echoes and asides, and obnoxious human smells, long years in the making.

Ward 4 was situated on the first floor, just above the porter and his newspaper, and just outside this ward there was a tiny side room which, in years gone by, somebody had decided to call an annexe. Annexe it remained thereafter. There was room for one bed, one bedside locker, and one very uncomfortable, bright orange plastic chair. The window overlooked the northern as distinct from the southern side street, and the doorway obliquely faced a small, irregular landing, a ward office, and a lift cage which had been stationary on that floor for more than an hour.

The chair was for Iris, and she sat in it day by day without uttering a word of complaint. In fact, she never said anything much, and, because she was silent and because she tended to merge with the background, no one ever paid much attention to her when she came and went from the building. Sometimes she was there, at other times she wasn't. Her presence changed nothing. No one watched to see if she might alter her position in the chair, no one noticed if she glanced out of the window, or read a book, or did a handstand against the wall. No one could remember a single thing that she had said, either to a nurse, a doctor, or a housekeeper. Not a word. Did she speak? Did she have a voice? Was she alive?

Where was the proof? And who cared anyway? No one. N
all. No one had the time.

She wore a drab, shapeless, brown coat which
wore buttoned right up to the neck, rain or shine, and she
drab, shapeless, brown hat which she skewered to her head with .
hat pin. On her lap she kept a drab, shapeless handbag which
contained her purse, two pension books, two sets of house keys,
and a packet of paper handkerchiefs she had bought in
Woolworths and never once attempted to open.

From time to time she looked at her husband's face and
studied it carefully. Her own face was always quite blank when she
did this. Carefully expressionless. Outwardly she seemed calm and
collected. Cool. Unruffled. It was her secret goal. When the
ambulance had fetched them both to the hospital on that sad, wet
Wednesday, Iris had set herself the task of always being calm and
collected – Leonard's phrase – even if the world was crashing down
around her ears, which it would be one day soon. "When all about
you…" he would often say, but without remembering the rest of
the quotation. So, calm and collected she remained, and if anyone
ever did pay her a moment's heed it was simply to think to
themselves, "Here sits a quiet woman, shapeless, calm and
collected. Drab and brown. A woman who makes no difference. A
woman who is soon forgotten." And then they would move on –
and soon forget her.

Leonard, her husband, lay in the bed, breathing very softly.
He had been lying in that same bed, breathing very softly, for ten
days now, without ever once opening an eye or uttering a single
word. He, too, seemed to have forgotten all about Iris. She
watched his chest rising and falling until the movement and the
rhythm became hypnotic, and in that way she passed the hours and
days. A drip-stand held a pack of intravenous fluid over his left
shoulder so that it could slowly dribble into his veins through a
bright yellow cannula taped to his wrist, and a syringe-driver
tucked under his pillow darted tiny jets of diamorphine into the
same tubing. Pain control. An organized retreat in the face of the
small-cell carcinomas that infested his lungs, now that they had
metastasized. A savage little war, lost almost as soon as it had

egun. Now there were no other remedial treatments left to try. Game over. He would die soon, hopefully without knowing too much about it, and his patient, drab, shapeless little wife would be allowed to sit there next to him and watch it all from her ringside seat. Counting the heartbeats, watching each rise and fall of his chest, wondering whether they would be his last.

The night sister stood in the doorway, a thick-set, muscular woman in late middle age, with long grey hair that she scooped back behind her cap each night in a no-nonsense ponytail. She, too, studied the old man's face and listened to the faint, dry sound of his breathing, noting that he was slipping away. She checked the dosage of the syringe-driver, smiled at Iris, and disappeared. She would repeat the ritual in an hour's time, and an hour after that, throughout the night, either until he died or until she handed over her bleep to the day sister in the morning. There was nothing else to do. Death always kept everyone waiting, handkerchiefs at the ready.

A little after midnight the switchboard bleeped very loudly, twice, the two sounds separated by almost a minute. The night porter jumped each time before answering the call. The first bleep was a call from another hospital wondering if an empty bed was to be had for the asking. The second bleep was the night sister waking the duty doctor in his basement flat across the road to tell him that she had accepted a new patient on his behalf. An hour or so, she said. Give or take. And it's raining. Hard.

An hour later an ambulance pulled up outside the front door and the porter tidied up his newspaper, straightened his tie, and searched for his bunch of keys. He pinned back the outer door with a metal hook, then he held open the inner door as the two half-drenched paramedics lifted the stretcher from the pavement and trundled it into reception. The porter could just make out a face among all the folds of glistening wet blanket. Without stopping to chat they pushed the stretcher along the corridor and then took the lift up to Ward 4.

The lift stopped opposite the annexe, and the paramedic nearest the gate pulled it back with such force that it screeched like a banshee, making Iris spring out of her chair. She stared at her husband until she was sure he was still breathing, and then she let out the breath she was holding. She felt light-headed, nauseous, but the night sister's voice and the sound of the stretcher scraping past the door reassured her and she slowly slumped back into her chair. A few minutes later the stretcher made its return journey and disappeared again, taking the two paramedics with it, and then the night sister went into the office to phone the doctor again. No rush, she said. A short, sharp check-in when you're ready. And a sleepy voice at the other end of the phone grunted softly.

Dr Kim Maskell rolled over onto his back, making the bed springs squeal as he scratched his bristly chin. He didn't want to get out of bed at this time of the night so he made his body slowly bounce up and down on the mattress instead. He had only been half-listening to the night sister's voice. She was far too chirpy for three minutes past two in the morning, when the rain was drumming a tattoo on the window. She had a knack of phoning him just as his dreams were getting interesting. She was like his mother; she could look down a phone line and see right through him. She could make him blush to the roots of his hair without even trying, even when she wasn't in the same room. While he still gently bounced up and down on the bed he tried to snatch his dream back, but his ravishing partner succumbed to the merest touch and vanished like gossamer.

Kim was a Berkshire boy, born and bred; son and heir of two Ascot-based G.P.s who would not be daunted in their quest for a clone of themselves. He progressed from prep school to red-brick university without having the least idea what he wanted to do or who he wanted to be. At which point the parents took over. They were in the business of treating symptoms, and he had symptoms, so they treated them. He was indecisive, he lacked ambition, and he played too much rugby, so they whisked him off to Medical School where he was three years behind everyone else of his age. Antidote duly administered. He would soon attain medical nirvana. Happiness and fulfilment would follow in due course, closely followed by a wife, several children, an Ascot home, and a fat pension. It was their bliss in new packaging. How could it fail?

Easily. Kim was still waiting. He was a giant of a man with a barrel chest, a beer gut and a savaged ear lobe. And he was bored. Incomplete. He told the bathroom mirror, and the mirror agreed with him. He wasn't happy and he wasn't fulfilled. He was nascent, unformed, unfinished. Inadequate. Timid, sometimes. Especially when a midnight phone call summoned him to an adult world. There was a child in Kim Maskell that was still naïve, bewildered and quite mystified by what was going on around him. He marvelled at his luck when the adults let him play with them, and he was filled with disbelief when they gave him costly toys to play with, like patients' lives. There was a part of Kim which was still a bleary-eyed, tousle-haired child, unwashed, ungroomed, who wanted someone else to take charge of him and tell him how to deal with each new day.

But, for now, Kim was cold and tired, and soon he would be wet, too. He had spent a long, dull morning in the Operating Theatre, and an even longer and duller afternoon in Shallcross's outpatients clinic, so now he was too tired to sleep, and too sleepy to be very polite to anyone he met halfway through a long dull night. He dozed between the two phone calls while he waited for the ambulance to arrive with the new patient. He knew that a crucial decision needed to be made. Should he get out of bed and dress himself fully, or should he just button his white coat over his T-shirt and boxer shorts and hope for the best? He reckoned that he could fall out of bed, dress, dart across the road, shake off the raindrops, reach the ward, poke the patient, read and initial the notes, refuse tea – who wants a mug of milky tea at this time of night? – and get back to bed, all in under fifteen minutes. If he was lucky, and if nothing else cropped up en route to scupper the plan. He rolled out of bed, groaned, and then said to himself, "Maskell, on your marks..."

"And whom do we have here, Sister?" Kim asked, sinking onto the bed beside the newly-arrived patient. Why doctors had to speak to new patients as though they were idiots quite escaped him, but it was a habit that had become ingrained during his training. Everyone else did it, so why shouldn't he? The rain and the cold night air were still clinging to him, and, thankfully, the patient was quite unaware of his huge, hairy knees jutting out from under his white coat.

"Stanley George Baker, eighty-seven years young, non-ambulant, due to the fact that he has severe ulceration of both lower legs. He's also diabetic, and a chronic asthmatic, probably as a result of about fifty woodbines a day, a habit which Mr Baker successfully kicked the moment he entered this ward!" And, sure enough, there was a crushed cigarette packet in the paper rubbish bag taped to the edge of the locker.

"Old, in other words," Kim muttered to himself. He was shivering under his white coat, and wondering what normal people did with themselves at this time of night.

"There's no mention anywhere in the notes of Mr Baker having defective hearing," the night sister added, giving Kim one of her old-fashioned looks as she closed the file and dropped it into his lap.

Kim blushed until his face resembled a beetroot. "Any pains at all, Mr Baker? Any discomfort of any kind?" Failing to elicit a response from the old man, except for a bewildered, frog-eyed stare, he stood up again and began to slowly bob up and down with his hands on his knees, as though he was warming up for a session in the gym. "Do you need me to write him up for anything?" He practised a slow backhand with an imaginary squash racquet, adding to the patient's bewilderment.

The night sister was sifting through the contents of a carrier bag filled with plastic pots and bottles. "You must be joking! He's got his own private pharmacy with him here. Either that or he's a Drug Lord, wanted in a dozen countries." She suddenly turned on Kim when he was in mid-swing. "Tea, young man! It's a non-alcoholic beverage, often partaken of by persons of a sober disposition."

"I'd prefer bed. If there's nothing else," Kim replied hopefully.

The night sister considered for a moment. "Well, as you're here, and as you don't like my tea, I would like you to have a quick look at Mr Blake in the annexe, before you go."

Kim's heart sank. "Worse?" He remembered Mr Blake. He was what he called a banker, a dead cert. Stiff by Sunday; written up for cremation by Monday; a cash fee in the hand by Friday, big enough to buy a pint or two and a takeaway.

"I don't know that he's any worse, necessarily," the night sister said thoughtfully. "Respiration's quite shallow. Steady but shallow."

Kim returned Mr Baker's anguished gaze for a moment. "Why disturb him, then?" he asked.

The night sister distilled all her years of nursing into the two words "a feeling" and Kim knew he was sunk. People ignored Audrey Kendon's feelings at their peril.

He tiptoed into the annexe and was momentarily taken aback to find Iris Blake still sitting at her husband's bedside in the middle of the night. She didn't seem to sleep. She reminded him of an owl; perfectly still, but possessed of wide open eyes that followed him everywhere. Kim sneaked a look at the window, hoping to find that his reflection was more presentable than it had any right to be. He smiled at Iris, and she accepted the greeting with a slight nod of her head and a slow blink of her owlish eyes.

Kim took out his stethoscope and began to listen to Leonard Blake's lungs. Nothing surprising there. They sounded exactly as he would expect them to sound in a man dying of lung cancer. He quickly lost interest, and his eyes began to sting with tiredness. He just managed to stifle a huge yawn by clamping his teeth together like a vice.

His father would be appalled if he could see him now, switched off, half asleep, going through the motions for the sake of it. But then Kim wasn't his father and he wasn't ever likely to be. In his heart of hearts he wasn't even a doctor. Not yet, anyway. He was a pretender. And all this was a pantomime, Kim told himself, prancing around a dead man in the wee small hours. It was an endlessly repeating performance, and, in this case, it was for the sake of an audience of precisely one. Iris the Owl. None of it was necessary; none of it did any good, but it was what everyone expected to see at a time like this, so the show went on. Give them their money's worth. Humour them. Play to the gallery. What do they know! So he checked the dosage of the syringe-driver with a frown of concentration, and then he fiddled around with the flow of the saline drip, because that was in the script, too. When he held the patient's wrist between his thumb and forefinger and consulted his watch, seeming to be counting under his breath, he didn't even calculate the pulse. It was… what was it? Scratchy. His pulse was scratchy. Write that in the notes if you dare, he thought. One day all doctors would be given a rubber stamp with the words Old & Dying embossed on it. Then people like Kim, with a warm bed to get back to, could simply stamp the notes and stamp the patient's forehead, and leave it at that.

He glanced up and realized that the night sister had followed him into the room and had been watching the pantomime. There was no fooling her. She gave him the same old-fashioned look again, and he buried his face in the notes to hide the next blush. Finally he shrugged and gave up. He couldn't find it. He couldn't pinpoint her feeling, whatever it was. There was nothing out of the ordinary with this old boy. He was running down. He was dying. End of story.

The night sister beckoned him out of the room and pulled the door to.

"I give in," Kim said. "What am I looking for? I can't see any significant changes in him since yesterday."

"But it's a different man!"

"What!" Kim said, feeling as though he had just been electrocuted. "It can't be!"

"And it isn't. Just joking. But it got your attention."

"Very funny. Ha ha." He made a mental note to bludgeon her to death when she wasn't looking. "He seems comfortable enough. Frail, but comfortable. There are no obvious signs of distress that I can make out. Mind you, if I were in his place I think I would want to kick off rather than just lie there with that old bat brooding over me like a vampire. I take it she's still alive and not just here to represent the undead? I could pop back in there and check, if you'd like me to."

"You leave her alone," the night sister said, slapping him hard, but in fun. "She's alright, is old Iris. Quiet, I'll grant you. You hardly ever get a squeak out of her, but that's not always a bad thing. She doesn't fuss. She's old school. Know what I mean? Polite. Faithful. Doesn't want to be a nuisance. If more of them were like her, my job would be made a lot easier, I can tell you."

"Great. She's an angel. So, back to your feeling."

The night sister studied the floor for a moment while she rocked backwards and forwards on her heels with her hands on her hips. "You know those times when you think something doesn't feel right, but you don't know why?"

It was Kim's turn to use the old-fashioned look. "At two o'clock on a cold and wet April morning, dressed in little more than a smile? No!"

"Go on, then!" Audrey said, her maternal instinct coming to his rescue. "Clear off. I'll call you if I need you."

At some point in the night all the nurses were entitled to an hour-long break. If they were quick off the mark, when their time came, they could usually manage to grab a nap of some kind, stretched out on the settee in the staff room. But Audrey preferred to read a book, and when her hour was nearly up she wrapped herself in her cloak and went in search of a cup of tea.

While she was waiting for the kettle to boil she looked in on Iris again and found her still wide awake. "Tea?" she mouthed silently, holding an imaginary cup to her lips. This time Iris was genuinely pleased and nodded.

The night sister wandered to the bedside and pushed her hand under the bedclothes, running her fingers lightly up and down Leonard's warm, thin body. His pyjama trousers were soiled again. It was time to catheterize him.

"Iris, I think I'd like to make young Leonard a little bit more comfortable, if you don't mind us pushing and pulling him around again. I know he's fast asleep, but he's due for a change of underwear, and, while we're at it, we might as well give him a change of sheets. I'm going to make the tea and then I'll grab one of the girls when she comes back off her break and get her to give me a hand." A pre-planned thought occurred to her. "Tell you what. Why don't you come along with me and have your tea in the office while we clean him up? That way you get a break and we get to hoick your chair out of the way."

Iris stood up very slowly, feeling the stiffness in her back. When she was upright she swayed for a moment with giddiness, then she steadied herself against the side of the bed, and finally followed the night sister out of the room. It was now just after three thirty in the morning.

With his wife out of their way the two nurses were able to get on with the job of cleaning up the sleeping husband. They brought a pile of clean sheets and blankets into the room, together with a bowl of warm water, some soap, a flannel, a towel, and a catheter bag and tubing, still sealed in a plastic bag. The night sister held the old man's arm clear of the bed and then picked up the syringe-driver and tubing. Her colleague pulled all the soiled sheets and blankets off the bed and stuffed them straight into a soiled laundry bag. Leonard Blake was lying on a plastic under sheet wearing just his ill-fitting brown nylon pyjamas which were soaked from his buttocks to his knees. Under his bottom there was a crumpled incontinence pad, stained with vile-smelling watery faeces.

Audrey screwed her nose up. "If I roll him towards me, can you pull the Inco pad out on your side, and then tuck your half of the under sheet beneath him? Then we'll swap round."

The nurse agreed and took the syringe-driver and the tubing from her. Bracing herself against the side of the bed, Audrey leaned over the patient and took a firm hold of his shoulder and hip. Then she began to pull him slowly but firmly towards her.

"You're heavy, young Leonard, me lad!" she exclaimed through gritted teeth. "Has someone nailed you to this bed?"

The nurse followed the tubing back to the bed, checking that it wasn't caught in the cot side. "He's clear, as far as I can see. Nothing's attached to him."

Audrey adjusted her footing and tried again. This time she took a deep breath and held it before putting all her strength into trying to heave the patient over onto his side. Still nothing happened. "I can't budge him," she finally declared, letting out her breath with a loud gasp.

"Do you want me to try?" the nurse asked, offering her the syringe-driver. "After all, I am half your age," she added with a sweet smile.

"You do what you can, my little angel," Audrey said with a sage nod of the head. "I'll clear up all the mess you make, as usual."

This time the nurse chose to grip the patient by his chest and hips. Then she, too, began to pull at him with a long, loud squeal. She managed to move his shoulder and his hip about an inch from the mattress before she gave up. The rest of his body stubbornly refused to move.

"This is ridiculous!" the night sister exclaimed with an incredulous laugh. "How much do you suppose he weighs? Ten stone? If that? He's wasting away, the poor old lad. He's as thin as a stick. So what on earth is stopping him from moving?"

Both nurses stood beside the bed with their hands on their hips, looking at Leonard Blake's long thin limbs and torso. The cancer had quite literally reduced him to a flesh-covered skeleton. Either one of them should have been able to lift and turn him with ease. Then the younger nurse reached down and pulled at the Inco pad with her fingertips. It sailed out from under his bottom.

The two women stared at one another.

2

George Shallcross was an angry man. His exasperated wife once told him he was an expert in the field of high dudgeon – which he looked up, and resented. If he had had friends, and if they had ever come together to think up a one-word name for him – which they never would, because there would never be enough of them to form a George Shallcross Fan Club – then that one word would be 'angry'. Red-faced, bull-snorting, chair-chewing angry. And yet he was a small, slight, short-sighted and slightly balding man who would pass muster as a provincial bank manager if he was noticed at all. He was the sort of person other people stood in front of without realizing it. To his annoyance. His late mother also thought he was permanently angry, but she could put a time, almost a date, to his outpouring of wrath. It was the day he stopped growing, just level with her forehead. After that he was angry. Always. It was a permanent condition. He could no more be nice than do a handstand on a telegraph pole. He didn't want to do the handstand in the first place, so why should he worry about being nice to anyone?

But, of course, anger left him isolated, always unsettled, always righteously indignant at life's many perceived slights and blows. It left him waiting for something that never seemed to arrive, something that would complete him, something that would give him happiness and justice, but he had no confidence in himself to recognize that 'something' when he saw it. Yet he went on waiting and hoping anyway.

He eventually became a wealthy man on the back of his professional accomplishments, which thrived on anger and hauteur, and he eventually fathered three tall, wealthy and accomplished children – none of which grew up to look or sound remotely like him – but none of this brought him happiness. Those other goals in life, which only other people ever achieved – goals like fulfilment, contentment, and inner peace – they always eluded him. And that made him angrier still.

If he had one genuine passion in life, then it was bees. Forty thousand loud and angry bees. They were querulous, dysfunctional and anti-social, and they were all crowded together into four hives that Shallcross had located in the middle of a small copse of birch trees right at the bottom of his garden, about three hundred yards from the back of the house.

They were his perfect companions. They didn't speak, so they didn't answer back; they didn't question him; and they made no demands of him. And they were short. What was there not to like? His arm's-length neighbours thought they were his soul mates: both were moody, both were solitary, both were given to frequent, unaccountable tantrums, and both jealously guarded their turf. They were a match made in heaven, Shallcross and his bees. He began each day with a visit to the hives. He inspected each one in turn and he muttered cooing endearments to its occupants; then he allowed himself to gleefully imagine the reign of terror they would impose on the neighbourhood while he was at work, keeping bikers, hikers, villagers – and his wife – at bay.

Of course, his wife hated the bees, but that was her problem. She knew nothing about them and was never likely to. She steered clear of the birch trees. Her turf, her kingdom, was the house and the front garden, the pond and the orchard – everything, in other words, except the hives – the whole plot of land that stretched all the way up to the lane. All of this land, she demanded, was a bee-free zone, and there must never be a repeat of the day when she and her friends were having tea on the lawn and a horde of Shallcross's chums called in uninvited and hogged the jam. The day of the kamikaze bees. She was convinced her husband had trained them, and so now she declared war. She badgered her twice-weekly cleaning lady to spray everything in sight with soapy water – every tree, bush, plant and flower on the property – having read somewhere that bees hated it, and in the summer she made it her business to festoon the house from top to bottom with sticky fly papers.

The house came with four acres of land, and the house and the land were all the fruits of Shallcross's medical career – and he often saw fit to remind his wife of that. He was a consultant – Stinger, or Attila the Hun to his peers – a demi-god in the field of healthcare, and he was a senior member of the Trust Management Team. All in all, he hadn't done too badly for the short, slight, balding younger son of a bus driver and a nurse, as he, too, often remarked to his bathroom mirror, set low above the wash basin. And in addition to all his other commitments he also managed to fit in a very lucrative private practice which just about paid for the running of the house and his wife's frequent holidays. But George Matthew Shallcross lived for bees.

For a busy, angry man to discover a love for bees was quite serendipitous, as great moments in life often are. One day he picked up a catalogue in his dentist's waiting room and found that it listed all the different uses for a wide variety of lurid plastic pet habitats. All at once he discovered how to keep rabbits, chickens, guinea pigs, hamsters, cats, dogs and... bees. He read on, entranced by a world of frames and foundations, honey filtration and storage, and queen-marking – and soon he was hooked. He stuck the catalogue in his pocket, and the first hive – and ten thousand bees – was ordered and delivered to the house within the week, and before he had said a single word about it to his wife. In return, she didn't say a single word to him – for a week. But when she thawed, and when she turned her mind to ousting the bees from her neat flowerbeds, the next three hives came along in swift succession, each one in retaliation for her growing opposition, until she finally grasped the merit of an embittered, smouldering silence.

Of course, Shallcross had to put up with occasional doses of venom, whether human or insect. When his new friends first saw fit to sting him the wounds felt like miniature myocardial infarctions, but he was totally unprepared for his first encounter with anaphylactic shock. One day, after a particularly determined flurry of stings from some very drowsy and suicidal bees during his morning visit, he hurried off to work, unaware of the amount of venom in his body. When he didn't arrive at the hospital, heated phone calls sparked a hurried search for the missing consultant, and he was found by a policeman, slumped over the steering wheel of his car in a shallow ditch on the outskirts of the village. The following day somebody left a small bunch of flowers at the exact spot where his car had rolled to a halt. A card attached to the bouquet read, "In loving memory of the bees." Now he carried phials of adrenaline – and the scars of humiliation – with him everywhere.

Today had started well. He had a quiet breakfast of home-produced honey on toast, and then he took a slow walk down to the hives and back. The swarm was quiet, breakfasting perhaps, or away tormenting his neighbours, either of which suited him well. And there was no reason why the day should not continue well. It was a Friday, after all, and Friday was his favourite day of the week. The weekend was close, almost within touching distance, and he would spend the morning in theatre – five, six routine endoscopies, nothing too taxing – and then have fish and chips for lunch in the hospital cafeteria, and the mellifluous aroma of those chips – that smell of childhood – would permeate its way into every corner of the building during the course of the morning. Bliss.

And then he arrived at the hospital and his mood instantly darkened. He was only a tad late by his own reckoning and yet the street was already filled with cars. Other people's cars. The most important man in the building and he couldn't get into it because he couldn't park his car. It was like being... Well, it was like being a patient! Reluctantly, angrily, he cruised around the nearby streets until he came across a very narrow slither of daylight between a white van and a rubbish skip, which he managed to reverse into at the fifth attempt. By the time he had locked the car, balanced his briefcase on top of a pile of notes, and then stomped all the way back to the hospital, he was well and truly late, and spoiling for a fight. He bounded up the steps, just able to see over the briefcase, and still managed to collide with the Head Porter's huge stomach.

"Good God, man!" he exclaimed, recoiling from the impact. "Diet, before you kill someone!"

The Head Porter, a morose man, stared at him without moving or blinking, and then he suddenly growled, "Morning!" in a deep, cavernous voice.

"Nowhere to park again!" Shallcross announced to a long line of startled outpatients queuing at the reception hatch. "I should have my own parking space, with cones, and chains!"

The Head Porter stared at him again for a moment without moving out of his way. Then he shrugged and held out his hands towards the consultant, palms upwards, as though he was beseeching a favour from him. "Won't you let me paint your name on the road for you?"

Shallcross seethed over the handle of his briefcase. "Where's your car?" he demanded. "I suppose you managed to park. I suppose you've got your own private space tucked away somewhere!"

"Don't own a car, don't drive," the Head Porter reminded him.

"Well, I do! And I should have my own parking space, and then I won't be late."

"Or..." the Head Porter said, brandishing his stubby finger like a baton, "you could just get here on time." He finally moved out of the way, but only far enough to make eye contact with the telephonist. "Jenny, phone the Lodge. See if anyone's free to come out and lie on the road and keep a space free for Mr..." (The consultant's office door slammed with a crash.) "...Shallcross."

———————

Shallcross needed more fuming time inside the office. The place was microscopic. It lacked parking places; it lacked room to swing a cat in. It was the smallest of the six hospitals scattered around the city, and it was squeezed into one street corner like a grocer's shop. It was one of the wonders of the age that any of the services in the building managed to operate at all – x-ray, physiotherapy, OPD, social work, surgery – they were all shoehorned into the place somewhere. Not that he had ever visited half of them. One day it would all be gone, he reminded himself spitefully, forgetting for a moment that the nose he was thinking of was on his own face. If the rumour-mongers were to be believed it would all be swept away and be replaced by a jumble of eccentric little flats that a clever architect would contrive to fit into the shell of the old building. Wouldn't that be fun! Living where the stiffs used to lie! Until then this cramped little hovel would have to remain the home of the Chest Unit, *his* Chest Unit. The perennial poor relation of the Trust's ramshackle healthcare empire.

The telephone rang twice in quick succession. Both times it was the theatre sister wondering when he would finally deign to grace them with his presence and cut up some customers. "Soon!" he snapped the first time. "Bloody well wait!" he shouted the second time, in a voice that rattled around the whole building.

At that precise moment there was a timid tap on the door. "What?" he screamed, his face turning purple with the effort. An unshaven face peered round the edge of the door and smiled at him. It was Kim Maskell, clearly very ill at ease.

"Got a moment?"

Shallcross waved at his empty desk with a clenched fist. "Why should I have a moment?" he demanded, as though he was inviting the young doctor to find one for himself. "I'm late! I couldn't park!" Then, after a pause, he added, "Why?"

"I've got a bit of a problem."

"Nothing new in that," Shallcross said unkindly, but he pointed to the empty chair across the desk. As Kim sat down the consultant peered over the top of his glasses at the frayed and faded Rugby shirt under the doctor's coat. "Just exactly what do you think you look like? You look more like a man who is going to empty my dustbin than take my pulse!"

Kim blushed. "Sorry," he mumbled. "Up most of the night."

"Comes with the territory," Shallcross advised him primly, suddenly propping his chin on a steeple of fingertips. "If you ever hope to be a doctor you need to start dressing and acting like one." Shallcross glanced aside to check his own reflection in a small vanity mirror set low on the wall. He was wearing his usual bow tie, knotted to perfection. Look upon my works, ye mighty! "What do you want? Be quick."

Kim took a deep breath and then plunged in. "I'd like you to see a patient for me…"

"Far too busy! Late for theatre. Shrew's nagging me already," Shallcross said shortly, pointing at the telephone as though the harridan in question was sitting on it.

Kim nodded at the telephone politely. "Okay, not urgent, doesn't have to be right now, but I guarantee you this one is well worth a look."

Shallcross inspected his fingernails for a moment, and then glanced at the clock. Three hours till chips. "Why?"

"There's something odd going on. Not something I've ever come across before."

Shallcross closed one eye as though he was lining the young doctor up in a gun sight. "Go on."

"An elderly male patient in the annexe on Ward 4. Leonard Blake."

Shallcross considered the name and then screwed his face up. "Don't recall him. What's he in for?"

"Small-cell carcinomas, both lungs. Terminal, of course, with enough diamorphine in him to keep a dinosaur in dreamland. He is one of yours."

"And?"

"And I can't budge him."

A gradual onset of anguish afflicted Shallcross's face like a rash. "What d'you mean, you can't budge him? On what? Matters of national importance? The plight of the pound?"

At times like this it helped Kim to remember the day they brought his boss to work in a police car, dosed to the gills with shame and adrenaline. Kim was there. He saw it with his own eyes. No one would ever be able to take that memory away from him. It was a warm, sustaining image that carried him through the dark days, and the sulks and the tantrums.

"I mean I can't move him. Simple as that."

Shallcross aimed a beetle-browed frown at the clock on the wall. "Not surprised with all that junk you're pumping into him. What do you want to move him for, anyway?"

"You don't understand," Kim explained patiently. "I just can't move him. Physically, I mean. Not by an inch. None of us can, and three of us have tried. It's like he's glued to the mattress."

Shallcross's head jerked back exactly two inches. It had taken him years to perfect that little manoeuvre, but it was worth it. "Bloody ridiculous," he said, languishing over every syllable like a Welsh preacher. "Big man?"

Kim shook his head. "Average build. Your size." He winced almost before the words were out of his mouth. And he had been doing so well.

The consultant stared at him in stony silence until his face felt like it was melting in the heat. Then with a sepulchral voice Shallcross declared, "I do not have an average build. I do not acknowledge the word 'average'." Then he thought for a moment. Theatre would just have to wait a little longer. He stood up abruptly, almost tipping his chair over. "Show me."

Kim led the way up the stairs and along the corridor, marvelling at the way everyone vanished at the little man's approach. Two theatre porters nearly collided with him, heading towards Ward 2 with their stretcher trolley, but this time it was Shallcross who chose not to see them. When they reached the annexe they found two sisters waiting for them at Leonard Blake's bedside, the night sister and her daytime counterpart. They also found the Hospital Manager, Liz Manners, a waspish, severe-looking middle-aged woman, waiting for them, perched on the windowsill like a watchful pigeon. And Iris Blake still sat at her husband's side.

"Right!" Shallcross announced, rubbing his hands together briskly as though he was sanding them smooth. "What's all this nonsense about?"

Everyone moved back and allowed him to see the comatose patient for himself. He peered down his nose at the syringe-driver and the drip and then stared at Iris Blake for a moment. "Who are you?" he demanded.

"This is Mrs Blake, the patient's wife!" the night sister informed him, shocked by the brusqueness of his question.

"Mrs Blake!" The expression on Shallcross's face changed at the flick of a switch to one of glutinous charm which slowly metamorphosed into an icy smile. "Dear lady! Perhaps I could ask you to step outside for a moment while my colleague and I examine your husband?"

The Hospital Manager took the hint and quickly air-brushed the old woman from the room, and the door had barely closed behind them before the consultant turned on the other people in the room.

"How can the three of you stand there and tell me you can't move a man who looks like he's just been liberated from Auschwitz? He's a stick insect. I could fold him up and post him to you, he's so thin. I could move him with one hand tied behind my back!" He narrowed his field of fire to the two nurses. "As for you two, the Sisters Grimm; you're trained in this sort of thing. What are we paying you for? To make tea?"

Kim finally lost his patience. It had been a long night and his eyes were burning with lack of sleep. He waved his hand towards the bed with an extravagant bow. "Be my guest. Use both hands. Pick him up, throw him over your shoulder, wind him, dance the tango with him, but move him just one inch in any direction at all and I will eat my hat."

This time Shallcross's icy stare made no headway against the young doctor's fixed, angry frown. His bluff had been called. He relented, took his jacket off, tossed it towards Audrey, and then examined the patient closely before roughly taking hold of him and trying to shake him loose from the bed. The result of his efforts was that Shallcross threw himself around like a rag doll while Leonard Blake remained exactly where he was, not moving at all.

The consultant drew an immaculately folded handkerchief from his pocket and mopped his brow. "Theatre will be wondering where on earth I've got to," he scolded himself in a loud aside. "Fetch a hoist," he added, staring into space majestically.

The day sister left the room without a word and Shallcross walked over to the window to await her return. While he watched the people and the traffic in the street outside he saw the Consultant Radiologist's car suddenly speed round the corner and stop in the middle of the road. It was a brand-spanking-new BMW, no less, and the gods smiled on it without hesitation. A car pulled away from the building and the BMW was free to park right outside the front door. Shallcross clenched his fists and briefly considered throwing something from the window, but there was only the chair and the locker to choose from. While he was still seething with disgust the day sister returned with the hoist, bumping it through the door like a dodgem car at a fairground. Kim snatched up the chair and shoved it back against the wall and then the day sister wrestled the hoist into position so that its wheels reached right under the bed and its two steel arms reached out above the bed and the patient like a sleep-walking robot. With a nudge of her hips the day sister edged two canvas straps and chains into place above the patient's shoulders and bottom.

"I'm not sure how this is going to work," Kim said cautiously. "If we can't move him then we can't get the straps under him, can we?"

Shallcross still had his back to the room. He folded his arms and watched the Consultant Radiologist wiping dust off his car with his sleeve. Where was a bilious pigeon when you wanted one? "Leave it to them. It's a perfectly simple nursing procedure."

Audrey snorted loudly, as though she had a heavy cold. When she realized that she was still holding Shallcross's jacket she held it up between thumb and forefinger and then dropped it on the floor. Stepping over it, she pushed Kim aside with a near perfect shoulder barge. "Stand back!" she ordered him. "If I were you, I'd take cover. I'm going to perform a perfectly simple nursing procedure, without the use of a safety net. Historians will write of this moment."

Oddly enough it was a simple matter to slip one strap under Leonard Blake's shoulders and then tuck it into his armpits, and another strap under his legs and draw that one up towards his thighs. It was done in a moment.

"There now!" Audrey announced, dusting off her hands. "Simple when you know how." She aimed a frosty stare at Shallcross's back and then turned to Kim. "Come on, Tarzan. Let's see if you have the strength to send old Lenny whizzing round the room, shall we?"

Kim took hold of the crank handle with both hands and then placed his feet well apart. He slowly turned the handle through two full revolutions until the hoist had taken up the slack on the chains and the straps, and then he stood ready to lift the old man himself from the bed. Kim turned the handle again and this time the back of the hoist began to rise slowly and unsteadily into the air. Thinking that the hoist was not level with the floor, Kim stood his whole weight on the base, and when he turned again, and while Leonard Blake remained exactly where he was, the hoist lifted all sixteen stones of the trainee doctor straight into the air.

Shallcross had turned from the window to watch with his arms folded. For what seemed like a very long time no one said a word, and then Kim simply reversed the direction of the handle and returned the hoist gently to the ground.

"Brake on?" Shallcross asked, starring fixedly at the patient.

"Brake on."

Shallcross plucked at his bottom lip. "Then how the…"

But before he could finish the sentence the day sister suddenly swooped down and peered at Leonard Blake's back with her face pressed against the mattress. "Take the straps off," she said quietly.

Kim and Audrey removed the straps and then the chains and finally the hoist itself. Then they watched in amazement as the day sister carefully inserted her hand between the patient and the mattress and wiggled her fingers on the other side. She slowly slid her hand up and down the bed. Then she stood up and pulled the pillows away and the patient's head did not move.

Kim's mouth opened and closed several times, making him look like a day-dreaming goldfish. Then he turned to the day sister for confirmation, and she simply nodded.

"He's not lying on the bed."

———————————

Shallcross sent Kim Maskell back to his flat to wash and sleep in that order. Next he ordered the day sister to place Leonard Blake in strict isolation, and finally he took himself off to the Operating Theatre, where he was by now more than an hour late for the start of the list. The smell of chips followed him up the stairs and for once he didn't notice it. On arrival he went straight into the changing room and pulled on his blues and his white boots. Then he scrubbed up and barged backwards through the swing doors into the anaesthetic room.

"And what time do you call this?" the sister snapped at him through her mask.

"Shut up!" he snapped back at her, and these were the only two words he spoke for the next three hours.

He completed all five operations in silence and then he quickly changed back into his own clothes, glanced into Recovery, and hurried back to his office on the ground floor. There he sat at his desk with his hands laid palm-downwards on the blotter until the clock on the wall reached 1.00 p.m., then he left the office again and this time headed towards the Hospital Manager's office on the first floor. When he arrived at her door he could make out several voices already in conversation, but before joining them he walked on along the corridor until he reached the annexe. The day sister had stuck a large cardboard notice to the door with a blob of blu-tac warning everyone who came near that barrier nursing protocols were now in force and that admittance to the room was strictly prohibited to all but a handful of authorized personnel.

Shallcross opened the door a few inches and peered inside. The blinds were drawn, even now, in the middle of the day, but he could still see Leonard Blake very clearly, just where he had left him three hours earlier, deeply unconscious and covered from chin to toe with a long blue eiderdown that reached all the way to the floor on either side of the bed. The ghastly orange chair was back in place but, for once, Iris Blake wasn't sitting on it. Shallcross quietly closed the door again and made his way back to the Hospital Manager's office.

They were waiting for him: Liz Manners, the day sister, and Kim Maskell. Kim still looked hung-over, but at least he had washed and shaved and changed into another rugby shirt. Shallcross sank into the armchair by the door and rested his feet on the spindly coffee table. Once he was comfortable he examined all three watching faces one by one.

"Who goes first?"

The Hospital Manager looked long and hard at the heels of his shoes on her frail little polished coffee table and then levelled the tip of her pencil at him. "You do!"

Shallcross hesitated. For some reason it hadn't occurred to him that he might start the proceedings. He had thought of nothing else all morning but he hadn't managed to get anywhere. He wanted to listen. He wanted answers. He saw that Kim had had the good sense to bring the patient's notes along with him. That was a starting point, but then another thought occurred to him.

"How many people know about this?"

"The people in this room," Liz Manners replied, touching the tip of her pencil on her pad very carefully. She knew she wasn't going to be home early today. That would mean her husband doing the weekend shopping on his own. A sobering thought.

"And Audrey," the day sister reminded her.

"And Audrey."

Shallcross's eyebrows sprang together like the springs of a gin-trap. "Who is Audrey?" he asked suspiciously.

The Hospital Manager's pencil crumpled into the paper with a loud snap and a shower of shattered graphite. "Who is Audrey?" Surely the man was joking. "Audrey is the night sister. She has been the night sister for most of the past twenty-five years. Until this morning, in fact, when, according to you, she was promoted to the ranks of the Sisters Grimm. All those years she's had to put up with your rudeness and you have the effrontery not to remember her name."

Shallcross was flabbergasted. "Rudeness? What rudeness? I am never rude. I don't know the meaning of the word." His wife's mother had called him rude on her daughter's wedding day, but then she was a witch and he had had the great satisfaction of chalking a pentacle on her patio before he and his wife had left for their honeymoon. Nevertheless, he blushed. "Why isn't she here?"

The Hospital Manager's voice rose by an octave and a significant number of decibels. "Because she is the night sister!" she exclaimed. "Could there possibly be a clue in the job title, do you suppose? She is a mere mortal. She sleeps by day because she works by night. She will be back on duty this evening when she will relieve Gill. Tomorrow morning Gill will be back to relieve Audrey. It's called continuity and team work."

Shallcross frowned. "I'm confused. Who are all these people? Who is this Gill?"

For a moment nothing happened. Liz Manner's face had completely frozen. Then she slowly sat back in her chair, blew out a weary sigh, and then pointed a finger at the woman sitting by his side, as though she was Miss Marple finally unveiling the murderer. Shallcross turned and gaped at the day sister, but wisely said nothing.

"How long can you keep that up?" Kim asked the day sister. "Turn and turn about, like that? It must mean twelve hour shifts. That's exhausting."

Gill turned the question over in her mind before answering. "The current rota extends up to – and includes – Sunday night."

"Three days from now," Kim said thoughtfully. "A lot could happen in three days."

"Or nothing at all," Liz Manners added quietly.

"Three days from now," Gill agreed. "Then we need to let someone else in on our little secret."

"Three days." Liz Manners took another pencil from the pot on her desk and made a note on her pad. She had compiled the rota Gill was quoting from, and she would need to make a careful study of it, now, before going home, if they were to appoint a new conspirator.

Shallcross tapped the file on Kim's knee. "Off you go. From the top."

Kim opened the file and scanned the front page. "I don't know if any of this is going to get us very far. Anyway, here goes. His name is Leonard George Blake, he's seventy-nine years old, married of course, and he and his wife have three children. He's C of E and five feet nine inches tall. His first date of referral is just over a year ago. Details of diagnosis. Records of all his radiotherapy and chemotherapy treatments. Lots of them, poor sod. He hasn't done badly, considering. He was most recently admitted ten days ago for what was intended to be a period of respite care, mainly for his wife, but he very quickly went downhill from there. Basically we've got him here now because there wasn't enough time to line up a bed for him at the Hospice. Too late now. The journey ends here."

"Current medication?"

"Standard fare. Diamorphine, sixty milligrams, four hourly, mixed with midazolam as a relaxant and sedative, all administered by subcutaneous infusion by syringe driver. I've made a note to myself here that if his breathing becomes laboured, if he's really starting to struggle, I'll try some hyoscine hydrobromide to dry up the lung secretions."

"Oxygen?"

"Not yet." Kim began to close the file.

"And that's it?" Liz Manners asked, looking up from her pad.

"That's it. What else do you want?" He held the file up between his fingertips as though he was weighing its contents. "There's nothing in here that's remotely out of the ordinary for a man in his condition. Quite the reverse. He's textbook all the way. It would help us no end if he turned out to be an alien from the Planet Zarg with a penchant for little old ladies in bungalows, but it just ain't so. Sorry."

"What did he do for a living?" Shallcross asked, racking his brains for a way in to the mystery.

Kim flipped the file open again and wiggled his finger up and down the page. "Postman. Retired."

"A postman." Liz Manners made another note on her pad. "How is that supposed to help us? We need him to glow in the dark. How does your utterly average everyday plodding postman end up with... what are we going to call this thing? A catatonic state? Some kind of pre-mortem rigidity?"

"No!" The day sister slapped the arm of her chair. "With respect, Liz, no, that's not what we're dealing with here. There is some very limited movement in both arms and legs, and the patient's head, neck and torso are all quite rigid. But... the simple fact of the matter is that no part of his body is in contact with the bed. Full stop."

Liz looked up again, pencil poised. "But that's ridiculous. That's just not possible. Some part of him has got to be in contact with something. Something is bearing his weight. It's got to be."

Gill shook her head. "Let me say it again so that there is no misunderstanding. No part of Leonard Blake's body is in direct contact with either the bed or the wall or the floor. Before I came to this meeting I measured the distance between his back and the mattress. I could put the whole of my hand under him without touching him. The gap is four to five centimetres."

Liz continued to make notes while she listened to the day sister, but then she paused and leaned her chin on her free hand. "So his head or his feet are bracing him somehow. They must be. Perhaps he's arching his back in some kind of spasm that..."

"No, Liz," the day sister said again, much louder this time. "You're not listening to me. I took his pillows away when I measured that gap between him and the bed. You can see daylight from every angle. I'm not suggesting we should, but I honestly think you could move the bed out of the room altogether and he would still be left just – call it what you will – *floating* there."

Liz put pencil to paper again but this time it refused to move. There was an embarrassing silence while everyone tried to think of something sensible to say.

"Leave the bed alone," Shallcross said quietly. "While it's there he still looks relatively normal. It helps to maintain the fiction. Buy time."

"For what?" Liz asked, still looking down at her pad. No one answered.

She was tired. Worn out. If any of her friends – and at least she had some – if any of her friends had wanted a word to sum her up, these days, they would all have opted for 'tired'. She was always tired, and that was sad, because that wasn't Liz, that wasn't the Liz that everyone remembered so fondly. She was the party girl, the serial good-time girl. She partied on when mere mortals fell by the wayside. She didn't just burn the candle at both ends, she blowtorched it clean in two. But now she was tired, and the secret portrait would no longer agree to stay hidden away in her attic. It trespassed across her bathroom mirror every morning, demanding tribute for all the high octane years that had gone before. Now she was the power-dresser, the hard-grafting career administrator. She had worked by day – a sister, like Audrey and Gill – and she had trained by night until, by dint of long years of trying, she finally climbed enough of the greasy pole to warrant this obscure little hospital for her troubles. It was a curio, a hospital in miniature, an oddity, but it was hers. Whether it was a dream come true or a wrong turning somewhere down the line she had yet to discuss with the mirror on the bathroom wall.

"Which reminds me," Kim suddenly said, "where is Mrs Blake?"

"I sent her home," Gill said simply. "She needed a bath and a change of clothes."

"And some sleep, I would imagine?" Kim added.

"No, she's put sleep on hold. Time for that later. She'll be back as soon as she can."

"How much does she know?" Liz asked, kicking herself that she hadn't tried to sound her out that morning.

"Difficult to say. Possibly nothing. It's amazing what you can miss when you're just sitting there watching somebody die. I certainly haven't spoken to her about it."

"But shouldn't she be here?" Kim asked, waving towards the empty chair. "Surely she must have a right to know," he suggested.

Shallcross leaned back in his chair and addressed the ceiling. "No. Not yet. Until we have some idea about how to deal with this, we can't risk anyone – even Mrs Blake – telling the rest of the world that we have a freak show going on in one of our wards."

Liz placed her pencil very neatly at the side of the pad. "Which brings us to my biggest headache. This place is a rabbit warren, and it's got little eyes and ears around every corner. Nothing is ever secret for long. How on earth can we hope to keep something like this to ourselves for more than five minutes?"

Shallcross pitched forward in his chair until he was sitting upright and looking straight at the Hospital Manager. "I don't know, but I suggest you find a way, and quickly, because if I hear of one syllable of this getting out, I will personally disembowel the culprit, whatever their job title or pay scale."

"That's a great help," Liz said coldly. "If only all our other problems could be solved that easily."

Shallcross ignored her and returned his gaze to the ceiling. Several moments passed.

"What should we be doing?" Gill finally asked of no one in particular.

"What *can* we do?" Kim asked. "I'm open to suggestions, but I warn you, folks, I'm going to follow the first white rabbit I see straight down the nearest hole."

Liz consulted her pad again. "Gill, can you and Audrey manage for now? Can you get us to Monday morning between you?"

"I'm sure we can," Gill said. "And what will the rest of you be doing?"

"Waiting."

"Waiting for what?" Kim asked.

Shallcross touched the young doctor's sleeve. "For him to die."

"How likely is that?" Liz asked.

Kim pulled a face for a moment, and then he simply shrugged his shoulders. "You tell me. He will die, and soon, of course he will. He can't survive. But will he die in five minutes' time or in five days' time? Who knows? In the last twenty-four hours he's been fairly stable."

"Since all this started, you mean?" Liz asked.

Kim flicked the notes open on his knee before he answered. "I hadn't thought of it in that way. Maybe. But we don't really know how long this has been going on, do we? It's not the sort of thing you check on, as a matter of routine. Heart rate, temperature, altitude."

Gill cleared her throat and then smoothed her clean white uniform over her knees. "I gave Mr Blake a bed bath on Wednesday. And on Wednesday he was lying on that bed. He was..." She searched for the right word.

"Normal?"

"Normal."

Liz pushed her chair back, stood up, and wandered over to the window. A double-decker bus was going by. People were walking in and out of the newsagent's shop across the road, talking, laughing. There was a patch of blue sky above the hospital, and a seagull was squawking on a chimney pot. That was normal.

"So. We get to nine o'clock Monday morning and Leonard Blake is alive and well and mastering the art of levitation. Audrey and Gill are off duty. What do the rest of us geniuses do then?"

"Meet again," Shallcross said simply, sitting up again and spreading his hands on his knees as though he was kneading dough. "We meet again, and we review what – if anything – has happened in the meantime. And we go from there."

The Hospital Manager's head was beginning to throb. "A date in a diary is not a solution," she said wearily.

"It's not," Shallcross agreed. "But it's all we have for now."

"Where shall we meet?" Kim asked, anxious to be gone.

Shallcross looked at Liz. "Here?"

The Hospital Manager reluctantly nodded her head. "Here."

3

Iris Blake had taken herself home in a taxi that morning, the first time in her life she had travelled in one on her own. When the driver stopped at the wrong end of the road and asked her where she wanted to get out, she waited for Leonard to answer him, and she was bewildered when the driver turned and stared at her instead. Her mind went completely blank for a moment, as though she had lost her place in the script, and then she very nearly clambered right over the passenger seat in her attempt to point to the little cherry tree in the front garden that identified their home among all the identical bungalows in the road. The driver watched her in the rear-view mirror while she explained when they had bought the tree and how they had planted it, although she was really talking to herself. They finally pulled up alongside the garden wall and the driver announced the fare like a bingo-caller, making no attempt to open the door for her. Now she missed Leonard again. She rummaged around in her handbag for her purse, and then she wracked her brains to remember how Leonard had calculated the tip whenever they had brought the shopping home from Sainsbury's. She didn't want to embarrass herself a second time in as many minutes so she gave him far too much, but he just shrugged and drove away, leaving her standing on the kerb staring at the cherry tree. How would she ever manage to prune it now, she wondered, without Leonard? How would she ever manage anything now, all on her own? She leaned on the garden wall to catch her breath, missing her husband, missing his steadying arm. She had always been the frail one. She had always been ear-marked as the first one to go. She wasn't built to cope.

She couldn't cope. And she didn't much want to try. The street was cold and grey and empty, and it made her feel alone, very alone.

She took a long, deep breath and began to walk up the path, reaching out towards an imaginary handrail, much like a tightrope walker, trying not to wobble, trying to keep her balance, filled with an old woman's fear of falling and snapping a bone. At the door she searched in her handbag again for her key, and then, once she was safely inside, she automatically checked to make sure that the place was secure. Did it feel right, look right, sound right, smell right? Was it safe? Was *she* safe? There was a bubbling cauldron of panic tucked away inside her somewhere, just waiting for the right moment to boil over and trash everything in sight. But for now everything was right. Everything was where she had left it. Neat and tidy. Untouched since her last departure. Beginning with Leonard's black shoes – his kept-for-best shoes – beautifully polished and placed neatly and squarely on a little piece of plastic matting to the left of the door. The shoes were left behind when they went to the hospital together in the ambulance. Leonard wore slippers and a dressing gown, and the shoes stayed behind to wait for his return. So how long would she leave them there, she wondered, now that it was certain that Leonard would never come back to claim them for himself? What was right? What was proper? What was normal, under these circumstances? A day, a week, a month, a year? What was too fast, or too slow? What messages did shoes give out to a watching world? What said she can cope, and what said she can't? It was like tipping the taxi driver. She had no one to ask now but herself.

Leonard had escaped. Leonard had fled the ugly bungalow and escaped into the void. Leaving it all to her, to dust, to sit in, to die in, for all she knew. She would sit and wait for her own ambulance, and she would leave her own scuffed and dirty shoes by the door for someone else to find and grieve over and throw away.

That morning she had asked the night sister how long it would take Leonard to die. She must know, she thought. She had seen this before. This was what she did: watch people die. She must know.

She had warmed to this quirky woman once she got her measure. She thought she was probably somewhere in her sixties. She wore no make-up and no jewellery, and her face was very plain and pale and deeply lined. Much like her own, she imagined. No wedding ring, of course, but there was talk of grownup sons and grandchildren, and Iris felt she wasn't alone, she felt that somebody somewhere was supporting her, sustaining her, lending her an arm, breaking the silences for her, so that she could spend her long nights in that hideous building watching other people's loved ones die.

The night sister had smiled when she had asked her. She had squeezed her, now that Iris thought about it. A gentle pressure on her arm. Then she had said, "Soon. Very soon." So let it be soon, Iris thought, the sooner the better; because she didn't want to spend another hour in that horrid little room. Why would anyone think she would want to sit there at her husband's side, watching him die, day after day, week after week? It made sense to let him go. It made sense to want him to die and be gone and set her free from all this waiting with a stiff back. If there were a switch to press, right here and now, a switch to end it all, to send Leonard on his way and release her into emptiness, she would push it, she would push it good and hard, and then hope that someone had the good sense to push her switch one day soon.

The telephone rang and she dropped her key. She hurried into the sitting room, snatched up the receiver and blurted out her name, still wearing her hat, coat and shoes. Had he been there, Leonard would have taken them all from her while she was speaking with the phone pressed hard to her ear, either to her sister, or to one or other of their children. This time it was Richard, not the hospital. Richard, clear as a bell, all the way from Adelaide.

"What time is it where you are?" she asked, because she always began their conversation that way.

"It's about ten o'clock, I think."

"At night?"

"Yes, Mum, at night," Richard said patiently. "How are you? How's Dad?"

"Much the same."

"No change at all?"

"No, not really. It's just a matter of waiting now. They said it won't be long. I've just come home to change. I'll go back in a while. How's Lucy?"

"She's fine. Kids are fine." Now there would be the customary pause, precise to the millisecond, before he said, "Mum, do you need me there?" As though he could wave a magic wand and make it happen, make all those thousands of miles just disappear at the drop of a hat.

Of course she wanted him here. What sort of a stupid question was that? He was the one child with enough gumption to cope with all this, with Leonard, with cancer, with her. Of course she wanted him here so that she didn't have to face all this misery, all this heartache alone. How could he doubt it? How could he even bother to ask it? Why didn't he just drop everything and come running when it mattered, when she needed him, when she cried out to him night after night? When he still could? Why bother to ask at all, now, when it was already far, far too late? Why bother to fly all the way home just to stand at a graveside and look jet-lagged?

"No, I'm fine. I'll manage," she said in reply, with exactly the right tone of weary patience in her voice that she intended his conscience to hear.

"Has Susan been in touch yet?" he asked, transferring the blame as usual. "If not, I'll ring her. It's high time I did, anyway. I have one or two things I want to say to her."

"She's busy. I'm sure she'll come when I need her."

"Yeah. Right. And I'm as sure that she won't. I'll call her. You shouldn't have to."

"No, you won't, Richard. Don't interfere."

"Yes I will! She should be there."

"She will be. She's not ideal, but she will be." If it suits her, Iris thought to herself. She's not ideal, Richard, she thought. She's not you, and you should be here.

Iris looked through the lace curtains at the grey street outside. Jeanette, her neighbour across the road, was heading up the garden path carrying what looked like an oven dish covered in foil. Whatever it was, she must have had it on a low heat waiting for Iris's return. She allowed Jeanette to ring the bell, knowing that Richard would hear it and end the call.

"What's that?" he asked.

"Someone at the door."

"Go and answer it. I'll wait."

"No, don't. It's Jeanette; you know how she talks."

"And talks and talks."

"Exactly. Don't wait. I'll ring you tomorrow, or as soon as there is news."

She opened the door while Richard was still saying goodbye and mouthed his name to Jeanette as she beckoned her into the hall. Jeanette bawled a hello at him, but he had already gone.

"I thought you might be hungry," Jeanette explained, filling the hall with the smell of shepherd's pie.

"That's a lovely thought and you're a dear, but I couldn't eat anything, really I couldn't."

"You need to. Keep your strength up," Jeanette said severely, heading for the kitchen. Iris followed her, amazed to discover that she was suddenly ravenously hungry.

"When did you last eat?" Jeanette asked, peering at her neighbour over her glasses as though she was measuring a dose of medicine for her.

"No idea. What day is it today?" Iris wondered absently.

"Friday."

"Friday?" She thought for a moment. "Wednesday, then. Breakfast time, Wednesday."

"You naughty girl!" Jeanette chastised her, pulling her coat off. "You sit down and eat that right now. I'll put the kettle on."

So Iris Blake sat at the little kitchen table and ate shepherd's pie straight from the dish, piping hot. And it was good.

———————

Kim got back to his flat shortly after five o'clock that afternoon. He took off all his clothes and left them in a heap on the bedroom floor, and then he sank into a hot bath and almost immediately fell asleep. No sooner were his eyes closed than he found himself for the umpteenth time right back in the middle of his worst nightmare. He was sitting in an examination hall, smack bang in the middle of the campus, on a summer's day, when it was unbearably hot and humid – just like a bathroom – and the paper he was trying to write on kept sticking to his hand and making the ink run. His heart was pounding and he could barely breathe. There was fear and loathing seeping out of every pore. He was convinced that somebody somewhere, just out of sight, wanted his essays. All of them. Hundreds of them, dating right the way back to his school days. Great, swaying piles of paper that didn't even exist outside of his imagination because he had never bothered to write them. It was a stress dream. A part of him knew that, but even so he was stuck with the pounding heart and the shadowy corner where the hidden tutor lay in wait for him. He looked up, wondering if he might find a way out, but instead the paper stuck fast to his sweaty chin, and, anyway, Leonard Blake was there, alive and well, quite naked, drifting around high above the heads of all the other students, munching a biscuit.

He woke up with a start, and shuddered. The water was stone cold.

He towelled himself dry and pulled on another old rugby shirt, this time a pink and white one with a faded university logo. Then he looked around the bedroom for a clean white coat, but he couldn't find one so he looped the stethoscope around his neck and left it at that.

He was feeling a little muzzy after the bath and the nap, so he took a slow stroll along the road to the Queen's Head, giving his head a chance to clear. He arrived right on the stroke of six, just as the landlord was chalking the evening menu on the blackboard. He stopped at the saloon bar door and looked back along the street at the hospital. He reached into his pocket and checked that his bleep was switched on. He was well within range, but it was as well to make sure. If the worst came to the worst, round about now – a knockdown, drag out cardiac arrest, for example – he could stampede along that road like a fly half with his britches on fire, and on a good day he would reach the ward in under two minutes and have the defibrillator plugged in, charged up and hovering over the patient's chest in under three. Any longer than that and he wouldn't even try. As Shallcross himself had once decreed, "They wouldn't thank you for it."

The landlord saw Kim and cheered, and then smiled and nodded when the young doctor ordered a pint and a large wedge of fatty steak and ale pie with chips. Kim sat by the door with his feet up on a radiator, positioning himself so that he could see the television on the wall above the billiards table. The news was on and Kim had a vague idea that he knew the man being interviewed on the green outside the Houses of Parliament. His sister, Clare, was the barricade-building activist in the family, replete with mother-baiting tattoos and dreadlocks like ships' hawsers. She was the one who could spot a tainted public servant at a thousand yards, and she would nail that smug smile in a second. She kept cuttings. She even kept dossiers on some members of the Cabinet. She could put the fear of God into Kim when she got up a full head of steam. Then he blushed. A caption appeared beneath the smug smile. It was the Secretary of State for Health. Clare would go mad and hit him with something. But she wouldn't know if he didn't tell her, and, anyway, he only wanted the weather forecast and the sports preview; the one to make him feel bad about working all weekend, and the other to whet his appetite for late evening football highlights.

But before the bulletin finished it showed an elderly patient in a hospital bed, and that caused Kim to wonder what might happen if Leonard Blake ever found his way on to prime time television. Panic, probably. There would be a deluge, a tidal wave of cameras and reporters, surely. All bearing down on that tiny little building along the road, ready to swamp it, ready to bring everything inside it grinding to a halt. One single solitary, levitating patient. One tiny little mystery and that would be enough. The thought made Kim shudder, as though someone had just walked over his grave.

What chiefly impressed Kim in all of this was the look he caught on Shallcross's face at lunchtime. He was an arrogant little man, everyone knew that, and he loved to humble all the sycophants and the flunkies who toadied up to him all the time. That was par for the course. That was the sort of thing that went with the territory, once you had slithered far enough up the slippery pole to be able to smirk at all the other wretches slipping and sliding around in your wake. But he knew his stuff. He was ace. Sharp as a tack. The main man. There wasn't much he didn't know in his area of expertize, and the great and the good would often beat a path to his door and do their obeisance before seeking his help. But what Kim saw on his face today was the look of a man who had run headlong into a brick wall and didn't know how to deal with the shock. He had found a mystery without a solution. He, the mighty George Shallcross, had to say out loud, to all the listening world, that *he didn't know*. He was stumped. He was mystified. He had feet of clay, after all.

Now, if Leonard Blake were to oblige them all by dying – better still, if he were to die and have the good manners to slump back down on the bed again – all well and good. Sorted. They could wrap him up like Tutankhamun, pack him off to the crematorium, and heave a great big sigh of relief. They could chalk it up to experience. Tuck it away in the back of their minds somewhere, where no one else would ever find it. The one that got away.

But what if he didn't die? Or, better still, what if he did die but just stayed up there somewhere, floating around the place like a barrage balloon? Would he stay there for ever? Would he still be there when everything else had moved on? When the hospital was a building site?

The landlord carried the steaming mound of steak and ale pie to his table and then took his glass away to refill it without being asked.

There were lots of things that could go wrong with the human body. Everyone knew that. Even Kim knew that, after six years of medical training. It was a marvel of genetic engineering; it was an awesome triumph of design. It could take abuse, lots of abuse – Kim had demonstrated that fact a time or two – in fact it could take a battering, a hammering, and it would still get up and brush itself down and come back for more. Sixty, seventy, eighty years or more. With just an oil change. Or, it could go wrong. Spectacularly wrong, sometimes, keeping people like Kim and Shallcross in very regular and lucrative employment for the rest of their lives. But what Kim had finally discovered, after all those years of training, was that there were only ever a thousand-and-one things that modern medicine could do about the million-and-one natural shocks that most human flesh is heir to. And this was one of those times. Here was the great big unknown. Here was a once-in-a-lifetime patient who had presented with something completely new, something that no one else had ever seen before, much less understood or cured. And there was nothing, absolutely nothing that Kim Alexander Maskell could do about it.

And that wasn't a very nice feeling.

By the time Shallcross got home that night there wasn't much of it left to call his own. He and his wife were due to meet some of her friends for a meal in the new Italian restaurant that had just opened in the village, so he would need to shower and change quickly and down a whopping great gin and tonic if there was to be any hope of him navigating his way through the evening politely.

His wife was a tall, elegant woman. She was tall to spite him. She towered over him, even without heels. Sometimes she reminded him of a Russian Empress, all bound up with pearls and polite and studied postures, and she seemed to choose her friends to match. And that always unsettled him. Prima donnas with attitude, all of them, and all looking down their long thin noses at him. He would need to visit the hives first. He would need to touch base with the bees and perhaps borrow a little of their venom from them in case he had to sting an odd baboon or two before the evening was out.

He stopped just short of the trees and contented himself with looking on from afar. He could see the hives very clearly. They looked white in the gathering dusk, but he knew better than to intrude upon their territory at this time of night. He had once watched a dog-fox make that mistake, sniffing and blundering its way right up to the hives at the end of a long hot summer's day. They had attacked him. Seen him off. In fact, they had declared war on him, total war; a war of annihilation. He had waited near the hives late into the evening, watching for the bees to finally reappear, and he often wondered what had become of the fox. Bees were like people: placid and tolerant one moment, savage the next. And just when you thought you knew all about them, everything they might say and do, just when your defences were down, that's exactly when they struck at you. Out of nowhere. And without mercy. People like Leonard Blake. An old man who could defy gravity and hover over a bed – and keep the secret to himself.

Of course, all his beekeeping plans for the weekend were in tatters. He had everything ready. He was going to smoke out the hives at the start of a full-scale spring clean. He even had a brand new full-length bee suit, bought especially for the occasion, hanging up in the garage. Now, instead, he would have to show his face at the hospital. Which was irritating, but necessary. Not necessary because it would have any effect at all on the treatment Blake was getting, but necessary because it might just help Shallcross himself to stop brooding over the man locked away in that stuffy little annexe on Ward 4.

With the exception of his wife's cooking, Shallcross believed that everything in life had an explanation, everything from angry bees to angry human beings. Earthquakes, tsunamis, wars, famines, even footballers earning more in a week that he earned in a year, they all had an explanation, however grim it might be, if you looked hard enough for it. And when it came to hunting down explanations, reasons, causes, effects, Shallcross was like a bulldog. He wouldn't let go, he didn't know how to let go, until he had found what he was looking for. In his line of business, if there was a symptom, there was a reason for it. If there was an ailment, then there was a cure for it, or at least an acknowledgment that no cure was possible, in which case his reputation and his determination remained untroubled. But now there was this bizarre old man, this stubbornly floating postman, who seemed to be able to defy all the known laws of physics; and try as he might, Shallcross could find no rhyme or reason for that. Newton was out the window. Gone.

Here, instead, was Leonard Blake, doing what everyone thought was quite impossible, and doing it without any fuss at all – and it was that that bothered George Shallcross most of all.

There was a bitter taste in his mouth tonight, and it had nothing to do with his gin or even his venom. It was the taste of ignorance, and it made him want to choke.

And that wasn't a very nice feeling.

———————————

Audrey arrived early for her night shift, giving herself time for a private chat with Gill Packer before the handover. She found her on Ward 2, in the office, smiling politely at two very earnest visitors. Audrey waved at her friend through the glass partition and then headed for the kitchen. By the time she had filled the kettle Gill had joined her and started to bang her head against a cupboard door.

"You have to love 'em," Audrey said with a smile.

"No, you don't! They're morons."

"What did they want? No! Don't tell me, I can see it in your face. A private room?"

"A private room. With an armchair and a telly."

"And a waiter with white gloves on?"

"Something like that. They said they would be willing to pay, if necessary, which I thought was jolly nice of them."

"What did you say? And don't leave anything out."

"I said no, we haven't got any private rooms or beds in a hospital this size. I told them they could take out a second mortgage and have their father moved to a private hospital where he would receive exactly the same treatment from exactly the same doctors, or they could leave him here, in the main ward with all the other members of the great unwashed, then they would have plenty of the legacy left after he's gone to go to Ibitha with."

"You didn't say that!"

"Of course not, but I wanted to. Anyway, some people are always going to be unhappy about something; they're just built that way."

46

"Change of subject. Any news on the annex?"

Gill poured hot water into two mugs. "It still has an occupant, if that's what you mean. We had a meeting at lunchtime."

"Who was there?"

"Liz, me, Shallcross, Kim."

"Iris?"

"No Iris. I sent her home for a break. She's back now."

Audrey considered for a moment. "Does she know what's going on? Has she said anything?"

"Not to me. I'm not sure she would talk to me, anyway, always assuming I could kick-start a conversation about her dying husband floating on a cushion of air. She likes you. She'll talk to you if she talks to anyone."

"Maybe. I'm not convinced. What about the meeting? Any big decisions made?"

Gill chuckled. "I'll give you one guess."

Audrey smiled as she sipped her tea. "Do nothing. Wait. Hope he dies."

Gill clapped. "Give the girl a coconut! But he's got to die before Monday."

"Why Monday?"

"You and I are both off duty, you to sleep, me to float down the Rhine, humming Wagner. If he's still around by then, they will need to recruit a new conspirator to help them keep the great secret safe."

Audrey snorted loudly. "If they keep a secret in this place, it will be the first time anyone has managed it."

"You haven't heard the best of it, yet. You and I are the only ones allowed in there. It's all barrier nursing from now on to scare off the natives. The notice was up for about ten minutes before the first nurse came to me and asked if it was still safe to work here."

"What do they think we've got in there, Frankenstein's monster?"

"Something like that. Everyone's getting mighty curious, I know that."

"Any change to the actual treatment?" Audrey asked.

"Nope. TLC, that's all we can do, really. Kim's on duty. He said he would call by, later in the evening."

After the formal handover, Audrey made Leonard Blake her first port of call. Iris had slotted herself back into place at his side, and so Audrey contented herself with checking the syringe-driver and the saline drip. It was then that she noticed that the patient's lips were dry and beginning to crack.

"Can't be doing with that, Leonard," she said good-humouredly, winking at Iris. "I'm going to get something to moisten his lips with, make him a little more comfortable. Tea?" Iris shook her head. "Have you eaten?" Iris nodded. No, Audrey thought, you're not the most talkative of women.

She collected a pair of latex gloves, a disposable apron, a bowl of water, some wipes, a towel, and a handful of swabs – absorbent sponge squares on lollipop sticks – and a new, unopened roll of cotton wool, and then she stacked all her wares on the locker next to the bed. Lifting up the coverlet, she placed the roll of cotton wool on the edge of the bed while she reached for a wipe. As she moved, her hip brushed the roll of cotton wool and sent it sliding across the mattress. Lifting the coverlet a little higher, she looked into the bed for a moment and then quietly settled the coverlet back into place.

Kim preferred the doctors' common room to his basement flat on a hot, balmy night like this. The flat felt damp even during a heatwave, and late at night the woodchip and magnolia walls seemed to close in around him like a shrinking prison cell, so he spent the evening sprawled in an armchair with one eye on the television and the other eye on the corridor.

So far it had been a quiet evening. No emergencies and no admissions to disturb the steak and ale pie, and just the one phone call, from his pal Tom over at the Children's Hospital. Tom was planning a 'beer and birds weekend' and was checking to see whether Kim was in the mood for fun, but when he heard that Kim had to work all over the weekend he tittered his sympathy very unconvincingly and rang off as soon as he could.

Just then a black silhouette filled the doorway. Kim shielded his eyes and saw the night sister beckoning to him with a long, slow hooking motion of her finger.

"I don't like the look of this," he said, heaving himself slowly out of his chair. "Where are you taking me?"

"Where do you think?"

They walked up the stairs side by side, and Kim could just make out that Audrey was humming a tune to herself. That and the absence of her usual dry banter was a warning sign that he had learned to note without comment. When they reached Leonard Blake's room the first thing that Kim looked for was the expression on Iris's face. It was unchanged, as far as he could tell, so they were still in the game for now. He glanced around the room. Everything was in its usual place. Then Audrey beckoned him to the far side of the bed and lifted up the coverlet.

Kim stooped down to conceal his face from Iris. "What am I looking for?" he whispered.

In reply, the night sister placed her hand under the patient's back and moved it up and down the bed.

"Not with you," Kim whispered again.

Audrey tugged at his sleeve and bundled him back out of the room and then marched him into the ward office and deposited him in a chair so that she could stand over him with her hands on her hips.

"Okay, so what did I do wrong? What have I missed this time?"

"Do I have to paint you a picture? I thought you were supposed to be bright, you young doctors. You must be blind not to see it. He's moved! Any idiot can see that."

"Well, this idiot can't. He doesn't look as though he's moved a muscle all day. All week, come to that."

"And that may well be true, Boy Wonder, but he has risen. He is higher above the bed than he was before!"

Now Kim understood the humming as they walked up the stairs. "Are you sure?" he asked as a surge of adrenalin collided with his bladder.

"Of course I'm sure! Gill told me she measured the gap at lunchtime, and I've just measured it again now."

Kim nodded. "I remember. She said the gap was about four to five centimetres. What do you make it now?"

Audrey picked up a ruler from the desk and placed her thumb and forefinger against it like pincers. "That's the gap Gill measured. Equal to the width of a hand minus the thumb joint. Four, five centimetres, give or take. What I was trying to show you just now is that I can put my whole hand under him. I noticed it when my roll of cotton wool went clean under him and out the other side. Twenty-four centimetres!" she announced proudly. "He's moved." She pointed at the ceiling with a wicked smile. "That-a-way!"

Kim plunged his fingers into his unruly hair and blew his cheeks out wearily. Then he looked at the night sister hopefully. "That is a King's Fund bed. It has a height adjustment mechanism."

But Audrey was already shaking her head. "Of course it does! And it was set at maximum height at lunchtime and it's set at maximum height now. No, Sherlock, it's not the bed that's moved; it's the patient. Our friend Leonard Blake is on the up-and-up."

Kim placed his hands on his head and swivelled backwards and forwards in the chair, thinking hard. "Okay," he said finally, "what do we do now?"

"We?" Audrey picked up the phone and graciously handed it to him.

———————————

Once Kim knew that Shallcross was on his way he flew down to the switchboard, begged the linen room key from the night porter, and quickly found himself a clean white coat to wear. Once he began to look the part he rushed back to the flat and brushed his teeth fiercely until his gums bled, and then he rinsed his mouth with a stinging antibacterial mouthwash until he was as sure as he could be that he had removed all traces of beer from his breath. Finally he retraced his steps to the ward office and sat down to wait for Shallcross to arrive.

Telephoning the Great Man at home at midnight on a Friday evening was just about the most nerve-wracking thing that Kim had ever had to do. When he pressed the last digit and actually heard the phone beginning to ring, his heart leapt into his mouth. He could picture the phone at the consultant's bedside. A four-poster bed, all pastel pinks and flowing folds of silk, edged with ermine. Shallcross and his wife slumbering peacefully. He winced as he imagined the shrill, harsh bell clanging in their ears, catapulting them awake and making them fumble around in the dark for bedside lights and glasses and alarm clocks, all because he, Kim Maskell, had decided to wet himself and cry for help. He was doomed.

Then a quiet voice answered the phone and Kim thought he had dialled the wrong number. Shallcross had to say hello three times before Kim could bring himself to answer him, but when he did, and when he stammered out his reason for calling him at this time of night, Shallcross listened carefully, said "I'm coming in," and then quietly replaced the receiver.

When Shallcross arrived in the flesh, the feeling of unreality persisted. Kim was reeking of spearmint mouthwash but even the medicinal haze all around him could not conceal the fact that it was Shallcross who was filling the room with the fragrance of garlic, and while the creases in Kim's white coat were still sharp enough to cut paper, Shallcross was wearing a shabby old jumper and a pair of jeans. Wasn't the Universe supposed to explode when matter and anti-matter came together like that? And then there was the voice. Shallcross was speaking quietly. And when the consultant even accepted Audrey's offer of a cup of tea, Kim nearly fell off his chair.

The two men sat facing one another while they waited for the kettle to boil. They were knee to knee. Kim felt like he was sitting with the Headmaster in a tiny study, waiting for the muffins to brown, and for somebody to pinch him awake. His mouth was bone dry, thanks to the mouthwash, and at this range Shallcross had to be dead to miss the hint of what Kim had been up to.

"I'm sorry I had to wake you," Kim muttered nervously for the third time.

Shallcross shrugged. "Not a problem. I wasn't asleep. You did the right thing." He even smiled when Audrey handed him his mug of tea. A Shallcross smile was probably a collector's item. "So, in old fashioned money, our man has risen by about eight inches in the last ten hours. That leaves me with three questions I want answered."

"How?" Kim suggested.

"And why. And when – or where – will it stop?"

Kim nodded. "I'll just settle for 'how' for the time being. There's a man in there that can just ignore all the known laws of science when he feels like it. What he's doing is a physical impossibility."

Shallcross smiled again. "Not anymore it's not. So let's stick with 'how'."

Kim thought for a moment and then took a deep breath and jumped in. "Off the top of my head, I don't think it's him. Not the man himself."

"Why not?"

"He's sedated. Unconscious. He's incapable of any normal voluntary physical movement. Ergo, he's not doing it intentionally, consciously, or by design."

"Fair enough, setting aside the word 'normal' for now. So, is it unconscious, or subconscious? Is it something that his body is doing all on its own?"

"Or is it the room?" Kim suddenly suggested.

Shallcross blinked extravagantly. "Why do you say that? How can it be the room? His wife has spent almost as much time in that room as her husband and she isn't clinging to the ceiling like a bat."

Kim's cheeks flushed as he tried to marshal his thoughts. He wasn't likely to keep Shallcross's mind company for long. "A human mind can't just decide to lift its host up into the air like that whenever the mood takes it. I know we haven't mapped out all the functions of the human brain yet but I'm pretty sure they don't include levitation."

"There are more things in heaven and earth, Horatio, than are dreamt of in your philosophy," Shallcross replied, amused by the look on Kim's face. "We'll leave science fiction well alone for now and stay with what we know best. And let's do what we should have done in the first place, if we'd had our wits about us. Let's do some simple, basic tests, even the ones we've done already. Let's start the process of elimination from first principles. Take some bloods – now, tonight – and get them over to the lab by taxi. Get them to drag someone out of bed and process them for us. Mark them urgent; use my name; tell them I'm waiting for the results. Then get hold of an electroencephalograph. Get Audrey to track it down for you. There's bound to be one around here somewhere. If there's anything untoward going on with his brain activity, that might be our starting point. All we need is a clue. I'll be content with that. Just one clue."

Kim would have been well advised not to think out loud as they both got up to leave the office. "Maybe the oxygen content of his blood? Or his bowel movements?"

Shallcross stopped in the doorway and stared at his young colleague. "Which do you want: human balloon or hovercraft?"

When Shallcross finally got home again that night he only managed a few more hours of sleep before he was awakened by the dawn. He got out of bed and stood at the bedroom window to watch the first faint traces of daylight beginning to appear in the garden through a dense white mist. At one point just the topmost branches of a tree appeared above the mist, seeming to hang motionless in the air forty feet from the ground, before the mist began to disperse and the huge trunk took form beneath it. The irony was not lost on Shallcross.

Nevertheless, whether he was short on sleep or not, the weekend began remarkably well for him, and it gave him no hint at all that he stood on the brink of a stunning personal defeat.

He and his wife took their breakfast out onto the terrace, and while he flicked through the pages of The Times she thoughtfully surveyed the newly planted borders. Conversation was desultory but there was nothing new in that. She critiqued last night's meal, and he critiqued the waiter who had tripped over his feet and deposited lasagne on Shallcross's shoes. His wife laughed, which Shallcross found oddly unsettling. She refilled the coffee pot, and then they munched on toast and honey while he exclaimed at the latest football transfer fee and she stared at the trees in the distance. Finally, deceptively demure, she asked him to describe how his morning would unfold, when, as she insisted on putting it, "he blew smoke up his hives". He should have been warned by her simpering smile, especially when she worried that the bees might all get cancer; but it was Saturday, after all, and he was rather tired, all said and done, and his defences were down.

After breakfast he dressed for battle, and his wife very nearly overplayed her hand when she waved him off to war and then swung her arms with a martial rhythm as he marched down the garden beneath his flowing gauze headdress. There was a brief pause for elevenses – another cafetiére of coffee and a batch of newly baked scones – at which point their daughter Caroline unexpectedly appeared on the scene. When he returned to the hives she sat with her mother and shared a whispered, tittering conversation with her that still gave him no real sense of his impending doom.

Shortly before lunch, and while he was still down among the trees and the drifting clouds of smoke, he heard a van approach the house and brake to a halt on the gravel. Then he could hear a man's voice in conversation with his wife and his daughter, and several times he heard loud, shrill laughter. He half expected someone to call him or approach the trees and the hives, perhaps a colleague in search of advice, or a neighbour coming to complain of the smoke and the smell. But, instead, nothing happened, and soon even the conversation and the laughter died away, until finally there was a long period of almost complete silence, at the end of which a door slammed and the van drove away again. Not a colleague then and not a neighbour. The postman? Not a hint or a clue until, loud and very clear, he heard his wife call out, "Charles! Oh Charles! Do come and get your lunch, dear!" at which point, when it was already far, far too late, he felt his blood turn to ice.

He walked slowly up the garden path, an instinctively beaten man, to view the scale of his wife's triumph. In the middle of the lawn – *his* lawn, proudly, meticulously manicured – there now stood a circular metal fence surrounding a squat, ugly, green and yellow plastic egloo. It was strategically placed right in front of the French windows so that he couldn't see the trees and the hives from the sitting room, but there was no mystery to this new acquisition. After all, it had been his catalogue first of all, and he knew even before he saw them strutting into view that his precious lawn had been invaded by three large, bright orange chickens.

"Come and meet our new pets, dear," his wife invited him warmly, while Caroline wiped tears from her eyes. "They've all got names, and the nice man who just delivered them said you don't even have to puff smoke at them."

And, as Shallcross looked on, quite speechless, one of the chickens excised a large piece of turf with a flick of its claw and with surgical precision.

5

"And, to make matters worse – you won't believe this when I tell you – she bought them from the same bloody place that sold me my bees! Using my own catalogue! Now, what do you think of that!" Shallcross hammered each word home by beating the arm of the chair with his fist, while his face was contorted with the shock of betrayal.

"I must be missing something," Gill Packer admitted frankly, while still managing to keep a perfectly straight face. "Why does that make matters worse?"

Shallcross couldn't believe his ears. "Why? Because it just does, that's why. All the business I've put their way and then they go and sell her... chickens!"

Kim Maskell chose this moment to blunder into the room without knocking. Gill Packer looked up at him and fired the first volley. "Have you heard?"

Kim's face froze. "Has he...?"

"Mrs Shallcross bought three chickens!"

Kim looked at Shallcross, uncertain of what to say or do next. The consultant seemed to be waiting for a response of some kind. "From the same people who sold me my bees!" he explained.

"Disloyal," Kim suggested.

"Disloyal! An act of sheer bloody treachery, the..."

"Right!"

Liz Manners had been sorting through some paperwork on her desk while Shallcross told them his sorry tale, but now that Kim had arrived she was keen to get on with the meeting. And bees and chickens were not on her agenda.

"Let's start. Thanks for coming, and thanks for putting off Sunday lunch. I thought there was no point in waiting until tomorrow, now that things seem to have moved on."

"Or up," Kim added just audibly.

"Quite." Liz took a deep breath and then sighed heavily before she spoke. "This problem isn't going to go away so we need to work out a strategy. And we need to do that now. Starting point? Twenty-four hours from now – assuming he's still alive – we will need at least one extra pair of hands to help us hold the fort. Any comments so far?"

"Must we?" Shallcross asked with a grimace. "Word is bound to get out if we do."

"Word is bound to get out anyway," Gill Packer said. "It's only a matter of time. This place is too small to keep anyone under wraps in for very long. As soon as you do anything out of the ordinary in this building, you invite attention. It's inevitable. Its human nature."

"Not if we choose wisely," Shallcross suggested. "Surely you have another sister you can call on?"

"It's not just nursing cover we need," Liz reminded them, pointing at Kim. "You will have been on duty all weekend. You need a rest as much as anyone." She sat back in her chair and tapped her pencil on the edge of the table. "I did think of covering the nursing side of things myself. I am, after all, a fully qualified Nursing Officer when I'm not pushing paper round this desk, but I would attract even more attention, and I've got a hospital to manage, too. So, step number one. We do indeed recruit a new sister, and I would suggest Pam Corin. Experienced, trustworthy, doesn't flap in a crisis."

"Sounds ideal," Kim said.

"The tone of your voice makes me curious to know what step number two is," Shallcross said warily.

"I'll come on to that in a minute. Let's deal with Pam Corin first. Recruiting her into our ranks isn't going to solve anything. She'll buy us a little more time, that's all. Gill's right, we're on borrowed time already. Tomorrow's Monday and the place will be heaving. Sooner or later someone is going to blunder into what we're trying to hide from them."

"I don't agree," Shallcross began, still nettled by his own secret demon with a beak.

"Well, you should!" Liz said crossly, cutting him short. "That's life. People are curious, people talk. As soon as anyone gets a whiff of what's going on, it will be all round the building like the flu. But that's not my primary concern."

"Here comes step number two," Shallcross said, gritting his teeth. "And I just know I'm not going to like it."

Liz ignored him. "Let me sum things up simply. We have a man in the annexe that is terminally ill, but rather reluctant to die. That same man is the subject of an extraordinary phenomenon which none of us can even begin to explain. Are these two facts related to one another? We don't know. In fact, that's pretty much our default position in all of this: we don't know. He should be dead; he isn't dead. Do we know why? No. Will he die anyway, and will he die soon? We don't know. And what happens if and when he does die? Does he stay there for good? We don't know. And how should we deal with this phenomenon when it is resolved? Hide it? Forget it? Report it, and get ourselves sectioned? I can spend the rest of the day finding questions that need answers, but I can't find any answers at all. Conclusion? We are floundering around in the dark, and we need help. We need to bring other people in on this. People who are capable of dealing with a crisis of this kind. We can't keep going on our own."

"No, no, no!" Shallcross exclaimed, just as she knew he would. "In one breath you talk about trying to keep it all hush-hush, and in the next breath you want to shout, 'Help!' from the rooftop. You might as well hold a news conference and be done with it."

The Hospital Manager aimed the tip of her pencil at the consultant like a rapier. "That's exactly what I don't want to do. It's all very well keeping a door shut and telling everyone to mind their own business, but we have a duty of care to uphold in all of this. It's our duty to care for Leonard Blake, his wife, and all the other patients – and the staff – in this building. We risk a disastrous breakdown in our function as a healthcare unit if we just wait until the rumour-mongers find their way into the Ward 4 annexe."

"So what are you suggesting?" Gill Packer asked, bemused, wondering where her boss was going with this.

"You obviously have someone in mind," Shallcross said, eyeing her darkly.

"Of course I have. God knows, I've spent enough time thinking about this. It's not just a name I plucked out of the air." She took another deep breath. This was the moment she had been dreading; the moment when she lit Shallcross's blue touchpaper and then ran for cover. "The Chief Executive," she said flatly.

Shallcross couldn't have roared more loudly if she had stuck the pencil in his eye.

"Who's the Chief Executive?" Kim Maskell asked.

"Paul somebody," Gill replied.

"Gravett, Paul Gravett," Liz corrected her.

"The most complete and utter moron ever to walk God's earth!" Shallcross proclaimed in a plaintive voice.

"And he wouldn't be my choice, either, if we had a choice, which we do not. Like it or not, he's the man in charge. He's the one with the grand-sounding title and the six-figure salary. He is where the buck stops. End of discussion."

"The man is without competence of any kind," Shallcross bellowed, grimacing as though he'd just swallowed rancid butter. "Paul Bloody Gravett! He's an accountant! I wouldn't trust him any farther than I could spit his entrails. He's not even a trained hospital administrator."

"I couldn't answer that, one way or the other. But I do know that *you* are not a trained hospital administrator either, and my training certainly didn't prepare me for anything like this. I'm not just out of my comfort zone, I'm out of my league." She paused, and then tried another approach. "Look, we keep the secret for another few hours, another few days, it makes no difference. Sooner or later word gets out and all hell breaks loose, and we will have the Press down on us like a ton of bricks. Everyone's Press. Every tuppenny-ha'penny newspaper from here to Istanbul that's got a spare inch of print space to fill will be camped on our doorstep. And that, folks, will be game over. We will not be able to function as a hospital anymore. When that time comes, we will need the man with the clout all prepped up and ready to go, and, whether we like it or not, that man is Paul Gravett."

Everyone looked at Shallcross and waited.

"I'd rather remove my own spleen with a fork!" he confided to the ceiling.

"Well, that doesn't help us at all," Gill suddenly announced, flapping at him like a bothersome fly. "Liz, I agree with you. Wholeheartedly. I can't think why we didn't do it in the first place."

Liz heaved a sigh of relief, grateful for her support. "And that's very likely what Paul Gravett himself will say."

Kim chose a spot on the carpet and studied it carefully, principally so that he could avoid Shallcross's glowering eyes. "I think I'm inclined to agree with you, too. I don't know the man, but if, as you say, he is the boss, then he seems the obvious person to turn to. You may not rate him personally," he added with a half glance towards his boss, "but he may be able to put us in touch with people who can help us, people who have the expertize to deal with this kind of thing." He paused for a moment and then frowned as a new thought occurred to him. "Up until now it seems to me we've been trivializing what we're faced with here. Maybe that's just our way of dealing with it. Keeping a handle on it. But whatever that thing is that's going on in there, with that old man, it's important. It's new. It's different. It's never happened before, that we know of. Liz, what did you say it was – an extraordinary phenomenon? It could just turn out to be one of the defining moments of our time, and as soon as I say that I can feel the hairs on the back of my neck standing up. And this cannot be just our secret, it really can't, you know. We have to share this with others. We have to understand it. Witness it – and understand it. All of us. So, Liz, yes, you make that call."

By the time he had finished speaking Shallcross had fallen silent. The consultant contented himself with gnawing at his fingernails and staring into space, shaking his head despondently from time to time.

"Then I make the call?" Liz asked the meeting.

"Yes, you make the call," Gill said immediately.

Liz looked at Shallcross and he merely shrugged. "I want to hear you say it," she insisted.

"Call him then. But don't expect me to speak to him."

"Oh, don't worry, I'll speak to him; I'm ready for that. That's the bonus that comes with my five-figure salary. I won't phone him now, not from here. I'll wait till I get home where I can speak more freely. I'll ask him to call in and meet with us first thing tomorrow morning."

"Why must he come here?" Shallcross demanded to know, crumpling his face up in a most unpleasant way. "The merest glimpse of the man offends me."

Gill exploded with laughter. It was a pure, exuberant, trilling outburst of mirth, and it left Shallcross completely mystified. "I really do think that's the funniest thing I've ever heard!" she said, trying to get her breath back. "Every time I go into that room I can't believe my eyes, and here you are, on the point of suggesting that we tell someone all about it over the phone! Priceless!"

"Will you still speak to Sister Corin?" Kim asked.

Liz nodded. "We still need her, at least until the Great Man gives judgement. I'll see her before I go."

"And Mrs Blake?" Gill asked.

"What about her?" Liz asked.

"Well, somebody needs to sit her down and talk all this through with her. It is her husband we're discussing, after all."

"Is that covered by your salary, too?" Shallcross asked with an unfriendly little smirk.

"I would hope it's covered by my humanity," Liz said honestly. She decided to stand up to indicate that, as far as she was concerned, the meeting was over. Shallcross pushed his chair back and marched to the door. With one hand on the door handle he turned to deliver his parting shot at the Hospital Manager but she was waiting for him and she judged the moment to perfection.

"Regards to your wife," she said warmly. "Tell her I'd love some eggs."

The door slammed with such a force that the papers on her desk lifted in the breeze.

Liz waited for Kim and Gill to leave and then she packed her briefcase, turned off the desk lamp and prepared to leave the room. She would make Iris Blake her first stop, and then she would seek out Pam Corin at the end of her lunch break. But when she opened the door she stopped in her tracks. Sitting just a few feet away from her at the hatch to the General Office was the Head Porter.

"What do you want?" she asked him curtly, standing with her hand on the doorknob.

Tiny Adams might have been studying a picture for all the attention he gave to her question. Of course, he had placed himself there quite deliberately, she could see that. He had engineered the moment. He had wanted to be absolutely sure that she would walk out of her office and all but trip over his huge, outstretched legs.

Her temper snapped the moment she set eyes on him, coming like a rush of bile to her mouth, bitter and nauseous. She loathed the man and he knew it, and he loathed her in return. She had often tried to describe him to her husband and she never quite succeeded in grasping what it was about him that repelled her. She always ended up referring to him as a dinosaur because he moved slowly, ponderously, because he was lazy and sly, and because he was the complete antithesis of everything she stood for. And she was stuck with him. He had come with the fixtures and the fittings of the place when Gravett had handed it over to her to call her very own. He opposed her in everything, turning sloth into an art form. But one day he would slip up, and when he did she would be waiting for him.

"I said, 'What do you want?'"

Tiny shrugged extravagantly. "Nothing."

"Then what are you just sitting there like a gargoyle for?" she asked him brutally. "Haven't you got any work to do?"

He was no more than ten feet from her door. She would give real money to know how long he had been there and how much he had heard.

"It's me lunch break. I'm taking a breather." And he slowly positioned his hands on his vast stomach and smiled like a Buddha.

"Why are you even here at all? You don't work weekends."

"Why are you?" he replied, sharp as a tack.

"I have work to do," she said, furious with herself for blushing. "Something you wouldn't understand." She decided to end the conversation before it had even started, and she turned her back on him and walked away down the corridor towards Ward 4.

She stopped at the lift and accosted a nurse who chose that moment to return to the ward from the cafeteria with her lunch in her hand. Out of the corner of her eye Liz watched to see which way the Head Porter would go. When he guessed that she was watching him he heaved himself out of the chair and slowly walked off in the opposite direction. Liz abandoned the nurse in mid-sentence and poked her head into the ward office.

Gill Packer had the phone to her ear, but she covered the mouthpiece with her hand when she saw the expression on Liz's face. "I take it you saw him."

Liz nodded. "Do you think he was listening?"

"Depends how long he was there."

"Has he been along here at all?"

"I don't know. I don't think so, but I could ask."

Liz hesitated for a moment. "Better not. Just keep an eye open for him. I don't want him anywhere near that room. He's not to be trusted."

"Understood." And Gill went back to her call.

Liz crossed to the annexe door, tapped gently, and stepped inside. Then she gasped and put her hand to her throat. She had been thinking of nothing but Leonard Blake for days. Day and night, pretty much her every waking thought was about him. But she hadn't found the time to go back to the annexe, and so nothing had prepared her for what she saw.

The curtains were drawn, keeping out the bright spring sunshine, and the room was warm, filled with rank, stale air. Iris was where Iris always was, at her husband's bedside, but Liz could only be sure of that when she stepped fully into the room because Leonard Blake now floated between the two women, more than a metre above his bed. He was still draped in the blue coverlet. It clung to his contours, accentuating them, before it plunged all the way to the floor on either side of him. Liz almost laughed. How could anyone keep all this a secret? She stepped back and leaned against the wall, grateful for the feel of something cold and hard and real. Whatever this thing was, it was mocking them. It might have been eavesdropping on their conversation in her office for all she knew. Perhaps it had drawn her here to goad her with her ignorance. To remind her of the vastness of all that she did not know, and perhaps would never know, even now. She could sense the laughter, the mockery. Or was that her? Was she laughing at herself, tucked away in this tiny little broom cupboard? Was she suitably reduced in size, now that her intelligence, her experience, her faith in a neat and tidy world had all been stripped away from her?

This was the unknown. And, for this moment at least, it terrified her.

She had been in the room for several minutes before it dawned on her that Iris Blake was watching her, studying every expression on her face, and probably wondering when she might finally get around to saying something to her. She took refuge in the first platitude that came to mind. "How are you?"

Iris raised one eyebrow. Was this all she had to say?

"Really. I mean, how are you? How are *you*?"

"I'm fine," the old woman said quietly. Then she looked away, seemed to make up her mind about something, and suddenly stood up. That way she could look at her husband's face. Liz thought that she looked suddenly very old and tired. Her shoulders sagged as though her coat was too heavy for her, her eyes had blood-red rims, and her cheeks were gaunt and hollow in spite of the face powder she still applied a dozen times a day out of habit. Her cheeks were stained, too, where she had been crying and then wiping away the evidence, not wanting to share the grief with anyone. Not wanting to show her weakness to anyone if they were watching. If they cared. Liz wondered how much more she could take of this heart-breaking, dusty little anteroom.

"He's not in any pain," Liz heard herself say in that irritating, unfeeling professional voice that seemed to spring to her lips unbidden at times like this. "You can at least be sure of that."

"Can I?" Iris Blake asked. "How?"

Liz hadn't heard that voice before. It was prickling with anger, sharp and hard and accusing, either on the verge of rage or collapse.

"He's very heavily sedated. He can't feel anything on a regime of medication as strong as that. He won't be aware of anything, I can promise you that."

Iris snorted with what seemed like disgust and then she very deliberately stood upright until she winced with the effort. Liz could have kicked herself that she hadn't thought of it before. The old woman wasn't just grieving, she was in pain – real physical pain – trapped inside this airless little cell with nothing to do but wait for death to come along and send her home empty-handed. No one had thought of offering painkillers to the one person in the room who still needed them.

Iris was looking out of the window when she spoke again. "They say patients still hear you, even when they are in a coma." It wasn't a question. She sounded like a schoolteacher addressing a class.

"I believe that's true, based on my own experience as a nurse."

"Do you?" Iris abruptly turned to face her. "Is that why we're all determined not to say anything of the least importance in this room? Because he might be listening to us? Because he might actually hear what we are all saying about him? About what's happening to him?"

Liz blushed deeply. "I'm not sure what you want me to say."

Iris wandered back to the bedside and looked at her husband again. "I don't suppose you do. I expect we've all got lots of questions, between us."

"And not enough answers to go round."

Iris grunted.

It was like meeting a different woman, a perfect stranger. Liz regretted thinking of her, when she thought of her at all, as a stereotype, a caricature, a thing of paste and cardboard, instead of a human being. She had made all sorts of assumptions about her. She had labelled her. Categorized her, because that was the simple and the easy thing to do. And then put her to one side. To that part of her mind where people didn't matter.

"I've come to tell you about our plans, such as they are," Liz said, aware of how arrogantly they had all discussed those plans without her.

Just for a moment Iris gave her the distinct impression that she was listening, not to her, but to somebody else, somebody who was in the room, but somebody that Liz could neither see nor hear herself. And when, suddenly, Iris said, "Your plans?" she seemed only then to fully return her attention to her.

It was time for the truth. Anything else now would be insulting. Liz pointed towards the patient in the huge, grotesque coverlet. Of course, it looked like a shroud. It made him look as though he was lying on some kind of dais, all trussed up like a sacrificial offering.

"We are worried about what will happen when word of this gets out, but we have to plan for all eventualities, so we are going to contact the Chief Executive, the man who heads up the Trust."

"What's the point of that?" Iris asked brusquely.

Liz decided to start again, and from a different angle. "Obviously, we can't move your husband, so whatever happens to him in the coming hours or days is going to happen to him here, in this hospital, and very likely in this room. These are our parameters and we can't do anything to change them. We don't know what's going to happen next, and we don't know what the consequences will be, but this is a hospital and we have a lot of people to think about, so we're going to brief the man at the top in case we need him in a hurry."

Iris sat down again and smoothed the creases out of her coat. "Mrs Manners," she said quietly, "you are not going to keep this a secret." She waved a hand at her husband.

Liz would always remember that moment. It was a curious mix of embarrassment, fear and excitement. The moment when she was sure that, sooner or later, something would happen.

"If word of this gets out… If we don't control how word of this gets out, then there's going to be chaos, Mrs Blake. We'll be swamped. Press, T.V., they'll swarm all over us. We won't be able to move!"

"I quite understand that the rest of the hospital is your first concern," Iris said, linking her hands together in her lap.

"That's not what I said. Your husband is in our care, Mrs Blake, and I want to make sure that we really do look after him. I don't want him turned into some kind of tourist attraction, or even an object of ridicule, just when he is preparing to leave this life."

Iris Blake glared at her, unable to stop her jaw trembling. If she cried now, she thought, it would never stop. "I didn't mean to imply that I was going to tell anyone. I haven't even told my own children about this yet." She saw the relief in the Hospital Manager's eyes. "I just said you will not keep this a secret."

And with that the conversation was at an end.

After the meeting Kim wandered back to the switchboard on his way to a sly lunch at the Queen's Head, but there was no way he was going to jump ship until he was sure that Shallcross had left the building. He glanced out of the door and recognized the consultant's car parked across the road so he decided to loiter at the kiosk. He poked his head inside, ready to smile at the telephonist, but it was Tiny Adams he found poring over a newspaper.

"Wow!" Kim exclaimed, pretending to recoil in shock. "You're not Jenny! If I didn't know any better I would say you are the spitting image of a certain Head Porter known to frequent these parts. But today is Sunday so I must be dreaming."

Tiny regarded him for a moment and then slowly smiled as though he was the villain in a horror film and Kim was his unsuspecting victim. "I can soon wake you up if you want me to. Waste-of-space Danny phoned in sick, the lying little toe-rag. I'll give him sick when I see him! Sitting at home with his feet up, watching the box, while I do all the bleedin' work!"

Kim smiled. "Why do bad things always happen to good people? Still, look on the bright side. You're not likely to die of overwork in this place on a Sunday afternoon, are you?" His guard dropped without making a sound.

"Not with all you lot here to help me, I won't. If you've got the time, of course, what with all the secret chinwags you have going on between you. What were you all talking about in Her Ladyship's office just now?"

"Don't ask me!" Kim said, taken completely unawares.

"But I *am* asking you," Tiny reminded him, standing up and emerging from the kiosk as though it was his shell. "Chapter and verse, and leave nothing out, if you don't want me to start logging your on-duty visits to the pub."

Kim was kicking himself. He should have had the courage of his convictions, Shallcross or no Shallcross. He should have marched straight out of that door and straight into the bar. He would have been sitting on a stool with a pint in his hand by now, instead of standing here blushing like a thief caught red-handed.

"Nothing to write home about. A couple of case studies we needed to chew over."

"Bollocks!" Tiny snapped at him, spitting out the word like a gobbet of phlegm. "A consultant, a ward sister, the Hospital Manager, and sweet little old you, all tucked up huggermugger in the old bint's office like a bunch of spies. Sunday lunchtime. Case studies! You must think I was born yesterday."

Kim started to back away, smiling and shrugging his innocence awkwardly. "Sorry, Tiny. That's all there is."

But as he stepped back, so Tiny stepped forward and took hold of his shoulder with an iron grip. "Know what? I think you're telling me porky pies. I think you're hiding a dark little secret, all of you. And I'm betting it's got something to do with that old codger and his missis on Ward 4." He looked fixedly at Kim, waiting for him to move a muscle of his face.

Kim tried to brush his hand away, still with an embarrassed smile, but when Tiny wouldn't let go he started to prize his stubby fingers off one by one. Quite suddenly Tiny released his grip and slid back into the kiosk. Kim looked round and saw Shallcross in conversation with Liz Manners at the far end of the corridor. When they saw him they both gathered pace, and as they swept by the switchboard and out of the front door, Kim fell into step with them and then heaved a huge sigh of relief as he reached the street.

"That was getting very uncomfortable," Kim said, wiping beads of sweat from his face.

"What did he want?" Liz asked, pulling Kim away from the open window behind the switchboard.

"I'll give you one guess. I'm not sure what he does know yet, but he's on the right track. He mentioned Blake."

"By name?" Liz asked.

"As good as."

All three walked towards Shallcross's car which was parked for once only a short distance from the main entrance.

"Don't tell him anything," Shallcross reminded him. He climbed into his car and lowered the window to speak to Liz Manners. "Ring me. Let me know what Gravett says."

"I will, if there's anything to report. He may not be in. He may just not answer the phone. It is Sunday, after all. In the real world," she added longingly.

Shallcross sniffed contemptuously and then started the engine. "He probably has all his calls diverted to a secretary, even at weekends. That or an answerphone telling everyone he's too important to talk to the likes of them."

Liz shrugged. "I'll settle for that. As long as I can get him here first thing tomorrow." She waited for Shallcross to engage first gear and start to move away, and then she quickly bent down to the window. "Don't forget the eggs!"

She jerked her head back as the car sped away. After Shallcross had disappeared from sight Kim walked Liz to her car and then waved her away, too. By now he was past caring. He darted straight across the road and then straight down the side street towards the Queen's Head. This time, he thought, it's medicinal.

Shallcross was wrong about Paul Gravett. True, he had never trained to be a hospital administrator, but neither had he ever been an accountant. Whenever he had need of either of those skillsets in the day-to-day running of a citywide healthcare trust that included six major hospitals and various other satellite clinics, he had plenty of fully qualified and highly experienced administrators and accountants and even lawyers at his beck and call. What Paul Gravett 'brought to the table' – one of his inexhaustible supply of clichéd sound bites – was himself; and the Chief Executive of the City Hospitals Trust was a work of art.

It had taken years to transform this supremely malleable man of the people into what he was today – a carefully cultivated and meticulously well groomed image of business acumen. And the image was so perfect in every detail that it had no need of substance at all, leading many people to believe that the man himself had no heart. What Paul Gravett was thoroughly schooled in was grassroots management of the thick-skinned, street-wise variety – the sort of management that left the scene strewn with bodies while the man himself remained impervious to either injury or blame. Like a conjuror, he could toss and scatter people and resources around a spreadsheet like spinning plates, sometimes managing to keep everything and everyone airborne at the same time, and sometimes breaking a great deal of crockery and careers, but always keeping all the detritus and the blood, sweat and tears well away from his Saville Row suit and his Teflon-coated reputation.

What he was in a nutshell was a chimera, a creature capable of infinite mutation and reinvention. He devoured sound bites and ideas – other people's ideas – and then spewed them all out again as fragments of wit and wisdom which he peddled as his own. He was a parasite, and that helped him to be a survivor in a grubby world. He became the embodiment of style and urbanity, and like all phantoms he could turn into a wisp of smoke in an instant if ever he was confronted in the clear light of day. When the time and the opportunity came along, it was so simple for a man like Paul Gravett just to segue into the plum new job of "bossing the doctors", because he could always rely on bluff and bluster – and the wits and hard work of others – to do the rest.

For the most part Gravett's working day was spent in a huge office in a huge tower block that rose up like a phallus out of the heart of the County Hospital. His office doubled as a conference room – dubbed 'the spider's web' by his detractors – and one way or another he usually managed to steer well clear of hospital wards and sick people. But his smile and his loose, limp handshake, or even the mere thought of them, could spread fear and uncertainty like a contagion into every corner of the sprawling organisation he controlled. To him and to the shadowy team of 'consultants' that seemed to people so many of his conversations, a fully-equipped ward with its quota of patients and staff seemed to be an unconscionable waste of taxpayers' money – an indulgence, something that needed to be modified (a favourite term), streamlined, rationalized, or squeezed, crushed and filleted, until the accountants who really did collate all the spreadsheets for him finally smiled with satisfaction.

One thing that Paul Gravett could always be relied upon never to do was to visit the smallest of his hospitals. It was, after all, a tediously long way away from his office, right the way over on the other side – the unfashionable side – of the city, and the seafront road was always a permanent traffic jam. It was little more than a street-corner hovel anyway, and whenever he did go there he always expected to bump into Charles Dickens taking notes. It was the National Health Service's take on The Old Curiosity Shop, with all its Victorian nooks and crannies, and its legions of coughing and wheezing denizens, who all belonged to that grotesque little Dickensian misanthrope, George Shallcross.

Gravett was damned if he'd ever set foot in the place again – unless, of course, it was to close it. That would be worth a traffic jam. To go there with the express intention of plucking that big, black, rusty key from Shallcross's sticky little fingers on the day that the whole building was finally emptied of all its goods and chattels, and then expunged from his precious balance sheets, taking with it a cost-per-patient ratio that his team of accountants thought was nothing less than obscene. Until then that sparky little wench, Liz Manners, could have the place to herself and be welcome to it. She wasn't going anywhere else in a hurry, so why not keep her there, in dusty obscurity, on a fairly long leash. She was the wrong side of fifty, she'd head-butted the glass ceiling of career advancement a long time ago as far as he was concerned, so why not let her hold the fort for him and play at running hospitals until the great day came when he could just snatch the whole dammed thing away from her again and smash it into neat little pieces!

So he wasn't best pleased when he reached for the telephone with a long, limp hand on that Sunday afternoon to find Liz Manners' voice at the other end of it. He hadn't the faintest idea how she came to have his home number – he would find out, and blood would flow – but even before he could gather his wits and fend her off, she was already telling him – *telling* him, mind you – that he was needed at The Old Curiosity Shop first thing Monday morning. Most urgent, she said. She even used the word 'imperative'. Now, quite aside from the fact that he never but *never* did anything first thing on a Monday morning, men on twice her salary knew better than to tell Paul Daniel Gravett what to do. Out of the question, he purred down the phone. Impossible. Unimaginable. She had to realize that he was such a busy man. His diary was managed for him – a tartar of a secretary – and it was always filled to the brim with meetings, conferences, appointments of every kind, for weeks, months in advance. He didn't have a moment to himself. No room to breathe. No gaps, no windows, much as he would have liked... Then, very distinctly, he heard her say the word 'Press'. Instant cold sweat. Completely ignoring him – talking over him, would you believe – she said the word 'Press'.

Newspapers. The carrion crows that followed him around everywhere, thirsting for blood, challenging his every word, pricking his every bubble of conceit, and haunting his secretary's office like spectres. Now the bitch had his attention. And he stalled. And she must have been waiting for him to stall, because as soon as the flow of excuses stopped she said, "Shall we say nine?" and then hung up. Cow!

And so to Monday morning and the start of a new week. Another threshold crossed. Days and weeks, old and new, cluttering up the landscape, indistinguishable from one another. A cracked record and a jumping stylus. New beginnings but with old intentions.

Gravett braved the seafront road, took his turn in the long, snaking queues of traffic, swore at traffic lights, shook his fist at the seagull that strafed his windscreen, and was there in plenty of time. But he couldn't park his car. It simply hadn't occurred to him that he wouldn't be able to park the car, the blessed Jag, where Shallcross would see it and spit tacks. They had obviously thought about ambulances – their right to hog the kerbs was painted all over the road – but no one had stopped to think what might happen when the gods themselves stepped down from Valhalla to rub shoulders with the humble souls they ruled over – and came by car. The whole street was filled with cars, but they were other people's cars, all parked nose to tail. There wasn't a glimmer of daylight anywhere. The next street was just as bad. And the next. And the next after that. Gravett drove around the whole neighbourhood in second gear but there wasn't room for a fag paper between the touching bumpers. Eventually he found himself back at the hospital, and he was just going to pop the Jag into the ambulance bay and claim blissful ignorance when not one but two taxis beat him to it, and smirked at him, too. And worse was to follow! The car in front of him suddenly stopped, double-parked, smack bang in the middle of the road, with its indicators flashing, and then he had to sit there and grin and bear it while the car's elderly driver extracted his equally elderly wife from the passenger seat and then began to creep towards the hospital with her, with a wave of his hand and a disarming smile, leaving his car abandoned behind him like a barricade, and with Gravett's Jag well and truly stuck behind it!

When he finally reached the switchboard, haggard and harassed, he was fifteen minutes late, a good five-minute walk from his car (which was parked on double yellow lines), and in a foul mood. He stood at the door of the kiosk, hands on hips, pointed to the road, and then began to address the telephonist in a booming street-trader's voice, even though it was perfectly obvious to anyone with a brain that she was in the middle of a call:

"I couldn't park anywhere! Why are there no parking spaces at this hospital? Is that too much to ask? How is one expected to function efficiently in a Third World environment like this! I'm now very late indeed for an extremely important meeting through no fault of my own, so will you kindly tell Mrs Manners that I'm here without any further delay!"

The telephonist went on with her call quite unconcerned, looking straight into Gravett's eyes as though he was a mannequin in a shop window. When at last she got around to him, she said very quietly, "Now tell me who you are, without shouting."

Gravett was genuinely taken aback. In the corridors of the County Hospital his face leered down upon the Great Unwashed like Kitchener. "Who I am?" he cried in disbelief. "I am Paul Gravett, Chief Executive of the very organisation that currently employs you, that's who I am. Now kindly tell Mrs Manners that I am here, and be quick about it. I think you will find that she is expecting me!"

"And I think you will find that 'she' is standing right behind you," Liz Manners muttered in his ear.

Gravett spun round to find himself toe to toe with the sparky wench. He quickly extended his long, limp handshake towards her at the height of his chest and almost level with her chin. "Liz!" he exclaimed brightly. "Good to see you!" Then, on the spur of the moment, he suddenly jettisoned the handshake and decided to grab her by the shoulders and peck her on the cheek, a departure from the script that left them both equally embarrassed.

"Thanks for coming," she said shortly, making a mental note to herself to wipe her face as soon as possible. "And don't bully my staff." She turned away before he could answer her and addressed the telephonist. "Mr Shallcross in?" she asked, and received a nod and a smile in reply. She approached the office door, rapped on it smartly, looked inside and said, "He's here," a piece of news which drew a long, low growl of displeasure from the interior of the room.

Shallcross emerged from his lair, frostily silent, and eyed Gravett up and down with a look of sheer disdain. He examined the long, limp hand very carefully before he agreed to touch it with his fingertips, and then he led the trio in a slow and stately procession towards the stairs.

When they arrived at the annexe, all was in readiness for them. Mrs Blake had been airbrushed from the scene again, and her chair with her; Audrey was hovering over the patient, still wearing her night cloak, like a bat on sentry duty; Kim Maskell had washed and shaved, and shocked everyone by producing a tie; and Paul Gravett walked into the room and instantly recoiled in horror.

"Good God, George! What on earth are you doing to the poor man?" he asked, his eyes bulging from their sockets.

Shallcross turned to look at Liz Manners with a cold, ironic smile. "I take it you didn't tell him, then?"

"Not over the phone, no," she admitted. "I didn't want to spoil the moment."

Another night had created a greatly altered scene. Blake had risen still higher into the air, and now the soles of his feet were roughly level with the top of Gravett's head. The Chief Executive seemed to be fixated by the sight of the patient's toenails, curved and claw-like, and stained the colour of nicotine. The drip-stand was now precariously balanced on a chair, and the syringe-driver now reached the patient with the help of a long, white extension lead which trailed down the wall to the socket.

Gravett began to laugh nervously. Kim glanced at him sharply, wondering for a moment if he was hyperventilating. Either way, the man suddenly couldn't stand still or control his features. "Come on, Charles," he prattled nervously, wringing his hands as though he was washing Duncan's blood from them. "Spill the beans! Tell me what in God's name this is all about."

Shallcross turned to Audrey and curtly nodded his head. "Get on with it, woman. You know you're dying to."

Reaching up, Audrey took hold of the syringe-driver with one hand and the long blue coverlet with the other, and then, with a flourish that she had clearly rehearsed well in advance, she pulled the quilt away in one sweeping, flowing, tumbling cascade of knitted blue wool, until Leonard Blake was left quite unsupported more than six feet from the floor.

Gravett bobbed and weaved his head from side to side like a shadow boxer. He seemed to be looking for hidden wires. "How on earth are you doing that, George?" he asked with a kind of feverish anxiety.

"Would you really like to know?" Shallcross asked him, calmly folding his arms and relaxing his weight against the wall.

"I would indeed!"

"So would I."

Gravett stared at him incredulously. "What do you mean?"

Shallcross scoffed. "What do you think I mean? Wake up, man! This is what we brought you here for, isn't that obvious? We don't know how he's doing this. We don't know why he's doing this. There are no hidden wires. There are no explanations. Your eyes do not deceive you. Why are you here? To help us to work out what we are supposed to do about it!"

Gravett's face registered utter bewilderment. He jabbed a trembling finger at the patient. "But that's impossible. He can't do that."

"Yes, thank you, we had already worked that much out for ourselves. Nevertheless, impossible or not, he seems to have got the knack of it, wouldn't you agree?"

Gravett stood on tiptoe and tried to catch a glimpse of Blake's face. "Is he alive?"

"Why don't you ask him?"

The suggestion seemed to terrify the Chief Executive and he shrank back towards the wall.

"Alive, but only just," Kim said, speaking for the first time. "He's quite clearly terminally ill. Whether or not that has any bearing at all on what you see is anyone's guess, quite frankly."

"But he's on the move," Audrey added in a sing-song voice and with a huge, beaming smile.

"What does that mean?" Gravett asked, now beginning to cower, ashen-faced.

"Well, now, let me see. He started off down here." And Audrey gave the mattress a hefty slap.

"You... mean...?"

"Yep! He's on the up and up. Far too slowly to be seen with the naked eye, of course, but most definitely, by infinitesimal degrees..." And she pointed towards the ceiling.

Gravett followed the direction of her finger. "But what if..."

"...he actually gets there? Exactly!" Shallcross said, like a teacher finally impressing a dim-witted schoolboy. "Your rapier-like intellect has seized upon the problem. What if?"

Gravett began to slowly slide down the wall until he was sat on his haunches. Still staring fixedly at the patient, he cupped his hands around his mouth and blew on them hard, puffing out his cheeks. It took a moment or two for the doctors to realize that he had fainted. Then everyone moved at once. Liz Manners filled a glass with water from the jug on the locker; Audrey smilingly opened the window and helped herself to a deep breath of air; Kim reached down and checked Gravett's pulse; and Shallcross helped himself to a large helping of derision.

"It must be said, you are a flimsy little man." He looked at the crumpled suit with complete detachment. "Come on," he suddenly decided, turning to Kim, "let's get him out of here before he makes a mess on the floor!"

The two doctors roughly pulled Gravett to his feet with a hand under each of his elbows, and then they frog-marched him from the room like a drunk at closing time. Liz led the way to her office, and once everyone was inside the Chief Executive was dumped into an armchair where he sat covering his face with his hands. Liz switched the kettle on and rattled some cups on a tray, and the two doctors stared at Gravett as though he was a body on a post-mortem slab.

"Not the best idea you've ever had," Shallcross said, talking to Liz, but still looking down at his nemesis with cold contempt.

Liz ignored him and went on making the tea.

Kim folded his arms. "We shouldn't be too surprised. After all, we've been in on this from the start. He hasn't. I'm not sure any of us would have taken it in our stride if we'd seen Blake for the first time this morning."

Shallcross rolled his eyes.

After a few minutes Gravett was beginning to pull himself together, but he spoke with a hoarse, wheezy voice and he still cupped his hands over his mouth like a mask. "What in God's name are we going to do?" he asked the room in general. "What in God's name are we going to do?"

"Don't worry, old chap," Shallcross said, bending over him with a grotesque smile. "We've called in reinforcements!" Gravett looked at him hopefully. Shallcross nodded. "Big Wigs! The Top Gun! The Man at the Helm! He'll tell us what to do. Won't you!"

Gravett shrank back in the chair and then turned to Kim. "You say he's terminally ill?"

Kim nodded.

"Well then he'll die, won't he? He'll die. That'll stop him."

"Or we could just shoot him and have done with it," Shallcross said breezily, taking his cup of tea from Liz Manners.

Gravett stuck with Kim and ignored the consultant. "You said he was dying. If he dies it'll stop all this. Won't it? Surely?" His face broke into a pathetic, pleading smile.

Kim took his own tea from Liz Manners and then stared into it as though it might contain the answer they were all seeking.

"Terminally ill? Yes. And normally at this stage in the proceedings we'd be concentrating on making him comfortable and waiting for the disease to take its course. And that's what we're still doing with Leonard Blake, to the extent that we're doing anything at all. Problem is, he hasn't died. Not yet. In fact, he's well overdue, given his condition; but all prognoses are based on normal or predicable circumstances, and, as you can plainly see, Leonard Blake's started writing his own rules."

"You've carried out tests?"

"Of course we've carried out tests!" Shallcross snapped scornfully. "And they don't tell us a thing. Old man, full of morphine. Don't plan for Christmas."

"Then what do we do?" Gravett demanded again as Liz inserted a mug of tea into his long, limp hand. "Do we just sit around and wait?"

"Yes," Shallcross said bluntly. "That's exactly what we do. Unless you have any bright ideas." He gazed placidly out of the window, sipping his tea, clearly not expecting an answer any time soon.

"Without knowing what we're waiting for..." Liz said, speaking for the first time as she took her own tea and perched on the edge of her desk. Everyone turned to face her. "He dies; he sinks back down on the bed. All well and good. Big sigh of relief all round. Mark it up to experience. Don't tell too many people in case they think we're insane. But..." She held up a finger. "...what if he doesn't die? What if, sooner or later, he gets to the ceiling? Then what?"

"So what do we do?" Gravett exclaimed again, spilling the contents of his mug of tea onto the carpet.

Shallcross suddenly marched across the room and bent over the cowering Chief Executive. "Give him a great big, shiny medal, and then shoot you!"

The amount of sugar Liz heaped into his second mug of tea finally gave Gravett the energy he needed to clear his head. He drifted back into the land of the living, aware that the conversation had been going on around him for some time. In a very dark corner of his mind he was just beginning to wake up to the fact that he had humiliated himself in front of George Bloody Shallcross. That would not do. That just would not do.

"What do you need?" he asked quietly.

"It's alive!" Shallcross declared with mock surprise.

Gravett ignored him. "What do you need? What can I do to help? What resources can I bring to bear?" he asked, seeking solace in the Book of Clichés.

Shallcross chuckled. "Looks like a Chief Executive, and now he even sounds like a Chief Executive. Cardboard King," he added savagely, half under his breath.

Without warning, Gravett suddenly snapped. He exploded with a sharp, shrill cry of rage, and Kim leapt between the two men to separate them. "Then you tell me what to say, if you know so much, you offensive little man!" he screamed at Shallcross. Tears started to his eyes and began to stream down his cheeks.

Liz gently backed him into his chair with her fingertips, and then waited for the moment to pass. "What we need is a contingency plan, something that will hopefully get us out of trouble if and when this situation really threatens to get out of hand," she said in a gentle, soothing voice.

Gravett was waking up quickly now. "Be specific. Say what you want."

"Say what I want?" Liz considered for a moment, chewing her thumbnail and staring at the wall. "Okay. Worst case scenario. Somehow or other, our star patient in there gets himself talked about. The next thing we know, we've got the whole world's Press corps camped on our doorstep. When that happens, we cease to function as a hospital."

"Surely, you're exaggerating!"

"In the time it takes to click your finger," Liz said confidently. "Stands to reason. It will be big news; big, big news. The situation will no longer be under our control."

"So you will need to provide us with somewhere to escape to," Shallcross said, pointing a finger at Gravett.

"Define 'us'."

"Everything and everyone in the building. The Chest Unit. The whole shooting match."

"And how am I supposed to do that?"

"I've absolutely no idea," Shallcross admitted, "but I'm sure you'll think of something, you and your illustrious team."

"Give me a timescale to work to," Gravett demanded, his mind beginning to go into hyper-drive as it found itself in familiar territory again.

"No time at all. None." Everyone turned to look at Kim. "I mean it. None. This story could break in the next hour for all we know. And if it does, Liz is right, we won't have any notice; we won't have any time to prepare ourselves."

"So don't let us keep you," Shallcross added, offering to pull the Chief Executive out of his chair. "Just go do that voodoo that you do so well."

Gravett, still unsure of his feet, was half-dragged, half-pushed to the door, but there he grabbed at the doorpost and held it tightly while he looked back at them all for a moment. But there was no punch line, if he was waiting for one. This wasn't an April Fool. No one had cracked a joke. No one was laughing.

When the Chief Executive finally left the building he no longer had the faintest idea where his car was. His schedule for the rest of the day was already in tatters, and it gradually dawned on him, as he stood there forlornly on the pavement, that the rest of his career might well be in tatters too, soon, if he didn't do something about it. But that was his concern. Staff and patients were coming and going all around him like busy little bees in one of Shallcross's accursed hives, and not one of them would spare a thought for the tall, gangly man with the pale face, dressed in an expensive but crumpled suit, who looked more than a little lost. Except, of course, those who made it their business to watch the world go by. Standing at the counter inside the switchboard, slowly sifting through a handful of letters, the Head Porter noted

Gravett's departure out of the corner of his eye. He glanced at the telephonist without the faintest glimmer of an expression on his face. The smile would come later, when he was alone.

As soon as Gravett got to his office he pounced on his secretary. He spun her chair away from her desk and held it firmly by its arms.

"Listen to me very carefully, and don't answer me back. Cancel everything. The whole day. Every appointment. D'you hear me? Nod if you understand!" So she nodded. "Then get me someone at the university to talk to. Some sort of boffin type. A scientist. Head of Physics, something like that."

"Do I get a name?"

"How the hell would I know his name? Show some initiative for once. Use some imagination, why don't you."

He retreated into his office and then slammed and locked the door. Then he began to march up and down the length of the conference table, staring at his feet, and then gazing impatiently out of the huge window at the rest of the city and the sea running into the beaches in endless rippling waves. This was damage limitation time. If he was to survive the day with his reputation intact and untarnished he needed to move quickly. He needed to reassert himself. He needed to take control of the situation and win back some of the lost ground from Shallcross and his cronies. He needed to be proactive. He needed to anticipate events, and not let himself be dictated to by a stuck-up Cough Doctor and a feckless wench on half his pay.

The phone rang. He snatched it up.

"I've got someone at the university on the line, and they can put you through to someone called Derek Harding."

"Who the hell is Derek Harding?"

"How should I know? Ask him, why don't you. Show some initiative for once."

Gravett bit his tongue, and then waited until a deep male voice at the other end of the line finished a quite separate conversation with a rather unpleasant chuckle and then said hello.

"Mr Harding?"

A pause, and then, "No."

"No?"

"No."

"I'm sorry. My secretary is at fault. Who am I speaking to?"

"*Doctor* Harding. Now, to whom am I speaking?"

Another smart-arsed doctor, Gravett thought. The day was filling up with them. "My name is Paul Gravett," he replied with steely politeness, gritting his teeth. "I'm the Chief Executive of the City Healthcare Trust."

"How nice for you."

Gravett waited a moment while Harding's voice picked up the threads of the other conversation again, not bothering to cover the mouthpiece.

"Are you still there?"

"Still here and still waiting," Harding replied dryly. "What do you want, Mr Chief Executive?"

"What are you? Head of Physics, something like that?"

"No."

"You're not in charge?"

"Would that I was. I am Assistant Head – repeat after me, *Assistant* Head – of the Department of Physics and Astronomy," Harding informed him pedantically. "Professor Turner heads up our little group," he added sourly.

"Then can I speak to Professor Turner, if he's there, please?" Gravett asked, imagining how much fun it would be to batter this man senseless with his own ego.

"No, you cannot. Professor Turner is in Chicago."

"What's he doing in Chicago?" Gravett asked before he could stop himself.

"If it is any of your concern, he is talking neutrinos with like-minded souls. What is it you want of the likes of Professor Turner, Mr Gravett?"

The voice at the other end of the phone was stamping heavily on Gravett's name each time it used it, causing him to bite his tongue. "I think I need your help," he answered carefully.

"Oh? What sort of help?"

For the first time Gravett sensed curiosity. If he wasn't very much mistaken, this would be the moment when control of the conversation passed to him. He spoke slowly and clearly.

"I have encountered a remarkable – I might even say an *astounding* – phenomenon for which I am certain that science has no rational explanation."

He must have sounded convincing because this time there was a long pause at the other end of the line. Then, more soberly, Harding's voice said, "Go on."

At which point the cat's paw reached up towards the top of the bag.

7

Iris had been awake for some time before she realized the phone was ringing. She sat bolt upright on the bed and then watched the room spin around her like a carousel. When she stood up the floor felt spongy under her feet, but she still hurried into the sitting room to snatch up the receiver before the ringing stopped.

"Mum?"

Susan. Not the hospital. So Richard had ignored her and phoned his sister, and given her a piece of his mind. Iris stood with the phone to her ear and her heart in her mouth. Next to hearing the news that Leonard had died, she dreaded a conversation with her daughter. The very thought of it exhausted her. Why bother, she thought? It won't get either of us anywhere.

"Mum?" Bright and breezy. So today it was going to be a bright and breezy – and brief – conversation. She didn't want anything today.

"Hello, Susan."

"How are you, Mum? And how's Dad? Any news?"

Gushing. Always gushing, at a distance. Where did she learn gushing from, Iris wondered? "I'm fine."

"And Dad? Still going strong?"

"Still with us."

"He's a fighter!"

Clichés, Iris thought. Silly, trite little clichés. Sound bites. Meaningless, empty phrases. Something, anything, to fill sixty seconds of time, after which she could reasonably end the conversation and hang up. "And how are you, dear?"

"Oh, I'm fine."

"Busy?"

"Always busy."

Busy making money. And friends. Money and friends; they made Susan's world's go round. It occurred to Iris to ask her if she was eating enough – she resembled a pencil – but that wouldn't make for a long conversation either, so instead she said, "How's work?"

"Busy, too." Which meant, keep off; you don't need to go there; I don't need your money today. "Mum, are you looking after yourself? You need to, you know. You need to keep your strength up, for Dad's sake."

No, Iris thought, I need to keep it up for mine. "I'm fine. Really."

"Listen, Mum. Do you need me to come down there and help you? Look after you? Would it help if I come to be with you?" The voice she would use to a child.

Yes, Iris thought, of course it would, if you meant it, and if you could ever be relied upon to keep a promise. Iris knew that if she came – and she wouldn't – she would expect to be waited on hand and foot. Pampered. Spoiled. Sent home again, petted and replete. All this was a game. Susan only wanted to ask the question so that it would be politely but firmly declined, and so that she could feel virtuous. Let's not waste our time with all this pretending, shall we?

"I'm fine. I can manage. I'll call you if I need you." And hell freezes over.

"Well, if you say so. Will you call me when there's news?" Susan asked.

When he's dead, you mean? When you can start mourning with your glamorous friends? "Yes, dear, of course I will."

"Love you, Mum," the voice added.

But I no longer love you, Iris thought, listening to the dialling tone. She looked at the clock on the wall: just under a minute. Now she could put a nice, neat tick by her mother's name on her to-do list in her nice, neat leather Filofax.

Every time Iris spoke to Susan – two, three times a year – the pain came back again, like a knife in her heart. The pain of losing her little girl again, the child who, once upon a time, had filled her life with love and exhaustion. The third child – the longed-for, prayed-for daughter.

When she was a little child they had both loved her, but Iris had never rivalled Leonard in affection for their daughter. To Leonard she could do no wrong. He indulged her in everything. Later, as she grew up, pert and headstrong, two messily failed marriages were cleaned up for her. Then her new business was launched with a bank loan that used their house as security; and when the business grew and flourished, and demanded new funds for expansion, they downsized into the dreadful bungalow and handed her the balance to enjoy with her fab new friends. And when, at last, she seemed happy, fulfilled, then they told themselves that they were happy too, even if, while making a success of her own life, she had almost entirely vanished from theirs. She became the voice on the phone, the kiss on the Christmas card. No longer someone they knew. No longer flesh and blood. And when Leonard eventually became unwell and then ill, the voice on the other end of the phone couldn't conceal the irritation.

Even now Iris couldn't look at Susan's photograph. It hurt too much. Jack and Richard, the two rough, larking boys, their faces grinned at her from picture frames all over the house. Their wives and children littered the house, too, even though none of them had ever been there. The place rang with their laughter. But Susan's picture lived in the drawer, where it couldn't hurt Iris anymore and leave her in despair.

When would Leonard go, Iris thought? When would he go? Slip away? When would it all be over and done with? When would there be no more hospital? When could she grieve? When could she cry?

The bungalow was cold. It was a collection of cold little boxes. Like ice. Like its occupants had been deep-frozen; put on ice. And yet Iris lived in one hot, stuffy little room now, with a plastic chair and a dying man. Leonard. The last, lingering remnants of Leonard.

Somewhere inside that cadaverous shell was the Brylcreem boy who had made her heart miss a beat when he stood on a park bench and whistled at her as she walked by. Somewhere deep down inside, under those tightly closed eyelids, was the self-same man who played cricket for the Post Office and turned every woman's head when he opened his shoulders and smote the full length ball out of the county. And somewhere beyond those dry, cracked lips was the gentle, greying baritone whose voice still thrilled her when he sang with the choir at the Church carol service. All the Leonards, still within reach, still at her fingertips. And that was all that mattered. For now. For today, tomorrow. Each hour, each minute that was left to be frittered away. Life, even now; life in all its fullness, as Leonard liked to say. Glorious life. Even when it was all about to turn into pink smoke and paper chains. Glorious life and love.

There was a sudden, shrill ring at the door. Jeanette. Lovely, kind and caring Jeanette, with just the one recipe.

Meanwhile, on the university campus just to the north of the city, a student studied his reflection in the mirror above the washbasin in the gents' loo and wondered why women found him so resistible. Christopher Pike's father, a merchant banker, called him a geek, so he dressed like a geek pretty much most of the time. It took very little effort, which appealed to him, and it saved him a great deal of time in the grooming department. Hair: mid-length, greasy, with an aimless, mind-of-its-own style. Dress code: anorak, grubby, greasy like his hair, worn on all occasions. Gait: hunched, slightly round-shouldered, as though his head was top-heavy and too full of brain.

Chris was a postgraduate student in the Department of Physics and Astronomy, researching neutrinos, majoring in Angela Harris's lustrous chest. He was nothing if not a serious scientist, so even his own sexual predilection had to be scrutinized with meticulous attention to detail, not least his own body's physical response to the stimulus of her presence. It wasn't exactly rocket science, it was a bit like elementary biology for beginners; but if you were a fan of *Blade Runner*, like Chris, then the methodology was a given. Blush responses, pupil dilation and, of course, an erectile function that you could strap a flag to. And right at the centre of his field of study were those two utterly bewitching and quite colossal breasts that she kept hidden away from the world behind an array of hard-pressed, tight-fitting T-shirts that became the stuff of his dreams. How to circumvent them, flank them, remove them from the equation, so that Chris could proceed right to the heart of the matter? The breasts, the famous breasts, the stuff of campus myth and legend. One intrepid but ultimately defeated former suitor had even given them a name. He had called them the Himalayas, because they were at once immense, beguiling, but to most people remote and inaccessible.

Chris craved them. He adored them. He imagined scaling them, conquering them, a dozen times a day from a dozen different directions, until they filled his waking and sleeping hours and pushed sanity to the margins of his mind. His greatest quest was to be able, one far distant day, to place his hands upon them and claim them as his own. But, while he squirmed with embarrassment and shortage of breath whenever she was nearby, he never once stopped to think what Angela's own body might be saying to him in reply. It was the self-same sequence of tests and whether or not it worked on Hollywood replicants it certainly worked on her. Especially the blush response. Whenever Chris was around her, complete with greasy thatch and grubby coat, a deep, fiery red hue ignited the whole of her neck and chest, and she, too, had examined in great detail how she would capitulate when he finally got around to scaling those precipitous heights and triumphantly planting his flag on virgin soil.

And today was Monday, and a warm spring day. The campus was bathed in sunshine, and the wood behind the library was a riot of colour. Tutorials had moved outdoors. Books were read under trees and hedgerows. Lovers lay in the long grass and stared up at the sky. And Chris and Angela found themselves in a hot, airless laboratory, staring at one of Harding's endlessly dull experiments. They had the whole science block to themselves. Near perfect silence; just the faintest sound of student voices permeating the heavy, still air.

90

Angela half-swooned, on the verge of sleep for much of the morning. Her eyes felt heavy and tired, and she swayed on the brink of a warm, embracing dream of sex in a sun-filled orchard. Then she woke up with a start and realized that Chris was staring at her fixedly. Perhaps it was the season, the sun, the warm, sultry atmosphere of the room, or perhaps it was because she knew she would grow old waiting for Chris to make the first move. She suddenly leaned towards him, tightening the T-shirt in all the right places, until their two heads were almost touching. She had never smiled at Chris like that before, and he had never been this close to the Himalayas before. For the first time he felt the warmth of her body; he detected the distinct, slightly sour odour of her breath; and he saw for himself the full extent of the great red flush that began just below her thrice-pierced earlobes and then disappeared deep into the foothills of his dreams. Suddenly it was so obvious. He would move another inch, and she would kiss him. So Angela moved six inches to be absolutely certain, and stopped his mouth up with her tongue.

He half-stepped, half-fell from his stool and threw his arms around her like an ape, discovering how much of her there was to enclose within his passionate embrace. He could feel her body – warm, plentiful, very firm – and his left hand moved to her waist while his right hand, relishing the moment, began that final slow, unhurried ascent, practised so many times in his dreams, which would bring it into perfect alignment with her left breast. At which point he discovered, with wild-eyed dismay, exactly what Angela's hands had always planned to do in reply.

The lab door flew open with a resounding bang.

"Unhand that man! It's rape. Put him down, you beast!"

Harding stood in the doorway for a moment watching the two students, and then he jumped up and hooked his fingers to the top of the door frame so that he could swing there like a monkey, grinning with delight.

"Chris, get hold of a recorder of some kind. Preferably something that works. Raid Turner's secret horde. Something top-notch, ultra sensitivity. For God's sake, check all leads and batteries. I want high definition, time-elapsed recording, twenty-four hours at least. Get a good tripod, too. No rubbish. Curvatious Angela, everything else please. If it makes a move or a sound, or if it rattles a window in Kazakhstan, I want to know about it. Throw everything – and your good selves – into my car and I will meet you there in twenty minutes.

"What's going on?" Chris asked, bewildered on so many fronts.

Harding stopped swinging and dropped to the ground again, rubbing his hands and smiling enigmatically. "A field trip with a difference. Something that might just drop a doctorate into your laps for you."

"And what do you get?" Angela asked, none too warmly.

"Nothing less than a Chair and a knighthood!" He took a deep breath and then unleashed a huge, toothy grin that she found revolting. "And a place in history!"

"Well, I'll be…" Chris said. But he wouldn't, at least, not for now. Not until much, much later, because Angela had already gone off in search of other equipment.

Five thirty was the perfect time to choose. By that time of the day most of the hospital was on the point of closing. The Medical Records staff had already gone home, and the radiographers from X-ray were determined not to be very far behind them. Both departments had pulled down their shutters and locked their doors. OPD had one last patient waiting to see the consultant, then that department, too, would shut up shop and head for home, with the pharmacists snapping at their heels. Most of Catering had long since gone, needing only to leave a small evening staff to transfer the meals to the heated trolleys, ready for delivery to the wards. Housekeeping and Portering Services, too, had only left skeleton staffs behind to clean the empty offices and finally put the building to bed. The corridors, busy all day, were almost deserted now, waiting only for occasional visitors and the night staff much later in the evening. Indeed it was the right time, the perfect time, to just turn up out of the blue.

The ancient rusty Volvo 850 pulled up right outside the front door, hard against the kerb, and low on its springs with its heavy load of equipment. Harding got out and leapt straight up the steps and into the building. The telephonist nearly jumped out of her skin when he suddenly appeared in the doorway and turned his toothy smile on her.

"Kindly point me the way to Ward 4, dear lady," he asked with a breathless and utterly false bonhomie.

The telephonist looked long and hard at his shoulder-length grey hair, the loud yellow waistcoat and the bright pink bow tie, and most especially at the piles of equipment that Chris and Angela were already staggering into reception with.

"Who are you, and who do you want to see?" she asked in the hard, sharp voice she reserved for anyone who called her "dear".

Harding's bucolic grin often gave strangers the impression he was about to burst out laughing and might therefore be stark, staring mad. "I'm here to see Mr Gravett, my dear. And my assistants, as you can doubtless see, have a mass of equipment to set up, so if you would be kind enough to point us in the right direction, we will be on our way. Eternal thanks."

The telephonist stood up, which did little to alter her height. "Mr Gravett I know," she said. "He was here earlier; he's not here now. You I do not know," she added, frost beginning to form in the air about her. "And you don't get past me until I've bleeped someone to come down here and deal with you. And that includes you, too!" she concluded loudly, stopping the two labouring students in their tracks.

Harding sensed an immovable object in his path and prepared to go round it. "Super! That is so very kind of you. And while we wait for your person with the bleep we'll crack on, shall we? Along here, is it?" And with that he began to shoo Chris and Angela ahead of him in what happened to be the right direction.

"YOU WILL WAIT!" For a small woman she had the lungs of a diva. It was, of course, entirely possible that she had some kind of alarm system tucked away in that tiny little hutch of hers, so prudence made Harding stop once again and elegantly pirouette on the tip of one shoe so that he could face her and expose her to more of his hideous grin.

"My dear lady," he sighed, dutifully retracing his steps to the counter and clasping his hands together in an attitude of prayer. "How to appeal to your tender nature? As I think I explained, dear lady, I am here at the express invitation of your Chief Executive. He contacted me and he asked me to meet him here, punctual to the moment, along with all the equipment you see before you, and my two faithful assistants. Alas, he appears to be late. Would it not make sense to at least begin the long and wearisome task of setting up this very sensitive and sophisticated technology whilst we wait for the Great Man to arrive and perhaps even chide you a little for the – how shall we put it? – the measure of your caution?"

"Call me 'dear' just one more time and I will start into some chiding of my own," the telephonist warned him quietly, and with a candour that made his idiotic smile drain from his face.

Just then the tiny sentinel glimpsed a huge and shadowy figure at the far end of the corridor, and she inwardly sighed with relief as the Head Porter lumbered slowly towards her. "Mr Adams!" she called out, invoking the use-of-surname code that was her only real alarm. "This man is demanding to be allowed to go up to Ward 4. He says he knows Mr Gravett, but as Mr Gravett is not here, I have no way of confirming that."

The Head Porter's speed remained the same, funereal, as he slowly padded towards her, step by step, like a somnambulant elephant. But his huge frame filled and blocked the corridor.

When he arrived at the switchboard he simply stopped, content to stand in the Physicist's way and stare at him without saying a word.

Harding, sensing the need for diplomacy, stuffed his shabby briefcase under his left arm and offered to shake the Head Porter's hand. "Delighted to meet you! Doctor Derek Harding, Department of Physics and Astronomy. Paul Gravett has arranged to meet me here. He appears to have been delayed."

Tiny calmly considered the newcomer's face and his wild grey hair, then the equipment piled in the middle of reception, and finally, and at considerable length, the welcome sight of the Himalayas. Then, to the telephonist's astonishment, he shook the outstretched hand and presented Harding with his own trademark mocking smile.

"In that case I'd better lend you a hand," he suggested.

"Shall I bleep the Duty Sister?" the telephonist asked, beginning to doubt her senses.

"Nah! Don't bother!" Tiny replied, dismissing her with a wave of his hand and beginning to turn back down the corridor. "I can handle this."

It so happened that Kim Maskell was on Ward 4 when Harding, Tiny and the two students arrived at the annexe and began to dump heavy cases of equipment by the door. Kim had been listening to Mr Baker's lungs spluttering and rattling in the earpiece of his stethoscope like a hookah pipe, wondering whether or not to tweak his medication a little. It wouldn't make any difference to Mr Baker, but it would give Kim something to write in the notes. Everyone read the notes, these days; it would be Kim's calling card, proof that he had passed this way. Mr Baker was dying, of course, and there was nothing Kim could do to prevent that, but he could tinker here and there. Not doctoring in its purest sense, perhaps. Well, not doctoring at all, if he was honest. It made him feel like his older brother. He used to tinker with old cars when he was a teenager. He was always thinking of things to do to old engines that would make them roar and growl, things that would keep him busy and plastered in oil for hours at a time. Of course, nothing ever did improve the performance of the engines because they were old, and their mileage clung to them like gossip. The mileage was irreversible, and sooner or later, as with all machines, the mileage proved to be terminal. You finally had to give up trying and turn your attention to a younger model. And that was Mr Baker's plight in a nutshell. He was dying of terminal mileage. Anno Domini. Too many years. One of their tutors at Medical School, a surgeon who used to change into fatigues at the weekend and play at being a soldier, summed up the duty of doctoring among the elderly as the difference between an organized withdrawal and a shambolic retreat. You could do nothing about the direction, only the manner of their going.

When his thoughts were interrupted by the sudden commotion in the corridor, Kim gave up on Mr Baker's notes, leapt up from his bed, and rushed out of the ward.

"Stay out of there!" he shouted in a thunderous voice, just as Tiny was reaching for the door handle.

"Mr Gravett's instructions," Tiny replied, making the mistake of treating Kim to a supercilious smile as well.

"You can stick Mr Gravett's instructions!" Kim shouted again, this time almost into the Head Porter's face as he thrust himself between him and the door. He jerked his thumb at the sign behind his head. "See that? I take it you can read? Authorized personnel only. Barrier nursing at all times. Do you want me to put that more bluntly for you?"

Harding tried to insinuate himself between the two men jammed in the doorway. "Doctor Derek Harding. Delighted to meet you," he said to Kim. "I am indeed authorized. I have Paul Gravett's blessing."

"But you don't have mine. Back off!" Kim snarled at him. "Where did you do your training?" he demanded, not taking his eyes off the Head Porter for a moment.

"Where did I what?" Harding asked, momentarily confused.

"Where did you do your medical training? Simple question."

"Oh, I see. Tedious pedantry, how dull," Harding said with a waxen smile. "I gained my Ph.D. in Advanced Nuclear Physics from Trinity College, Cambridge. I specialized in biophysics and nanoscience. Mention my work on the CERN project to anyone of substance in that field and they will soon disabuse you of any notions of intellectual superiority you might be harbouring at this moment. Clear enough for you?"

Kim scoffed. He had been insulted by experts in his time. "So you're not a medical doctor, then?"

"I am not." Harding chose that moment to form a steeple with his fingers, oddly reminiscent of Shallcross.

"Then you don't go in," Kim said flatly.

"I have all the authority I need," Harding said, matching the tone of Kim's anger, syllable for syllable.

"I've asked you nicely. Now I'm telling you."

"If you think I'm going to listen to the thuggish ranting of a backstreet sawbones, you are very much mistaken," Harding said in little more than a whisper, close to Kim's face. Then Harding saw something in Kim's eye. Perhaps instinct told him it was the right moment to retreat, before the rugby player in the younger doctor floored him with a single blow of that undoubtedly muscular forearm. Either way, he stepped backwards and trod straight onto Chris's foot. Chris yelped, giving Tiny Adams just the distraction he needed. Kim sensed a movement and spun round just as Tiny started to open the annexe door. He snatched at the Head Porter's arm and wrenched him backwards with all his strength, causing Tiny to grab at the half-open door with his other hand. Just for a moment a part of the room's interior was revealed.

It was a bad maul and Kim knew it. He was off balance now and out of position. He quickly improvised and snatched at the lapels of Tiny's jacket, pulling them as hard as he could. The huge man lurched forward, and when he did Kim threw the whole weight of his own body behind him, so that he could grab the door handle and slam the annexe shut. It was all he could think of. There was no knowing what, if anything, either Tiny or Harding had managed to glimpse in that moment.

Now, too late, the battlefield began to fill with reinforcements. Liz Manners rushed from her office at the sound of Kim's voice; Sister Corin appeared at the top of the stairs to block the way to Ward 5 like Horatio at the bridge; and now Iris Blake chose this precise moment to step out of the lift and confront the scene. Finally, Paul Gravett strode along the corridor with a vast beaming smile, holding up his hands in a gesture of surrender, and clucking like a mother hen.

"Oh dear, oh dear, oh dear!" he said cheerily. "I think I can explain. Put down your swords, gentlemen. This is an acquaintance of mine, a most distinguished scientist by the name of Stephen Harding…"

"Derek!"

"…Derek Harding, from the Department of Physics…"

"…and Astronomy…"

"…at the university. Quite so. I have asked Doctor Harding to assist us with our investigation into Mr Blake's…"

At which point Liz Manners landed a stunning blow right in the middle of the Chief Executive's chest and then shouted, "Stop!" Then she turned to face the Head Porter and stabbed an accusing finger at him. "Why are you here?" she demanded.

Tiny was still recovering his breath after wrestling with Kim. "I was giving this bloke a hand," he said hoarsely. "That's my bleeding job!"

"We don't need you. Go away." When he didn't move quickly enough, she held out her arm, pointing along the corridor like the Grim Reaper. "Go. Go."

"I do hope I haven't caused..." Harding began.

"Shut up. You can go," Liz repeated, holding her hand up to silence everyone until the Head Porter had entirely disappeared. Then she turned to Sister Corin who was still guarding the stairs. "Pam, call the switchboard. Get them to track down Mr Shallcross and get him here fast."

"I hardly think that's necessary," Gravett protested, but the ward sister had already vanished.

Finally, Liz turned to Iris Blake and appealed to her. "Do you know anything about this? Has anyone had the decency to ask you?"

It was her trump card. When Iris slowly shook her head, Liz began to herd everyone along the passageway towards her office, leaving just Kim and Iris to go into the annexe together and shut the door.

Liz, on the other hand, slammed her door as hard as she could, making the window rattle, and then stormed over to the window to fume at the street until she could trust herself to speak coherently.

"Are you completely out of your mind?" she demanded, without turning her head. It was clear that she was addressing the Chief Executive. "What part of the notion of trying to contain this situation did you not understand? You might as well have taken out a full-page ad in The Times as bring in people like..." This time she glanced at Harding. "...this!"

Gravett offered to surrender again. "Alright. I give in. I've said I'm sorry. I should have brought you up to speed first, but there wasn't time. We needed expert advice – you agreed with that – and so I moved quickly. I'm sorry if you feel I trod on your toes, but these are the scientific disciplines..."

"Rubbish!" the Hospital Manager snapped at him furiously. "Your job was to prepare for the worst, not bring it about!"

Gravett was stung. The look on his face hardened, and the tone of his voice changed. "My job? You're going to tell me my job, are you? Shall we compare job descriptions, while we're about it? Shall we hold them both up to the light, side by side, and see which one of us has the authority here? Don't you bloody lecture me, woman! You were losing it. It was obvious to me that I needed to be proactive, so I was. I took action. I did what I thought was necessary, and I didn't need your bloody permission, either!"

The gloves were off and Liz Manners was having none of it. "Gosh, I'm impressed. You must have thought of all of that even as you were sliding down the wall, pissing your pants at the sight of our little secret." Harding started to close in on Liz, reaching out his hand towards her. But he snatched it back again when she glanced at it and looked as though she might bite it off. "Last time I looked, Leonard Blake was still a living, breathing human being, and not a lab rat in a cage! He's a patient. He's the person we're here to look after, even when we can't cure him. He has a right to the very best we can do for him. Not to be poked around like a specimen."

At which point the door flew open and Shallcross arrived with all guns blazing. "What in God's name is going on here? Behold, the moron returns. We give you one damned thing to do, and you foul up big-time." He turned aside to Liz Manners. "What has he done?"

"May I?" Harding asked.

Shallcross flinched from the outstretched hand and then recoiled with horror from what seemed like a mirror image. Apart from the fact that Harding was wearing a pink instead of a red bow tie, they might have shared the same tailor. "Who the devil are you?"

"Harding, Doctor Derek. Assistant Head of the Department of Physics and Astronomy," the scientist replied with a bemused smile, clearly finding something very entertaining in Shallcross's appearance. "Hopefully my colleagues and I will bring a measure of scientific objectivity to the proceedings." He smiled at Liz again, but this time from a safe distance. "I understand what you are saying, Mrs... Of course we will respect the fact that Mr Blake is your patient, and we will be sensitive to all aspects of his medical care. We won't get in the way. Promise. Scout's honour. But you must understand that we have equipment to hand that will help us to investigate this man and his condition in a way that you could not envisage within the – how shall I put it? – the constraints of NHS resources. You can only monitor the man. We can monitor everything, the whole environment. Ours is an holistic approach, if you will. Clearly, something is responsible for this extraordinary phenomenon. We need to find out what that something is, identify it, and investigate it. This may very well prove to be a seminal moment in modern science, Mr... er..."

But Shallcross ignored the grinning stranger and turned on Gravett with an explosion of rage. "You told him! You complete and utter idiot, you told him! You couldn't wait, could you? After everything we said, you just couldn't wait to get out there and blab your mouth off to Dr Who here and his grubby little chums! Do you have any moral integrity left in you at all? But what am I saying? Of course you haven't! The only thing that motivates you is the thought of a knighthood for services rendered to the cause of errant stupidity!" At which point it would have been as well for him to be monitoring Harding's blush responses, but Shallcross had never seen the film.

"Don't lecture me, George. I took what I deemed to be a sound and sensible decision," Gravett said stubbornly.

"You wouldn't know a sound and sensible decision if you tripped over one. And don't call me George!" Then the consultant rounded on the Physicist. "And as for you, you have no dress sense, but do you have a code of ethics of any kind in your line of work? Something like our Hippocratic Oath? Feel free to use words of few syllables, if you can."

Harding's fingers fluttered towards his bow tie nervously and stayed there. "I'm not sure that I quite follow you."

"Do we or do we not have a way of ensuring your silence?" Shallcross shouted at him, making the veins on his forehead stand out like tattoos.

"Oh, I see!" Harding said when the penny dropped with a loud clang. "Of course. Of course, yes! We would hardly wish to share... to discuss..." Harding stopped for a moment so that he could entirely disengage his brain from the conversation he had

had with Gravett that morning. Then he took a deep breath and began again. "You can rely on my professional integrity at all times." He turned to Chris and Angela and raised his eyebrows.

"Likewise," Chris said.

"Ditto," Angela muttered with a baleful look at the whole company.

Shallcross glanced across at Liz Manners to check on her mood, but she clearly had nothing more she wished to say. Various things came to mind, like horses and stable doors, but there was little point in saying any of them now. The sands had just shifted under all their feet, and there was nothing she could do about that.

The moment of silence lengthened until all the anger seemed suddenly to have gone from the room. Then Shallcross spoke again. "Then our next step would seem to be a conversation with Mrs Blake."

Liz immediately headed towards the door, determined to be a part of that dialogue, and the rest of the gathering slowly filed out behind her. As Angela approached the door she found Shallcross hovering in wait for her.

"And do they make you dust the Tardis?" he asked.

To everyone's surprise Iris Blake agreed to Harding's equipment being deployed in her husband's room. Her one caveat was that it should not be allowed to get in Kim's way. Liz added a condition of her own and insisted that nothing be done until all other visitors had left the building. And so it was very late indeed when Harding, Chris and Angela themselves finally left the hospital, walking very quietly to Harding's car.

All three of them were still shaken by what they had seen, and their conversation on the way back to the campus was desultory at best. Chris stared out of the window but he wasn't looking at city streets. He brooded deeply, even while his mind felt like it was spiralling down a vortex, as though it had been flushed away. He thought of Sunday School miracles, childhood fantasies; he remembered the teenager within him turning from science fiction to science fact in a mood of veneration. It was all there, from dreams to doctorates, but nothing could prepare him for what he had seen in a tiny hospital ward. Science always needed the capacity to dream, to leap boldly into darkness, before it could find something new to keep, something from the heart of creation that it could dust off, polish, and place upon a shelf. This was how the facts of science were compiled – slowly, carefully, painstakingly, tested over and over again. But nothing had ever pointed to this. This was something that had been waiting for them in the darkness. And no one had seen it coming.

Angela, too, was quiet, keeping her thoughts to herself, as she usually did. What bothered her now, as they bumped and shuddered along in the back of Harding's car, was an intense feeling of sadness. Where it came from, she could not say. From Leonard or Iris Blake, or both; from that crowded little room; from her own remembered secret places; something made her want to weep from her heart. And she didn't know why.

Chris looked across at her and knew better than to press her. When he looked away, Angela stole a glance at him, and chose not to speak. Harding watched them both in the rear-view mirror and had nothing to say to either of them.

When they arrived at the campus and got out of the car the cold night air seemed to stir them awake, and the two students walked off towards the Hall of Residence together, holding hands. Harding watched them go and then drove on to his home in a village on the outskirts of the campus. There he parked the car, let himself into the cottage with a latch key, and proceeded to cook himself an omelette while he whistled a jaunty tune. As he sat at the table and ate his supper it occurred to him that he hadn't reminded the two love-birds to keep mum about the evening's events, but then he remembered the passionate embrace he had delighted in spoiling for them earlier in the day and thought they would have other things to do to keep themselves occupied before the night was out.

Supper over, he pushed his empty plate to one side and flipped up the lid of his laptop. His own smug features greeted him when the screensaver loaded, and as always he paused for a moment to study himself. This was his favourite self-portrait, but there were several others kept on file, and from time to time, with his changing moods, they too would have their day. But this one was the real Harding, he felt. Aloof, mocking, self-aware, without a care in the world for anything except his own ambition. Harding the man.

He wasn't what people would call a pleasant man; he knew that and he could live with it. He lived alone, anyway, unmarried, and not very often befriended, so he was free to create whatever kind of man he chose to be, and very often he chose to be a man who made other people dislike him intensely. He was a little like Gravett, without knowing it, another self-made man who had a face, a persona for every occasion, every situation that might serve him or progress his glittering career. He wanted success in life. More than friends, or love, or good opinion, he wanted success. Success in his chosen field. Adulation even. That was not too strong a word. He wanted to triumph where others had miserably failed, and he wanted adulation... but from whom? He was never quite sure. Parents? Teachers? Ghosts from the past? He had long since forgotten, but the motivation played on inside him, like a programme on a loop. As a result he was only a shell of a man. A carapace. All the extremities – the smile, the gushing insincerity, the features that twisted and contorted into any attitude or emotion he might need – they were all fixed in place. But inside? Inside there was nothing. He was damaged goods and he didn't even know it. Damaged, unformed; functional, perhaps, but conceptually incomplete. A man who could be heartless because he had no heart; just an insatiable hunger and a consuming greed.

Harding waited for the word processor to load on the computer, and then he selected a heading style. But what heading should he give to his notes, he wondered, so early in the investigation? What name could he give to that weird little tableau in that drab little broom cupboard of a room? History chose such strange places for its defining moments.

He could call it pretty much anything he liked. It was a phenomenon without a name. It was new. Different. Unknown. Unchartered. There had been many times down the centuries when human knowledge had taken a great leap forward like this – a great leap into the dark – and every time that happened a man would come forward to claim the fame and book his place in the annals of history. Einstein, Newton, Hawking, take your pick. Sometimes they were the ones who had the courage to leap without knowing where they would land. And sometimes they were simply the ones who had the presence of mind to leap up out of a crowd of onlookers and claim that fame by right of conquest. By right of snatching it away from others who saw it first and said nothing.

Harding had not been the first person to set eyes on Leonard Blake, but he was determined to be the one people remembered when the phenomenon was talked about in the future. Harding, the man who... what? The man who worked out how Blake hovered in the air instead of climbing into a coffin? The man who stepped in front of Darwin to take the applause.

He decided to type in the word 'UP'. That would do for now. It was a working title. The rest of the legend would come later, along with its own vocabulary, its own new language. Everything would be new by then. The New Age. The New Science, by Doctor... by *Professor Sir* Derek Harding. Now that had a ring to it.

When he had finished making his notes he spent some time mulling over that careless promise he had made to Shallcross, to mind his Ps and Qs when it came to pussyfooting around the business of patient confidentiality. Harding had no idea whether there was any codified system of ethics that covered moonlighting like this, but it might be worth finding out, and soon. After all, he didn't want to have to drag the rest of the university around on his coattails for the rest of his life. Their salary bought his services as a teacher, as a researcher, and that was all as far as he was concerned. It didn't buy his intellect, and he certainly didn't see why it should buy his discoveries, especially when he acquired them outside of the campus. No, they could bask in his reflected glory if they wanted to, but he would not accept a reversal of those roles, and neither would he tolerate any arbitrary, jealous constraints being imposed upon him by that pompous little popinjay Shallcross, either! The Devil take the man! Harding knew what he was about, and no mistaking. He wanted the glory, too. All for himself. Poor, self-deluded little man. Didn't he know? Didn't he know the rules of the game? It was everyone for himself in the race to win the biggest prize of all. Of course it was. But Harding would win. Be certain of that. Harding would win.

He clicked on 'Shut down', and the grin faded away as the screensaver disappeared into darkness.

Kim sat with his bottom jammed against the window ledge next to Iris's chair. Behind them the drip-stand had now been balanced on top of the locker, and the syringe-driver had been joined in Leonard's lap by the catheter bag. And Kim had leaned a small stepladder against the wall behind the door so that he could still meet with his patient face to face when he wanted to.

But now there was a camera positioned at the bottom of the bed, perched on a huge tripod so that it too could stare at the sleeping patient. A second locker had been pressed into service to hold a stack of other recording and monitoring devices, and one way or another the intention seemed to be that everything that happened in that room – every sound and every movement – would be captured for posterity. Every moment of time, and every human emotion, however intimate.

At the end of another warm spring day the room was unbearably hot and humid again, but Iris insisted on keeping the curtains drawn to fend off the rest of the world from her husband's bedside. The door opened and Audrey Kendon poked her head in and smiled.

"Just saying hi, and bad luck, you're stuck with me again." Then she hesitated for a moment and allowed the door to swing open so that she could plant her hands on her hips. "What in the name of sanity is this?" she demanded to know.

"Don't ask," Kim said. "It's a long story!"

"Your idea?"

"You must be joking! We made the mistake of asking the man at the top for help, and this is the consequence."

"Always fatal," Audrey muttered, slowly closing in on the camera and its consorts. "Asking men, I mean."

"We are now being closely scrutinized by a team of mad – and I mean *mad* – scientists!"

"Are we indeed?" Audrey cheered up at once. She began to inspect the new equipment and then started to poke all the knobs and switches she could reach. "What does it do?" She smiled coyly. "It reminds me of the time I was abducted by aliens. Did I ever tell you about that? I was probed twice nightly. We did a swap in the end. I came back to earth to be a night sister and the real Audrey Kendon went off to be Queen of Saturn's third largest moon. We write every Christmas. Does it make tea?"

"It does everything except the washing up, apparently. It records sound, movement, even undetectable seismic anomalies, so I'm told."

"Does it, does it indeed..." Audrey said thoughtfully. "Have we had many of those on Ward 4 since I was last on duty?"

"No."

"No. I thought not." She loomed over what appeared to be a small microphone. "But if any of this junk gets in my way, I will be responsible for a seismic anomaly of my own, you can be sure of that. And all you little cogs and wheels and wires will end up in the street by the shortest route." She suddenly turned on Iris, frowning. "Did anyone ask you for your permission before they did all this, Iris, old girl?"

"Yes. They did. They said I could say no if I wanted to."

"So why didn't you?"

Iris shrugged and considered for a moment. "I couldn't really think of a reason for saying no. It's not really doing any harm, and, who knows, we might even learn a thing or two from it."

"And pigs might fly," Audrey said with feeling. "Have you slept at all today?"

"I had a nap."

"Eaten anything?"

Iris suddenly became very animated and nodded her head keenly. "Oh yes!" she said. "Believe me, I've eaten!"

Audrey winced. "Not another shepherd's pie!"

"'Fraid so."

"You'll end up looking like one. Remind me to buy your neighbour a recipe book for Christmas. This calls for the kettle to be plugged in. Do you want a cup of tea up there, Leonard?" she asked loudly, and then winked at Iris. She started to leave the room but she couldn't resist growling into the microphone again. "I'll give you anomaly. Window to street in three seconds tops! The last thing to go through your microchipped little brain will be the pavement." Then she was gone.

Iris chuckled, and then a very different expression flittered across her face. For the first time Kim suspected her of holding back tears.

"Okay, Ma?" he asked a little shyly, aware that she was old enough to be his grandmother.

He was right. Her defences were slowly eroding. She took a deep breath and then her lips began to tremble. She seemed to shudder for a moment, as though she was trying to shrug off a black mood before it could claim her thoughts, much like she might start at a sudden chill breeze.

"That's the first time anyone has spoken *to* Leonard, rather than *about* him, in a very long while," she said quietly.

"I think he knows you're here," Kim said gently, stepping very carefully this close to her feelings.

She patted his arm. "I'm fine. Really, I'm fine. Let's not…" She hesitated but then chose to let the unfinished sentence drift away from her.

"Can I ask you a personal question before I go, Mrs B?"

"Yes. As long as you let me punch you if you call me Mrs B again."

"Why did you let them do all this? It won't help you, and it certainly won't help Leonard, you know that. It won't make a scrap of difference to his condition."

"But it won't do him any harm, either, will it? Let me ask you a question, Dr M," she said, shifting her chair so that she could see his face.

"By all means. Ma."

"Aren't you curious? Don't you want to know?"

"Of course I do." He pushed himself off the window ledge and wandered towards the door, stopping to look up at his patient before he answered her. Sometimes Leonard Blake looked rather absurd, stuck up there, all alone in his own little world. And sometimes he seemed quite sublime. "More than anything, Mrs B. More than anything."

Then he left her alone with her husband.

9

Liz Manners hated her bleep. Sometimes she called it her little brat, because it behaved like one, and because it clung to her and went everywhere with her. It wanted her undivided attention, and it was a jealous offspring. If she tried to grab a half-hour lunch-break in the cafeteria, it twittered her away before she could even sit down to eat. If she stopped to speak to someone in the corridor, it would twitter her away before she got to the end of the first sentence. And whenever she was rash enough to venture into the ladies' toilet, first the bleep then the invective would be heard for miles around. She even suggested that a telephone be fitted in the cubicle, and when the engineer started to smile he quickly realized that she wasn't joking.

Today the brat had already scuppered both her lunch and her comfort break, and now it lay in wait for her, determined to go for a hat-trick. Liz had squeezed herself into Ward 2's tiny office along with no fewer than six nurses in the hope of sorting out their conflicting and overlapping holiday plans. She sat with a Year Plan on her knees which she had covered with scribbles, crossings-out, and a cluster of duty rotas. It was then that the brat struck, sending the Year Plan and the rotas cascading onto the floor and Liz's temper rocketing into high altitude. She swore at the brat and the papers, and then she snatched up the phone and snarled at it.

"Mrs Manners!"

"Outside call for you." The calm and detached voice of a smiling telephonist.

Liz heard a click and then for a few moments nothing happened. "Hello?" She banged the phone on the table. "Anyone there? Speak!" But instead of words she heard the sound of somebody breathing steadily, close to the mouthpiece. A man, she was certain of that. "Hello? Who is this?"

"Are you the one in charge?" She was right. Deep voice. Not old. Middle-aged? Just possibly younger. Hesitant. Guarded.

"I'm the Hospital Manager, yes. How may I help you?"

Another long pause. More breathing. Then, "What's going on on Ward 4? That's what I'd like to know."

"I'm sorry, I don't quite understand you. Can you begin by giving me your name, please?"

"I don't want to give you my name."

"Then I'm afraid I'm unlikely to be able to help you, am I?"

Another pause. "Is it dangerous?"

"Is what dangerous?" The wrong thing to say. Now she had an attentive audience of nurses in the office, straining their ears to hear more.

"Is it a disease? Is it harmful? Would it kill people if it got out? Into the community?"

Now it was Liz's turn to hesitate. Where did that word 'community' come from? It didn't fit the profile, not if this was supposed to be a concerned member of the public. She didn't like it. It jarred. Liz had received phone calls from some of the wackiest people in the world, and she could categorize them in her sleep: the hostile ones; the confused ones; the loopy ones; the just plain rude or bombastic ones. She could see them coming a mile off. They all had their own speech patterns, their own vocabulary, and this one no longer fitted any of them. Not with that word 'community' thrown in at the end of the sentence for good measure. The caller was a worried man; he was hesitant, nervous, responding to a garbled rumour. Little tremors of fear spiked his conversation, because he was shy, intimidated to be crossing swords with someone who spoke in joined-up writing. All that was plausible. All that fitted the profile, but not the word 'community'. Her defences clicked into place.

"Can you give me your name, please?"

"I've told you, I don't want to give you my name; I want to know if it's dangerous." The voice was careless. It had just shed twenty years and learned the art of grammatical speech.

"If *what* is dangerous? What are you talking about?"

"You know what I mean. You know what I mean. You've got a patient in there you won't let anyone go near. I know. I'm not stupid. It's true, isn't it? People are saying he's got a tropical disease of some kind. They say you're worried it will get out; be released into the neighbourhood."

'Isn't' pronounced without crushing the alveolar fricative, and now the word 'neighbourhood'.

"If you don't give me your name, I can't help you. I can assure you, however, that there is nothing of the kind you describe anywhere in this hospital. You have nothing to worry about." She winced as the six nurses all exploded into whispers.

"So you're refusing to tell me. That means it's all true!"

"It means nothing of the kind. Oh, and by the way, you're getting younger and younger as this conversation goes on."

The caller hesitated again. When he spoke again he had aged alarmingly. "People are going to panic. I know they will. It shouldn't be allowed. You people, you take too many risks. You think you're above the law."

"Let me ask you a different question."

"What?"

"Which comic are you reading from?"

The line went dead.

"Wow!" the Charge Nurse exclaimed as soon as she put the phone down. "Come on, out with it, spill the beans! What was that all about?"

"I have no idea," Liz said, certain that she wouldn't tell him anyway. She jumped up and headed for her office before the interrogation could get into full swing. Halfway along the corridor the brat twittered again. On the tiny LED screen she could see the letters 'INC CALL'. Something told her that it would be the same man. She rushed into her office, slammed the door shut, and picked up the phone.

"Liz Manners."

"Another call for you. You're popular today."

"Wait! Did the caller give a name?"

"No. Male. Polite, well spoken."

"Young, old?"

The telephonist paused to consider. "Young… -ish."

"Put him through." She waited for the click, half expecting to hear more sinister breathing.

"Hi! Can I speak to the Hospital Manager, Liz Manners, please?"

"Speaking."

On the face of it, very different to the other call. Polite, confident, business-like. Was she right or wrong?

"Mrs Manners, hi, I'm Greg Hallows. I don't think we've met. I'm on the staff of the Evening Herald. I wondered if I might just have five minutes of your time."

"For what?" Liz asked warily.

"For a meeting. I'd be more than happy to come to you. What time would suit you best?"

"You won't be surprised to hear me say I'm busy, Mr Hallows. And you also won't be surprised to hear me say that you should be speaking to the Press Officer at the County Hospital, rather than to me. You know this Trust's Press Policy as well as I do."

"Yes, I know, and I did try her, but she said she had no information on the crisis at your hospital."

"Hardly surprising, Mr Hallows. Neither have I. Is someone playing games, do you think?" Starting with you?

"I would hope not, Mrs Manners. I'm calling you because we have received quite a number of calls from members of the public who are becoming increasingly concerned about rumours coming out of your hospital. Word is you have a mystery patient who's fetched up on one of your wards with an undiagnosed, possibly highly contagious disease."

"What rot!"

"I think you owe it to other members of the community to take this matter more seriously than that, Mrs Manners."

There it was again. Community. The tone of the voice was very different, but there was enough in its cadence to convince her that she was indeed speaking to the same man.

"Mr Hallows, we never comment on individual patients, least of all to a stranger over the phone, and never to a reporter fishing for idle gossip!"

"A meeting would be helpful, Mrs Manners."

"A meeting would be a complete waste of my time, Mr Hallows."

"You leave me no alternative but to think you're being deliberately evasive. Doesn't it worry you that people in the community are starting to fear coming anywhere near your hospital?"

"You seem keen enough."

Hallows laughed. "Touché. My job takes me into all sorts of odd places. When may I come and see you?"

"You can't."

"But, Mrs Manners, if this does turn out to be an undisclosed public health risk, and it came to light that you had refused to discuss..."

"Mr Hallows, if we were to find a public health risk in this hospital, no one would be more surprised than me. Now, pin back your ears. There is no crisis. There is no mystery patient. There is no public health risk. And please do not add fuel to a smouldering fire by suggesting that any of these things is true. Unless, of course, I find out that it was you who started the fire in the first place."

"I'm sure, if we met, we..."

"Goodbye Mr Hallows." And she banged the phone down again, this time aware that at least part of her closing denial had nearly stuck in her throat. She waited for the call to clear and then she picked up the phone again and waited for the telephonist to answer her. "No more calls until further notice." Then she put the phone down again without waiting for a reply.

The return of the Black Death could not have made her move faster. She flew out of her office and tore down the stairs and along the corridor, reaching the switchboard just as the startled telephonist completed her next call.

"Any idea where Mr Shallcross is?" Liz asked breathlessly.

The telephonist pointed to the consultant's door. "He went in there a short time ago. I've just put an outside call through to that office and it hasn't bounced back yet, so I assume he's still there."

Liz nodded and crept towards the closed door, tapping it lightly, and then pressing her ear to the wood to hear what was going on inside. She could hear Shallcross's voice suddenly call out, "Come in!" She opened the door a few inches and peeped inside. When Shallcross saw her he waved her into the room excitedly, waving at the receiver he was still holding to his ear. He snatched up a pen and scribbled the word 'Press' across the top of his pad of prescriptions before tossing the whole pad across the table to her.

"Will you be pausing to catch your breath any time soon, Mr Hallows, so that I can say, 'No comment,' for a fourth time?"

Liz snatched the pen from his hand, wrote, "Officer" under the word 'Press', and then heavily underlined both words. Shallcross nodded.

"Mr Hallows, you have a colourful, not to say overwrought, imagination. Seek therapy, I beg of you. Now, if you want to discuss any other half-baked rumours your paper might have unearthed, then please feel free to telephone our charming Press Officer. She is paid to have nothing better to do than speak to the likes of you, leaving people like me free to deal with serious and genuine health issues." At which point he, too, ended Hallows' call.

He turned to Liz anxiously. "What do you make of that? Is word out, do you suppose?"

Liz puckered her lips thoughtfully, but finally shook her head. "Hard to be sure, but I don't think so. He called me before he called you. Twice, I think. Playing silly games. I think he's been speaking to someone who has got hold of part but not all of the story. And now he's fishing for the rest."

Shallcross sat bolt upright. "Whom has he been speaking to?" he demanded, instantly hot under his collar.

Liz opened her arms wide. "How on earth should I know?"

"Is this another aberration on the part of your chum Gravett, do you suppose?"

"No. And he's not my chum."

"Harding the Hideous?"

"No..." Then she hesitated for a moment. "No. I don't think so. What would be the point? He wants his name up there in lights when the time comes, but he isn't going to ask the likes of Greg Hallows to flick the switch for him. He'd phone Paxman."

"Who, then?"

"My guess is someone much closer to home."

"A cleaner?"

"Why on earth a cleaner?"

"A nurse, then?"

"No. Why not a doctor?"

"Why not Mrs Blake!" Shallcross seemed pleased with his detecting skills.

"Good grief, no!" Liz exclaimed. "That's absurd. We just don't know. And, until we do, we're going to have to be a lot more careful, and keep our eyes and ears open."

Shallcross moodily drummed a tattoo on the prescription pad, and then he snatched off the top copy and tore it into tiny pieces. Liz thought for a moment that he was going to eat it. "Not much else we can do, I suppose," he said grumpily, when she got up to leave. "Keep me posted," he added.

When the Hospital Manager had gone, he stood up, walked to the far side of his desk, walked back to his chair, sat down, stood up again, and then stared unblinking at the clock on the wall. He watched the second hand tick its way through sixty seconds. One minute. One whole minute. And it seemed like an eternity. Why wait, he thought peevishly? Why not just get on with it and die! He started for the door and then stopped again, catching a glimpse of himself in the mirror and blushing with shame. "In a bed," he added aloud. "Like normal people do."

When she left Shallcross's office Liz headed back to the cafeteria, determined to grab a salad at the second attempt, even if it meant eating it in her office in solitary confinement. She joined a queue of people and waited for her turn to pay, and while she waited she studied the occupants of the different tables, looking for the mole.

There was the porters' table, always full, always noisy, and always presided over by Tiny Adams, her number one suspect, her odds-on favourite. Tinker, Tailor, Soldier, Fat Man.

Next came a table full of medical secretaries. Gossips one and all, but about each other. They had little direct contact with patients, and they would barter their wares with doctors before they troubled themselves with newspaper reporters.

Then came the radiographers. Leonard Blake had been x-rayed when he first arrived. The mobile had been trundled up to the annexe to take an only halfway decent snapshot of his corrupted lungs, but that was long before he started going up in the world.

Next came a table occupied by four elderly women who had followed the smell of food all the way from the waiting room into the basement cafeteria. They didn't seem to be trembling with fright at the thought of a public health risk, although the quiche had been known to claim the occasional martyr, and they put Liz in mind of Iris Blake, locked away up there in that hellish little room with the man of the hour. It couldn't be her. It just couldn't. She barely left his side now, except to pee.

The next table was shared by engineers and physiotherapists – subterranean creatures that rarely ventured far above ground – and the last table was filled with doctors and nurses, the loudest company by far.

Right on cue a bleep went off somewhere in the room. Not the brat this time. She waited to see who moved. A number of people reached into pockets to see if they were the intended target, but it was Kim Maskell who dropped his knife and fork with a clatter and stomped towards the telephone on the wall just by the cash register. He took the call just as Liz's turn to pay arrived, and he stared at her with a glazed expression while someone spoke to him at length. He frowned, replaced the receiver, and at once began to leave the cafeteria. As he passed her he whispered, "Blake," into her ear. Liz dumped her salad on the counter and followed him up the stairs.

Sister Corin was waiting for him outside the annexe. So, too, was a huge ladder, all of ten feet long, lying on its side and stretching almost all the way from the lift to the door of Leonard Blake's room.

"Who left this dammed thing here?" Liz asked angrily, kicking it with her foot. "Somebody's going to break their neck on it, if they're not careful."

"Well, it's sort of mine, for now," Sister Corin confessed with a blush. "Took quite a bit of persuading to get the engineers to lend it to me, but I won in the end. I told them we wanted it to reach some cupboards in the sluice. Spring-cleaning, I said. There aren't any cupboards, but they didn't think of that. They offered to help at first, but then they remembered the poo. Few men will give you an argument when poo is involved. Neither would you get a ladder like that into the sluice in a month of Sundays," she added thoughtfully.

"So what do you want it for?" Liz wanted to know.

Sister Corin gave her boss the look she normally gave her teenage son when he was being particularly dim. She nodded towards the annexe and touched the side of her nose. All three of them entered the room, and Kim and Liz both shared the same sharp intake of breath. Leonard Blake was almost touching the ceiling.

"Oh my God!" Liz said when she got her breath back. "When did this happen?"

"Quite recently. Within the last ten minutes."

But Sister Corin wasn't referring to the patient's proximity to the ceiling. The blue coverlet was still in place, the drip stand had been abandoned, and the syringe-pump now only reached all the way up to Leonard Blake at the end of a long white cable. Harding's precious camera was staring at a blank patch of wall. And Leonard Blake was no longer dying peacefully.

For the first time in many days he was struggling to breathe. When he coughed his whole body went into spasm, making him lurch and convulse from head to toe, but well beyond the reach of

118

those who might help him. Iris sat on the edge of her chair, her hands at her mouth, petrified that the moment had come.

Kim reacted quickly. Somewhere in the back of his mind he had been rehearsing for this eventuality and he knew what to do. First of all he gathered together all of Harding's equipment and shoved it out none too carefully through the door. Then he began to inch the huge stepladder into the room, twisting and turning it over Iris's head and even poking one end of it out of the window before he was able to stand it upright and lock it into place. Then he quickly tested it with his own weight and scampered up the steps to Blake's side. Liz threw his stethoscope up to him when he waved for it, and then she and Iris waited nervously for his verdict. From the top of the ladder the burly young doctor began to look all around the room.

"What do you want?" Sister Corin asked him.

"Oxygen. I can't remember, is it piped to this room?"

Liz roared with laughter in spite of the urgency. "We haven't even got oxygen piped to the building, let alone to this one little side room."

"Blast! He needs oxygen. How do we get it to him?"

"The old-fashioned way," Sister Corin assured him. "From a G-size cylinder on a trolley. There's one in the ward. I can get it for you in a moment."

"I'm at the top of a ten-foot ladder," Kim reminded her.

"That's not a problem," Liz chipped in. "Narrow gauge oxygen tubing comes in fifty-metre reels."

The Hospital Manager and the ward sister looked at each other and then went their separate ways in search of what Kim needed. Meanwhile Kim came back down the stepladder to wait with Iris. He curled his vast arm around her gently.

"Hang on in there, Mrs B. We ain't beat yet."

"But he's worse," she said. "Much worse."

"He's finding it a bit harder to breathe. We expected that to happen, didn't we. We talked about it more than once. Hopefully the oxygen will settle him down in a moment or two, and then after that I've got another clever trick up my sleeve called hyoscine hydrobromide which will help to dry up that cough. And don't forget, he's still deeply sedated. He knows a lot less about what's going on here than you do."

"You don't understand," Iris said fretfully. "I don't want him to struggle. I want him to go peacefully. With..." She looked up at her husband. "With dignity."

Kim squeezed the poor woman until she could hardly breathe herself. "And he will. He will. And perhaps that might not be very far away now," he added, looking up at Leonard as well. When Iris didn't answer him, he looked down at her face. Her eyes had closed and her dry pale lips were tightly pressed together. Kim had the distinct impression she was praying.

The oxygen and the change of medication worked, as Kim said they would, and Leonard Blake almost immediately stopped coughing and lapsed into silence. By the late afternoon the crisis had passed and the open-ended waiting game had resumed its course. Liz was reluctant to go home, just in case matters were beginning to come to a head, and so she busied herself in her office, waiting on events. She phoned her husband, Phil, and told him that a bug had thinned out her night staff, and then she guided him to a remote and mysterious grotto called a kitchen where she promised him he would find a miraculous white box called a fridge.

She glanced at the clock as she put the phone down. Not quite five o'clock. Nearly time to unlock the prison gates again and let the inmates go free, but there was one little chore that she could tick off her list and this was the perfect time to do it. She picked up the phone again and asked the telephonist if she knew where the Head Porter was hiding.

"It just so happens that he is standing right next to me, coat on, ready for the off."

"Oh, is he indeed?" Liz said, relishing the chance to tug his lead. "Tell him from me his watch is fast. Tell him to take his coat off and beat a path to my office. And be sure to say please."

There was a brief delay while the telephonist had a muffled conversation with her hand over the mouthpiece. "He says tomorrow will have to do. He's going out by the back gate, via the mortuary, so that he can release a body to an undertaker at the same time."

"Did you see the undertaker?"

The telephonist hesitated and then dropped her voice. "No."

"Is he standing there with the mortuary key in his hand?"

"No."

"I thought not. Tell him, 'Five minutes.'" And she put the phone down.

But it was twenty minutes before Tiny Adams finally arrived at her office door, preceded by the creaking of the floorboards that always betrayed his approach. She had just begun to think that he had deliberately ignored her and gone home when a single dull, heavy thud on the door made her jump. Nearly a minute had elapsed between floorboards and fist. Did the man always listen at keyholes?

"Come in."

He walked into the room with a heavy, weary sigh and immediately took a long, hard look at the clock on the wall. Then he jutted out his massive chin, squinted at his watch, shook it hard, and held it to his ear.

"Save me the pantomime," Liz said flatly. "Your duty finished ten minutes ago. I asked you to come to my office twenty minutes ago. You work it out."

"I had to see a body out."

"So I heard. Patient's name?"

A look of irritation flashed across the Head Porter's face. He had forgotten that information of that kind passed across the Hospital Manager's desk. Instead of answering her question, he sat down heavily in the tiny occasional chair she kept on the far side of the desk for her visitors. Every time he used it, Tiny made the chair groan, and Liz was convinced that one day it would collapse under him like matchwood. It would almost be worth losing the chair, she thought.

She allowed the silence to lengthen. She was in no rush. When, finally, she grew tired of simply staring at him, she said, "We have been contacted by the Evening Herald."

"Have you now." he replied. A neutral statement? A question? Either? Neither? No, she thought; there was no trace of surprise in that face. He knew. She would bet her mortgage on the fact that he knew.

"Yes, both Mr Shallcross and I received calls from the paper earlier today. A chap called Hallows, Greg Hallows. Ever heard of him?" she asked, pressing her luck a little.

"No."

"No?" She floated another long silence across the table between them while she studied his face. Sullenness? Always. But indignation? Anger? None to be seen. He had expected the question. "They've got it into their heads that we're keeping some kind of dreadful secret from them."

"Imagine that."

"They say the whole neighbourhood – the whole community – is up in arms, terrified that they're all going to catch the plague and be dead in a week."

"Do they." He stared back at her, dull and expressionless.

"Silly."

"You tell me."

So her temper snapped first. "Don't be so stupid!"

At last, a reaction of a kind. He folded his arms and glared at her balefully. "I like being stupid. It means I don't have to worry about all those secret meetings I don't get asked to. And it means that I don't have to be secretive all the time, because no one has told me any secrets to be secretive about. Have they? I am clearly not the trustworthy kind. But that's up to you. You know how to keep all the secrets. Good luck to you. You want to keep Jack the Ripper cooped up in that poxy little annexe for a month of Sundays, you go ahead. See if I care!"

"Why did you mention the annexe?"

He looked away from her, breaking eye contact for the first time. Then he crossed one leg over the other and brushed an imaginary speck of dust from his knee.

When he didn't answer her she pretended to be surprised. "Are you a nurse? A doctor? A social worker? Then why should you concern yourself with what goes on in the annexe? It's not your business."

"Barrier nursing not my business? Tut-tut. A hazardous place for ancillary staff to go. Gosh, next thing you know we'll be having loads more rumours flying around the place."

Liz paused. She wasn't sure if he had just landed a blow. In fact, she wasn't at all sure what he had just said. Her voice hardened. No more word games.

"The sole purpose of barrier nursing is to prevent the spread of infection, as you very well know. And infection passes in both directions, in or out of any given environment. We have invoked a very necessary but also a very commonplace code of nursing practice. We are trying to safeguard the wellbeing of frail and elderly patients and our own members of staff, if that's quite acceptable to you." She paused for a reply but none was forthcoming. "Someone around here is trying to cause a lot of trouble. That someone has called the Press and deliberately given them an unsubstantiated rumour, knowing that they will go to town on it, knowing that they will put two and two together and, as usual, come up with ten. Motive? Money? Kicks? Who knows? You tell me. But here's something I can tell you: the person who made that call acted in a grossly irresponsible manner. That person deserves to be tracked down and disciplined. Don't you agree?"

She paused for effect, and when he still didn't answer her, she asked him in a very matter-of-fact voice, "Tiny, did you make that call?"

"Me?" For a moment he looked as though he might heave himself out of his chair and lunge at her.

"Because, if you did, if I ever find out it was you, I will personally eviscerate you and give your body to the crows." She could have leaned forward at this point, smiled, waved her own words aside, eased and reduced the tension between them. Instead, she chose to sit back in her chair and fold her arms, deaf to entreaty. "We work as a team in this building. We live and work together as a family much of the time. We all pull together and we look out for each other. And the sole reason that any of us have for coming into this building is to serve the needs of the sick and the dying. There is nothing else. And when one of us lets the rest of the team down, he – or she – lets everyone down: staff, patients, all of us, but themselves most of all. And for what? Greed? A few pieces of silver? A moment of fame? That'll keep you nice and warm on a winter's night after you've been sacked! Betray this team, betray the trust of the people we serve – patients and their families – and you will earn the contempt of us all. Do I make myself clear?"

Tiny Adams was breathing very deeply, clenching and unclenching his huge fists, and then squeezing the arms of the chair as though he wanted to crush them. Or her. "Are you giving this little speech to everyone?" he growled malevolently.

"No. Just you. You can tell the others, if you want to. After all, that's your job, isn't it? That's what you do. Tell others what you think they should know."

He suddenly pushed down on the arms of the chair, snapping one arm clean in two as he lifted himself up and turned towards the door. She expected something else – a parting shot, a look, perhaps even a veiled threat – but instead he simply opened the door and walked away, leaving the door wide open behind him. When he had gone she looked down at her hands and saw that they were shaking.

What had she just done, she wondered? Had she put out a fire before it began to burn out of control? Or had she just started a separate blaze of her own?

10

Don arrived in good time to begin his night duty at 10.30 pm. He relieved the late duty porter, locked the front door behind him, and then settled down at the switchboard with a huge, half-finished paperback novel to read. Don was Old School. He might well sit at the switchboard for the whole night, neither seeing nor speaking to anyone, but he wore his regulation uniform, neatly ironed, and he wore his tie, knotted firmly to the throat. He was sixty-three years old, rapidly approaching retirement, and as keen as ever to do his job well. He was polite, considerate, genuinely caring, and reliable. Nothing was too much trouble for him, whether it was for a patient or another member of staff. He was liked and trusted by everyone. Cloned in sufficient numbers, he would have won back the Empire. But the mould had been broken a long time ago.

When Don heard the key turn in the lock of the side door, the street door used by key-holders, he expected to see the on-call doctor creeping into the hospital, half-asleep. Instead he saw Tiny Adams standing in the middle of the dimly lit corridor trying to remember who his night man was.

"Oh, it's you. Donald Duck!" He slowly walked over to the switchboard and lifted Don's novel out of his hands to inspect the back page. "What rubbish are you reading now? Porn at midnight?"

"I didn't expect to see you here at this time of night," Don replied pleasantly, careful to retrieve his book from the Head Porter without losing his page.

"I'll bet you didn't," Tiny's voice rumbled from the depths of his chest. "I was passing. I remembered I'd left my pen in the mortuary. Good pen. Didn't want to lose it, so I thought I'd call in and get it back before some tea-leaf in the Lodge has it away. Bung us the keys."

Don reached up to the keyboard above his head and took down the long, black mortuary key. He tapped the open notebook on the counter and half-seriously invited Tiny to sign the key out. "Time for an autograph? Lead by example?"

The Head Porter stared at him for a moment, then took the key from him and wandered off down the darkened corridor without saying another word.

Don listened to the courtyard door bang shut, then he watched the little screen of the black and white security monitor until Tiny's huge shadow suddenly filled it as he passed under the camera above the rubbish shed door and then walked down the alleyway towards the gates at the back of the hospital. Halfway down the alleyway he stopped at the mortuary door, fumbled with the key for a moment, and then disappeared from sight. The mortuary window lit up, illuminating much of the alleyway, and revealing the gates and the oxygen store where all the gas cylinders were kept. Then the light disappeared and the Head Porter emerged into the alleyway again and locked the door. For a moment he seemed to check each of his coat pockets in turn, and then he held up what looked like a pen so that the camera could see it. Before heading back into the hospital Tiny decided to walk on down to the gates and shake them to make sure that they were securely locked. Satisfied, he retraced his steps and disappeared from the camera's view. A few moments later the courtyard door banged again, and then Tiny was back at the hatch, waving his pen in triumph. Don might have been mistaken, but it looked like the biro that lived in the spine of the mortuary register. Hardly worth a detour at this time of night, Don thought to himself. Tiny threw the mortuary key onto the notebook and immediately headed towards the side door.

"See you tomorrow," Don called after him.

"Whatever," Tiny muttered, and then that door, too, slammed firmly shut behind him.

An hour passed without any more interruptions, and Don managed to read a whole chapter of his book without being disturbed. Then he yawned and nearly cracked his jaw. It was the signal to make that first mug of tea of the night.

Just then the doorbell rang, and he marked his place in the book and went to open the front door. In the porch, key in hand, he stopped when he saw a face peering in at him through the grubby glass of the outer door. A man was standing on the doorstep. Clean-shaven, not above middle-aged, quite well dressed. Don went through the checklist every time he found a stranger at the door. What was the likelihood of drugs or drink? Were there any signs that pointed to irrational behaviour? Was there a perceived danger of any kind? That old, heavy Victorian front door was the first line of defence for all the patients and staff in the hospital, and once it was opened, everyone depended on Don's judgement.

The man at the window was not a regular. Don knew them all after twenty years in the job – their nights, their times, their pleas, their excuses, their habits, their needs. Very few were allowed in. Most were turned away. This man was bleary-eyed. He was grinning and blinking stupidly at the bright porch light. Drunk, Don thought. Pound to a penny, and on my watch. When he opened the door he decided to leave the security chain in place.

"Can I help you?" he asked politely through the narrow gap left by the chain.

A giddying wave of beer fumes made him jerk his head back from the door. The man on the doorstep belched and then wobbled, and then steadied himself again, as though he was teetering on the edge of a great precipice. "Can I come in?" he asked in a thick, slurring voice.

"No, you can't."

"But I need to. It's cold." And right on cue he shivered violently and then pulled the lapels of his jacket up to his chin.

"Go home then and get warm."

"I need a pee!"

"Have a pee by all means," Don suggested, without offering to open the door. "I'm not stopping you."

"I need the loo!" the man insisted, suddenly perfectly steady on his feet.

"Better not hang around then. Off you go."

"I need to use your loo."

"You're not going to use my loo. Head for home. Use yours."

"Come on," the man whined. "I'll pee in the street. I'll piss myself, I will!"

"Fine. Don't let me stop you." And the door remained ajar, the chain pulled taut and clearly visible.

The stranger thought the matter through for a moment. Nothing about him rang true. He reeked of booze but he wasn't drunk, not falling down drunk like he would have Don believe. He seemed to wobble and stagger when it suited him, or when he remembered to. He seemed to be going through the motions – and all the clichés – of what he thought a drunk might do at a hospital door at the dead of night. Shifting his weight from foot to foot and then plunging his hands into his trouser pockets, he announced, "I need a taxi. I need to phone a taxi."

"Phone box on the street corner," Don answered him, as he had answered a hundred other men through this same crack in the door over the years.

"I haven't got any money."

"Then you won't get a taxi, will you? They're free tomorrow night!"

"Lend us a few quid. I'll pay you back. Honest I will."

"In your dreams."

The man suddenly lunged at the door. The chain held fast and the man bounced off the door, and while he recovered his balance, Don slammed the door in his face, locked it, retreated through the inner door, and switched off the light. The man kicked the door as hard as he could and then he stumbled backwards onto the pavement. Then he took himself off and decided to stagger again as he turned into the main road and wandered slowly past the front of the hospital. Don tiptoed into Shallcross's office and watched his progress from the window. When he drifted out of sight Don gave up on him and walked along to the Porter's Lodge to switch the kettle on. At the next street corner the drunk stopped at the kerb, glanced quickly behind him, and then took a long hard look down the side street towards the gates at the back of the hospital. There was no one there, so he stood up straight, took his hands out of his pockets, walked on for another block, and then turned into the next side street and let himself into a parked car. Once there, he sat back to suck a mint and wait.

Hallows had waited for his decoy to ring the doorbell before he darted down the back road to the hospital gates. He found them unlocked as promised, and when he touched them with his fingertips they swung open silently to admit him. Once inside he closed and locked the gates behind him, then he tiptoed quickly and quietly down the alleyway, past the mortuary, until he was out of sight of the camera. He next found himself in the courtyard, surrounded on all four sides by the sheer walls of the hospital building, and, above them, a starlit night. A few inadequate security lights flickered off and on for the benefit of the moths, but their pale yellow glare only served to accentuate the deep black gloom that surrounded him. He stood under one of the lights for a moment and consulted a piece of paper he drew from his coat pocket. It contained a roughly sketched map of the interior of the hospital, showing the position of two portacabins in the courtyard and the foot of a steel fire escape that was hidden away behind one of them. He was glad of his rubber soled shoes. He quickly ran up the first flight of stairs to an exterior gantry that was level with the rooms inside. He pressed himself up against the wall between two windows and listened carefully. There wasn't a sound to be heard anyway. No one was awake; no one was moving around the building. Still with his back to the wall he crept along the gantry until he found a door. According to the map he was now standing one floor above an empty waiting room, one floor below an office, and right outside the fire escape to Ward 4. He knelt down and tried the door handle very gently. The door was a little stiff, but it opened without a sound. The bolt on the inside had been drawn back, as promised. Satisfied, he closed the door again and crouched down to wait.

The minutes passed slowly. Don, at the front door, was still occupied with his early-morning caller, but something suddenly appeared near one of the ward windows, banging against the glass. Hallows shivered from head to foot, wondering for a moment if he had been seen, but the object was a pillow, tossed onto a window ledge by a nurse tucking a patient back into his bed. Hallows watched carefully as the shadowy figure moved from bed to bed and then left the ward. When she had gone Hallows quickly opened the door again and this time stepped into the ward and crouched down on the floor behind two large cylinder trolleys. He could hear two voices in conversation in the office on the landing, and he could hear a dozen old men snoring for England, and that suited him perfectly. He crept into the passageway that led to the annexe and stopped by the entrance to the sluice to check on the nurses again. They were both still in the office, beyond the lift, with the office door pulled to. From there, assuming they stayed there, they would neither see nor hear him.

Hallows took a deep breath. If the map was accurate in every detail then the door to his left was the door to Leonard Blake's room. He reached out and turned the handle.

If they caught him now, he thought, he was as good as dead. Up against the wall, last fag. There wasn't an excuse in Wonderland that would explain away a newspaper reporter found wandering round a men's ward at two o'clock in the morning. But, if it came off, he would be a made man. He would write his own contract. Choose his own job title. Run the whole shooting match. All for having the nonce to worm his way into a hospital at the dead of night to take a good long look at a very strange patient.

He looked into the room. The infamous annexe. It was empty.

His information had been faultless. The back gate, unlocked as requested; the fire escape, located on the map as requested; the bolt on the fire escape door, pulled back as requested; the room itself identified by the notice stuck to the door. He was in the right room. So where was the star patient? Where was the mystery? Where was Leonard Blake?

Actually, the room wasn't empty at all. There was a bed, but the bed was empty. It was covered by a huge blue eiderdown, all crumpled up, as though someone had just thrown it aside. Sticking out of the eiderdown was something that looked like a large syringe inside some kind of clamp. On the far side of the bed was another oxygen cylinder bolted inside a trolley. There was a long, untidy coil of green tubing attached to it which trailed along the ground, hissing gently. Best of all, there was a drip-stand perched up on top of a locker, and a huge great stepladder, towering over the bed like a Martian War Machine. There was even an old lady, fully dressed, slumped in a chair by the window, with her head thrown back and her mouth wide open, fast asleep, and snoring like an express train. It wasn't an empty room. It was a weird room. But there was no patient.

Then Hallows nearly had a heart attack. The door behind him began to open very slowly. He threw himself against the wall and held his breath. In about three seconds he would be discovered, somebody would be bound to scream, they might even kick out an alarm, and then all hell would break loose. Blue lights, bracelets, goodbye cruel world. Instead, a loud, urgent voice called out for a nurse from somewhere inside the main ward, and the pressure on the door eased and the door itself slowly closed again.

There was no point in staying here any longer. It was time to get out of here while he still could. He slipped out of the room, tip-toed straight back to the fire escape door, barely a dozen paces behind the nurse, then darted through the door and took off down the steps and into the courtyard like a bat out of hell. There was no point in being cautious now. If anyone saw him he would be moving at speed, he would have his back to them, it was pitch dark, and he wasn't going to stop for anything, least of all to tell anyone why he was there in the first place. But first of all he ran straight into the side of the first portacabin and nearly knocked himself out. Without waiting to get his wind back, he dragged himself to his feet, ran down the back alleyway, pulled back the gates and fled into the street. And, to his immense relief, nothing happened. No dogs, no searchlights, no machine guns. Just the crash of the hospital gates slamming shut again. He walked round the corner to the waiting car, climbed inside, and swore.

Don was too far away to hear the gates, and he didn't look up at the right moment to witness the flight of the Evening Herald's finest, scurrying for home.

Iris woke up very slowly and found Audrey Kendon standing over her. When the night sister was sure that she was fully awake, she squeezed her shoulder gently and then bent down and kissed her on the cheek, and that told Iris all that she needed to know.

"Is he gone?" she asked softly, still fearful she might wake him.

"Oh yes," Audrey said. "He's gone."

When Kim got the long-awaited call he said he would dress and come at once. Shallcross had asked to be informed if Blake died that night, too, and he also said he would dress and drive down to the hospital straight away. And when Audrey learned from Don that Liz Manners was still in her office, she called her to the annexe, too, assembling all the original players in the drama for one last curtain call.

Kim, Audrey and Liz all stood around Leonard Blake's widow, wanting to comfort her and yet not finding the right words to say between them. It was hard. The room seemed so empty, now that there was no longer a dying man clinging to the ceiling high above their heads.

"Dear God," Liz said wearily, her eyes stinging with tiredness. "So he really *has* gone, this time, hasn't he? No body? Nothing?"

"So it would appear," Kim said softly, half to himself.

"How does that work, then?" Liz asked.

Kim stared at her incredulously. "You're asking me?"

"Sorry. I'm just... curious. And very tired."

"I'm embarrassed."

"Embarrassed?"

"Yes, if I feel anything at all, I feel embarrassed. As though I'm solely responsible for losing him."

"Well, I'm just glad," Audrey said honestly. "Relieved and glad. I'm glad for his sake most of all, because I didn't want him to end up like some sort of freak peep show, with all the world and his dog bowling up to look at him. And I'm sure you didn't want that either," she said to Iris, resting a hand on her shoulder again. "I'm relieved for the rest of us. Sanity is restored."

"I wish I could be as sure of that!" Kim said with some feeling, struggling to control his emotions.

Liz had been staring at the empty bed. "What on earth are you going to put on the death certificate?" she said, turning to Kim with a look of dismay.

"You ask me that now!" Kim exclaimed. "How should I know? Probably something that won't intrigue the coroner too much, if I still want to have a medical career after all this has blown over." Iris looked at him blankly. "Coroners have the right to call in bodies for post mortem examination, and I haven't got one to give them."

"You'll have to write something," Liz concluded.

"Yes," Kim said. "Thank you, Liz. I will indeed have to write something. Just let me go and read up on my Arthur C. Clarke first."

"I need to sleep," Liz said with a barely stifled yawn. "About a week should do it. Then you can all take it in turns to tell me it was a dream. I'm sorry if that sounds insensitive," she added for Iris's benefit, "but, quite frankly, I was beginning to find it very hard to focus any part of my mind on normal things. Like the rest of my life, for instance. All because of this." She pointed at the empty bed. "This thing we haven't even got a name for."

Kim had stopped listening to the Hospital Manager. Instead, he was watching Iris's face, trying to gauge how she was feeling, in the midst of this madness, now that it seemed to be over. "What are you thinking?" he asked her quietly.

His words broke the spell. She suddenly stood up, brushed herself down, and picked up her handbag. "I'm thinking it's time to go home," she said, in a loud, hard voice. "I feel tired. And I feel relieved. And that's all that I can feel for now." Audrey's hand reached towards her again. "So help me, I do believe you are going to offer me yet another cup of tea!" Audrey nodded, and Iris glared at her for a moment as though a great torrent of anger might spill out of her and engulf the entire room. Then she sighed and relented. "One last cup of tea, then. If it will make you happy, one last cup of tea."

Despite the lateness of the hour – Kim wrote in the notes that Leonard Blake's death occurred at 1.00 a.m. – they all sat in Liz's office drinking tea. When Shallcross arrived he roused Don from his novel and then he, too, joined them, even accepting a mug of tea as well. Alas, he had a speech prepared.

"Mrs Blake," he said, alarming everyone by suddenly snatching up Iris's hand and stroking it fondly. "My condolences. I find myself in part relieved and in part sorry, and yet you, of course, are facing your loss under very trying circumstances. But..." And he held up an arrow-straight finger, in case anyone should think of interrupting. "...except for those last few hours, your husband was peaceful. He did not suffer. There was no pain. But neither was there any quality of life. And so it was the right time to let him go, and he will be at peace now. And..." Another finger. "...if it is any consolation to you, I think I may safely say without fear of contradiction that your husband will not be forgotten."

"That much is true!" Kim said aloud, before he could stop himself.

They were all exhausted and they had all used up their limited store of platitudes for occasions like this. Nothing new could be said about death, and what they did say made not a scrap of difference to the woman who just wanted to go home and sit at her kitchen table.

While they sat through the awkward silence that followed Shallcross's speech, Liz looked down at her pad and saw that she had scribbled, "Body – Funeral?" But it was far too late at night to deal with that conundrum. It would have to wait. Hymns, readings and eulogies and the hereafter, it would all have to wait. She needed to go home now that there was nothing to keep her here anymore.

As Shallcross had his car with him, he chivalrously offered to drive Iris home, but both Liz and Audrey worried about her going into a cold and empty house all on her own.

"Is there anyone we can call for you?" Audrey asked. "Any of your children?"

"No!" Iris said very firmly. "None of them lives locally, but please don't worry, I'll be fine. I have good neighbours. I'll be okay. Remember, I've had a long time to prepare for this."

She didn't terribly much care what she said now, as long as she could get out of there soon. She just wanted to breathe fresh, untainted air again, and to walk ten feet and not encounter a magnolia-coloured brick wall. She stood up again and began to shake them all by the hand. Finally, turning to Liz, she said, "I will of course be in touch with you about the formalities. Audrey has kindly given me a pamphlet which explains what I have to do."

She stepped into the corridor and waited for Shallcross to lead the way. Just then a nurse hurried along the corridor and whispered something in Audrey's ear. For a moment the night sister looked at her as though she couldn't understand what she was saying.

"True! I'm telling you. Come and see for yourself, if you don't believe me," the nurse insisted.

Audrey hurried away with her, and although no one else spoke a word, and no one suggested it, everyone remained standing exactly where they were until she returned. When Audrey did come back, she walked towards them slowly, like a sleepwalker.

"You'd better come and see this," she said. "All of you."

She led them, not to Ward 4, nor to the annexe, but to the steep wooden stairs that led to Ward 5. There they crossed another landing – the lift to the left, a kitchen to the right – and then Audrey led them into a small side room exactly where the annexe itself was situated on the floor below. Putting a finger to her lips, the night sister showed them a white-haired woman lying fast asleep in an old metal bed. There was a locker at the bedside, the ubiquitous jug of water and plastic beaker on top, and next to the locker there was even an empty orange chair identical to the one Iris had lived in for endless days. But they had not come to see the room or its occupant. Audrey pushed the door back as far as it would go so that they could see the floor under the bed where, dressed in the same pair of nylon pyjamas, there lay the body of Leonard Blake.

11

Shallcross won. Shallcross always won. They might have spent the rest of the night arguing about it, but Liz insisted on spinning a coin, and Shallcross always shouted heads before anyone else could, so that meant Liz lost and Shallcross won. He would get to make the phone call. He would get to wake Gravett up at four o'clock in the morning.

They were like children with a catapult. It was entirely possible that they would ring his number and then run and hide. Liz knew where to put her hands on the number so she was allowed to dial, but when the faint tribbling sound began at the other end of the line, Shallcross snatched the phone away from her and listened with glee.

The telephone rang and rang, and then at last it was answered by a quiet, wakeful voice.

"Yes?"

And now Shallcross couldn't think of anything to say.

"Hello? Anyone there?"

"Who's that?" Shallcross demanded.

"Isn't that *my* line?"

"Gravett?"

"Who else would answer my phone at this time of the morning?"

"I shudder to think!"

"My goodness! George? Is that you? I hardly recognized you."

"Did I wake you?" Shallcross asked hopefully.

"No, I was in the kitchen making a cup of tea. I'm in my study as a matter of fact. You know how it is. Much to ponder. I'm sorry if I kept you waiting," Gravett added.

Shallcross sniffed into the phone noisily. "That's hardly the point," he said, staring down Liz's disappointment at the same time.

"What can I do for you?" Then Gravett suddenly thought to ask, "My God, is he dead?"

Shallcross grunted. "Well, he was for a while, but he isn't now!"

Gravett gave that piece of information a moment or two to sink in, and then he said, "Doubtless you will explain what that means to me in due course. In the meantime, I assume your call is urgent as it's not yet dawn."

The conversation was far too cordial for Shallcross's liking. These opportunities came along very rarely in life. He decided to tighten the screw a little.

"When you get to your palatial Valhalla-by-the-Sea, sometime before lunch today, I want you to set about transferring Ward 5 from this building to anywhere that you can find a niche for it. I'm sure you must have a spare ward or two in your sumptuous seaside folly."

"All of it?" Gravett asked. "The whole ward?"

"All of it." Shallcross smiled at Liz.

"When?"

"When?" This was the moment he had been waiting for. "When? When? As soon as you get to work, my good man. Action this day! Action this day!"

"No, when am I transferring them?"

"Damn it man, I'm *talking* about transferring them! Today. At once! Before the close of play!" He winked at Liz and she closed in on the earpiece.

Gravett was quiet again for a moment, and Shallcross could hear the sound of a pen scratching on paper. When Gravett finished writing he simply said, "Okay."

"Okay?" Shallcross looked at the mouthpiece and then shook it. "What do you mean by okay? I said now. Today! At once!"

"Okay. I heard you. I'm not deaf. All the arrangements are in place. Egremont Ward is ready, or will be by the time you get there. It's equipped with beds, lockers, all the usual paraphernalia. I'll order a rapid deep-clean as soon as I get in. We can start to receive patients from midday."

"That's eight hours' time," Shallcross said.

"Yes, that's right, George. I do have a watch."

"That's…"

"Impressive? Yes, I know. It's called contingency planning, George. Wait a minute. You said Ward 5. Why Ward 5? I thought he was on Ward 4."

"He was, but he isn't now. That's the crux of a long story. I'll fill you in later." All Shallcross could do was watch the disappointment forming on Liz's face. He was facing defeat. "Of course, it goes without saying that the costs of all this will come out of your budget and not mine."

"Funding isn't a problem."

Shallcross achieved the perfect double take, mystifying Liz still further. "I'm sorry; did I just slip into a parallel dimension? I thought you just said funding isn't a problem. It's always a problem with penny-pinching people like you."

"I said funding is not a problem and it isn't. We keep a sizeable war chest for emergencies of this kind."

Shallcross's frustration began to boil over. "War Chest! You sound like Genghis Khan!" But he was out of ammunition and the fun had long since gone out of the game. This time Gravett had won. "Very well, then. I'll let you go back to sleep."

"I said I was up. I think I'll head into the office and make an early start. Doubtless we will speak later." And the line went dead.

Shallcross was left listening to the dialling tone. He put the phone down slowly and turned to Liz Manners.

"Bugger!"

––––––––––––––––

The first ambulance arrived at ten o'clock precisely, nine hours after Leonard Blake's recorded death, seven hours after his resurrection, and just six hours after Gravett had received the news. The other ambulances followed one another throughout the day, and by early evening Ward 5 stood empty of staff and patients. Two ladies had been allowed to go home; the other ten patients would wake up the next day to an unaccustomed view of the sea, the shriek of gulls, and the incessant roar of seafront traffic.

But long before even that first ambulance arrived at the hospital's doorstep, and immediately after the call to the Chief Executive, there was the little matter of Amy Roper to deal with. Amy was ninety-four years old, and for that reason she spent much of her time soundly asleep; and when she slept she left her hearing aids in a denture pot on the locker to ensure that nothing short of a world war would disturb her. Fast asleep, therefore, Miss Roper had to be carefully removed from the room that Leonard Blake had now chosen to occupy.

It was time for Don to put his novel aside and bring himself, a stretcher trolley and two long wooden poles to the landing outside Miss Roper's room. When he arrived he found a welcoming committee waiting for him. A consultant helped him to pull the trolley from the lift, a Hospital Manager held the lift door open for him, a doctor offered to carry the poles for him, and a night sister greeted him at the patient's bedside.

Audrey smiled and silently clapped her hands. "I'm glad it's you, young Donald," she said quietly to the man whose birthday she shared. "We're going to attempt a little piece of legerdemain with an old biddy or two, and you are just the man for the job."

"Should I take that as a compliment?" Don whispered, unaware of the hearing aids in the denture pot.

"Compliment intended. Here's the plan. We need to get Amy, here, out of this room and into the annexe downstairs, where we have a nice new bed waiting for her. The trouble is, Old Sport, we can't move the bed she's lying on – and, no, you can't ask me why – so you and Tarzan here will just have to lift her out of the bed, using the canvas and the poles, and then carry her out to the trolley in the corridor, without dropping her and without giving yourselves a hernia. Possible?"

Don nodded and smiled.

"Good boy! Right. She's already on the canvas so it's over to you."

Anyone else would have begun by looking under the bed, but Audrey was right: Don was the perfect man for the job. He concentrated his attention on the bed itself. It was old – it almost looked as if it was made of cast iron – and it was soldered into one piece. Unlike the King's Fund beds, it could not be dismantled, so Don decided to just leave it where it was and work around it.

He brought each of the wooden poles into the room and stood them up against the wall. Then, taking one pole at a time, he raised one end of the pole until it almost touched the ceiling, then he inserted the other end of the pole inside the stitched sleeve that ran the length of the canvas that Amy Roper was already lying on. When both poles were in place, Don moved the locker out of the way and nodded to Kim to take up a lifting position at the bottom of the bed. The young doctor was twice Don's size and half his age, but from the bottom of the bed he would only lift one third of Amy's weight, whilst from the top of the bed Don would control the lift. It came in two stages. Firstly Don leaned his left elbow right over Amy's head, braced it on the mattress and then, with Kim's help, simply shifted the whole canvas and the sleeping patient about eighteen inches down the bed, bringing the ends of the poles out from under the fixed head of the bed. That done, the two men prepared themselves again, took a firm grip on both poles, and this time lifted Amy straight up into the air. Slowly Don stood up, never once letting the canvas dip or sag, and then, with Audrey holding the door and Liz holding the trolley, the two men shuffled the stretcher slowly and carefully out of the room and landed Amy safely on the trolley in the corridor, where she sighed contentedly.

"Well done, gents!" Audrey said softly, patting them both on the back. "When we have delivered Amy to her new home, can you get rid of the trolley, Don, and then come back to us, please? We have another little job for you, one that will not be quite as straightforward as this."

Don never forgot the next half hour, but neither did he ever mention it to a living soul. When he returned to Ward 5, having returned the trolley to its home outside the lift on the ground floor, he found Shallcross waiting for him again, and this time Kim had taken off his white coat and rolled up his shirt sleeves. Liz Manners had moved over to the window, and Audrey had returned to the head of the bed, and between them they all looked like fielders at a bizarre game of cricket.

Shallcross was clearly in charge now. "Gentlemen, this bed must go, but we can't move it across the floor, we can only lift it upwards. It was built in the reign of Canute; it weighs a ton. Suggestions?"

Don stood with his hands on his hips and gave the bed a long, hard look. Out of the corner of his eye he saw Audrey kick the edge of a blue coverlet out of sight under the bed. That, he knew, was none of his business, and so he studied the length of the bed and the width of the room. Shallcross followed the direction of his eyes.

"What are you thinking?"

"I'm thinking that we tip the bed up on its end," Don said. "We lift the head of the bed, pivot it on its feet, turn it through ninety degrees and then stand it up on end against the wall by the window."

"No, no," Shallcross insisted, shaking his head. "You don't understand. It must leave the room. It's too tall, stood on end. It won't go through the door."

"Let him finish," Kim said quietly, reading Don's polite smile. Shallcross might be a demon with a scalpel but he had never worked for Pickford's.

"Phase Two of our Master Plan will be to lower the bed – on its side – so that the head of the bed is nearest the door. Then we should be able to lift the bed out through the door by feeding the head of the bed through the door first and then swinging the whole bed to the left as we go. With any luck we should end up with the bed resting on its side on the landing. Remember the removal man's motto: if it went in in the first place, it must be able to come out now!"

"You've just given me a migraine," Shallcross admitted, rubbing his temples sourly.

But Kim seemed to know instinctively what Don intended to do. This time he was determined to provide the muscle, so he gently pushed past the porter, took hold of the top of the bed and lifted it up into the air with a deep, guttural roar. Don jammed his shoe against the foot of the bed to stop it from sliding away, and in a moment the two men had the bed standing on its end between them. And, as the bed rose, so Audrey quickly knelt down and adjusted the blue bedspread over a familiar shape on the floor. But Don had deliberately turned his head away.

With a few more stertorous grunts, and with Shallcross directing traffic, the two men inched the bed out of the room and onto the landing exactly as Don had described. Once on the landing it was a simple matter to stand the bed upright again, push it into the lift, and speed it on its way to the engineer's workshop in the basement. Then the lift stopped at the ground floor and Don prepared to leave Kim and return to the switchboard.

"Anything else you need?" he asked, with his usual smile.

"No, Don. Thank you. We're done." Kim held out his hand and Don shook it warmly. "You are the best of the best."

Don blushed, and then walked back to the switchboard where he flicked off the call-divert switch, checked for incoming calls, then sat down, puffed out his cheeks, and returned to his unfinished novel.

By the time Kim got back to the room, Shallcross was already kneeling on the floor with his stethoscope to Leonard Blake's chest. The only piece of furniture in the room was an orange chair, and Iris was sitting on it.

Kim knelt at Shallcross's elbow and scrutinized the patient's face. "If it's not a silly question," he began hesitantly, "is he alive?"

Shallcross gathered up the stethoscope in his hand and shrugged. "You tell me. No medication, no saline, no oxygen and, as far as I can tell, no pulse and no respiration. And yet..." He took Kim's hand and placed it on Leonard Blake's cheek.

"He's warm!"

Shallcross nodded. "He's warm."

The young doctor touched one of the patient's eyelids and gently teased it open. The pupil immediately dilated in response to the bright light. Kim looked up at Iris. "He's alive!"

And Iris nodded.

12

Liz sat in her office and rubbed her neck ruefully. On days like this she could just about believe that she was beginning to get old. Liz the party girl used to be able to dance till dawn and then boogie through a bright new day on caffeine alone. But not now. The wear and tear was beginning to tell. She was like Mr Baker on Ward 4. Her mileage was beginning to slow her down.

She hadn't been able to get home at all, and now she had fallen asleep at her desk twice in the space of ten minutes. She didn't need coffee or fresh air; she needed a new body and twelve hours' uninterrupted sleep, and not necessarily in that order. In the last two hours she had waded through a list of phone calls as long as her arm, trying to explain to nurses and then to next-of-kin why they should suddenly expect to find their jobs and their loved ones in other hospitals. And, no, she didn't know how long it would be for; and, yes, it would take longer to get there; and, no, there wouldn't be anywhere for them to park. Much did she care!

She had also telephoned her husband – again – and this time she had to invent an outbreak of spring flu, which he didn't believe for a second. But he could sense the struggle that lay behind the shabby pretence, and he chose not to add to the pressure and the desperate weariness that he could hear in her voice. She loved him and she hated lying to him. She missed him and she told him so. She missed his no-nonsense approach to life in general, and to her working life in particular, especially when it took her away from him.

Of course, they both knew perfectly well that all the secrecy, all the subterfuge, was intended to protect the hospital and its staff and its patients. A thing called integrity was at stake, and the hospital – that amalgam of brick, mortar, flesh, blood, and hard-won expertize – needed to go on serving and protecting everyone who needed it for their survival. But now one of its wards had gone, and a bond of trust had gone, too – broken, shattered, trampled on – and all for the sake of a truth too ludicrous to put into words: an old man quietly making his way to heaven by an unconventional route.

And now matters had gone from bad to worse, after what Kim had decided to call Round Two: The Resurrection. Were they simply to accept that Leonard Blake had left one room and then appeared in another room a few moments later, passing through a ceiling and a floor as though they weren't there? And were they now simply to accept that he was alive, and yet not alive in a way that made any sense to them or to the so-called wisdom accumulated by medical science? If this was life, then it was certainly life as none of them had ever experienced it before. And Liz knew exactly what her feet-on-the-ground husband would have to say about that. "It's new? It's different? Great! Why the secret?"

Meanwhile the empty ward was strictly out of bounds. There were two notices – one in the lift, one perched on an artist's easel in the middle of the landing – telling everyone that they could still reach Ward 6 at the top of the building, but that they were forbidden to go anywhere near Ward 5. And to make sure that their curiosity didn't get the better of them, the door to the ward was now locked. Kim had one of the three keys, and it was Kim who announced the beginning of Round Two as soon as he established that Leonard Blake was on the move again.

He was kneeling at the patient's side, and he tried to push his fingers under the old man's back, but he seemed to be securely anchored to the floor. Kim listened to his chest, searched for a pulse, pulled back his eyelids, and measured his temperature, all to no avail. Then, still on his knees, he looked up at the ceiling and listened to Ward 6 thudding around up there in the real world. How long before that ward needed to be moved out of their way, he wondered? How long before they found themselves on the roof? What then? Would it all stop there, among the seagulls and the chimney pots? Where were they all going, he wondered? Where was 'journey's end'? Then, as he stood up, he dropped his stethoscope, snatched at it, and managed to send it spinning away across the floor, under Leonard Blake's body and out on the other side. No obstruction. Movement in a matter of minutes.

Business as usual. Round Two.

Chris was shocked to wake up out of a deep sleep and find his heart palpitating wildly. He hammered Angela's alarm clock with his fist and then tried to snatch back the remnants of his dream before they drifted away. He was standing on a mountaintop. No. Wrong. He was clinging to a mountaintop. By his fingertips. He was scrambling for a foothold, slipping, sliding, desperately trying not to fall. Leonard Blake was just above his head, and just out of reach. Chris wanted to touch him. More than anything he wanted to touch him, touch his clothes, make contact with any part of him. But he couldn't. He would fall if he tried. Fall all the way. All the way back to the bottom of the mountain, where the rest of the world watched, utterly enthralled. A world full of people, and all of them watching Leonard Blake, etched against a never-ending sky.

And then the dream disappeared.

Chris waited for his heart to calm down, and then he realized that he was no longer dreaming of mountains but looking at them. The much-feted Himalayas, to be precise. In the flesh, so to speak. Angela lay asleep next to him, wedged between him and the edge of the bed, her contours silhouetted black on blue against the window behind her, and the panoramic view of the Downs beyond the trees.

Given the choice, Chris would have stayed where he was until the goddess stirred, but the alarm had been set for a reason. Harding's Volvo would be waiting outside the Hall of Residence by now; accurate to the second, knowing its driver. So Chris carefully climbed over the mountain range, retrieved his clothes from the floor, scribbled Angela a note, and then let himself out of the room and hurtled down the stairs three at a time.

Just as he thought, the car was parked with its engine running, and before Chris had a chance to close his door, Harding had his foot on the accelerator.

"Tell me all about yesterday!" Harding demanded without any other greeting, keeping his eyes on the road as he began to dodge jay-walking students.

"Yesterday?" Chris blushed to the roots of his hair when he thought about yesterday. How did he know about yesterday? The man was unnatural. He had a sixth sense. "Yesterday?" he said again, waiting for the fog to clear from his mind.

"The hospital, you numbskull! Big building, full of sick people. One of them flies. Remember?"

"Oh!"

The Volvo juddered to a halt and Chris's face bounced off the windscreen.

"Tell me you went to the hospital."

"No, I didn't. I thought you were going. I told you I couldn't go. I had a lecture. I had two, actually." And missed them both.

"Oh, sir, sir, please sir, I had a lecture," Harding said with a mocking leer. "Forget the lectures! I told you that I would be in London. All you had to do was get your sorry self down there, show your face, check and realign the equipment, and bring away any fresh data with you. So simple a monkey could have done it. In fact, I should have sent a monkey to do it, because you were too busy shagging the pneumatic Miss Harris all day long; and don't bother to deny it, it's written all over your face. And your neck!"

Chris fingered his neck guiltily and blushed again. Harding had shouted at him and, thanks to the open window, several heads turned at the mention of the Himalayas finally being conquered.

"Sorry," Chris said lamely. "A misunderstanding."

"Misunderstanding, my Aunt Fanny!" The Volvo slowly rolled forward again. Harding stared at the road ahead without blinking, occasionally flicking his eyes at the mirror and seeing his own reflection staring back at him. And there was his sin, if you did but know where to look.

"One day soon they will have to start rewriting most of the current laws of physics. I would like to be a part of that process.

Hell, I'd like to be a part of what they were writing *about*, wouldn't you?"

"I think so," Chris said hesitantly.

"You think so! You think so!" He looked aside at Chris for a moment. "You'd better wake up and get in the game, young man, before it leaves you behind. The rest of your life's a bloody long time to regret not keeping your jeans zipped up. Stay focused on what we are doing. This is history. Do you hear me? This is history!"

Chris blushed yet again, wondering why every oblique reference to Angela made him feel so guilty. "What was so important in London that it tore you away?" he asked boldly.

Harding hugged the steering wheel and smiled knowingly at his reflection. He tapped his coat pocket, crackling a thick white envelope. "I went to see an old friend about some back-up, in case those dimwits in the hospital start queering the pitch."

"What on earth does that mean?" Chris asked, wishing not for the first time that he had never clapped eyes on the man sitting next to him. "What kind of back-up?"

Harding pulled the edge of the envelope from his inside pocket. "This kind," he said. "The kind that comes on *very* good quality paper."

The Right Honourable Colin Chiltern was in the Strangers' Bar when his P.P.S. found him. He had promised himself just one drink to steady the ship before the afternoon's debate began, and he was nursing a half-pint of Top Totty when Turner appeared at his side.

"What do you want?"

"Oh, well, if you're offering."

"Which I'm not."

Turner, new to the Commons, called himself the Minister's bag-carrier. As he saw it, his job was to keep his ear to the ground, in and around both Houses of Parliament, and then report back to Chiltern on the gist of what other people were saying about him, friend and foe alike. He saw himself as Al Pacino's Consigliere, the right-hand man, the trigger man, the Chief of Staff, the one always on the shoulder of the Godfather, seated just off centre of the web of power. It was his favourite film, especially the moment when Pacino settled all accounts.

Chiltern, on the other hand, thought of Turner, when he thought of him at all, as a house-trained puppy, and he often spoke to him as though he was one. Either way, Turner gleefully chased down the bouncing balls of gossip, took them to his owner, dropped them in his lap, and got an occasional pat on the head for his troubles.

As the newly appointed Secretary of State for Health in the last Cabinet reshuffle, Chiltern wasn't terribly much concerned with Party tittle-tattle anymore, but his ears pricked up whenever Turner hinted that the Party grandees were whispering his name about the place. If the whispers – and Turner – were to be believed, then Chiltern was regarded as a possible, indeed a potential, Leader-in-Waiting, one of three currently in the frame. He ticked the boxes with Eton and Cambridge, but apparently he still needed to "man up" on immigration, stand firm on Europe and, above all, stay squeaky clean on the Home Front, especially when the next round of spending cuts brought forth the expected howls of anguish from left of centre. "And he'd do well to make sure that any skeletons are buried deep, my boy, very deep. Tell him so. From me, laddie. In bloody duplicate." In a world that was only ever one drear and monotonous shade of grey, Chiltern had to demonstrate that he was whiter than white, even if no one believed it for a moment.

"Your Constituency Office called," Turner said, still eyeing the glass of beer hopefully.

"What the hell do they want?" Chiltern asked angrily.

"They're sending some chap over to see you. They said you need to see him before you go into the afternoon session."

"They said what!" Chiltern thundered, fully intending to turn every head in the Bar. "Since when did they appoint themselves keepers of my diary? Who is it? What's his name, this oh-so-very-important-little-oik that can't be kept waiting?"

Turner consulted a slip of paper in his hand even though he had committed the name to memory. After all, balls bounced in all sorts of different directions. "Harding."

"Never heard of him, never want... Not Derek Harding?"

"That's him." Turner said, committing the look on his chief's face to memory, too. "Greta said you would know him."

Chiltern stared at the half-finished drink for a moment and then thrust it towards Turner. "Get rid of this!" When Turner started to raise the glass to his lips, Chiltern pressed hard on the rim until the contents started to drip on the floor. Then he took hold of Turner's lapel between his thumb and forefinger and tugged it hard. "Never mind what Greta says, you little toad, you listen to me! When he gets here, you make good and sure that you find us somewhere very quiet. You got that? Somewhere *very* quiet."

———————————

The Volvo pulled up outside the front door of the hospital, right in the middle of the ambulance bay, and Harding jumped out and rushed into the building. This time he ignored the switchboard and made straight for the stairs, confident that no one would try to stop him. At the door of the annexe he stopped just long enough to tear down the notice and rip it into pieces, and then he kicked open the door and discovered that his patient had gone.

"If you're looking for Miss Roper," a friendly nurse remarked, pushing past him with a vile-smelling and very full bedpan in her hands, "she was transferred to the County Hospital about an hour ago. Shame you missed her."

"And whom might the entirely inconsequential Miss Roper be?" Harding demanded, screwing his nose up at the sight of the bedpan.

"The old dear who was in that bed until an hour ago? Who are you, her nephew?"

"I am not! Where is the man who was in here? Mr Whatsisname?"

"Blake," Chris said, finally catching up with him.

"Blake! What have you done with Mr Blake?"

"Roper, Miss. Trust me, I'm a nurse. I can spot the difference.

"Blake, woman! Blake, Blake, Blake!"

"Listen, dear, I'm an agency nurse and this is my second day, so don't start having a go at me! I have seen precisely one old lady in that bed in the time I've been on this ward. Amy Roper. Dear old thing, nutty as a fruit cake and deaf as a post, and now to be found on Egremont Ward at the County Hospital. Take it or leave it."

Harding suddenly stepped forward menacingly. "Listen to me, you stupid woman. I want... I *demand* to see the man I left in this room, hovering in a state of grace nine feet from the ground. And I want to see him... NOW!"

The nurse flinched as Harding loomed over her, slopping an appreciable quantity of urine on the floor at his feet. "Are you a doctor, or do you just need one?"

"I'll deal with this," Liz Manners said, coming up behind Harding and pushing the nurse and the bedpan into the sluice. She turned on Harding in a seething rage. "Why don't you just shout your mouth off a little louder? That way everyone can hear you!"

Harding took her at her word. "What have you done with my patient?" he roared.

"He is not your patient!" she bawled back at him, and then, for good measure, she jabbed him in the chest with the pencil she was holding.

Harding was taken aback and began to rub his chest ruefully. "He is my subject," he said in a quieter voice. "And I demand that he be returned to me."

"Along with our equipment," Chris suggested.

Harding turned on him. "Our equipment? Where is our equipment?" He grabbed his hair with both hands and tugged it hard, growling with anger.

"Out of the way. Unlike you," Liz informed him.

Harding let go of his hair and stood toe to toe with the Hospital Manager, breathing deeply. Suddenly it occurred to him to pull the envelope from his coat pocket and wave it in her face.

"Read this."

"I don't want to."

"I insist you read it."

"Insist all you like."

"I can make you read it."

"I'd like to see you try!" Liz had no intention of touching the envelope, but then she saw the House of Commons watermark. That changed everything. "What is it?" she asked.

"Read it and you will find out."

She snatched the envelope from his hands, drew out the carefully folded sheet of paper inside, and read the contents.

Harding enjoyed the moment. He knew he would. "Doubtless you recognize the signature of the Secretary of State. Capo di tutti capi. I also have his private number, should you wish to add still further to your humiliation."

Liz read the whole letter in silence and then handed it back to him.

"Good. Now we'll start again. Where is Mr Blake?"

For the third time in as many minutes, Shallcross looked the Chief Executive straight in the eye and said, "This is your fault. You know that, don't you? Your fault."

"Yes, George, it's my fault. I admit it. How many times do you want me to apologize?"

"I'll tell you when you get close. How do you come to know this man? What dank, dark little corner of your seedy underworld did he inhabit before you inflicted him on us?"

Gravett shifted in his seat uneasily. "Truth is, I didn't know him," he said quietly.

"Then what on earth is he doing here?" Liz asked in amazement. "He's your man. You said as much."

Gravett looked down at his feet. "My secretary phoned the university. He was the one who answered."

"That's it?" Shallcross demanded incredulously. "You stuck a pin in a phonebook and came up with Dr Strangelove? What possessed you, man?"

"You were getting nowhere fast. We needed fresh input, we needed a scientist, I went in search of a scientist."

"And came up with Quatermass! I always thought you were stupid. Now I think you're certifiable! You are a complete and utter moron!"

Gravett held up his hands in a vain attempt to ward off the consultant's anger. "How was I supposed to know that he would go running off to Westminster to buddy-up with someone in the Cabinet?"

"How indeed? It's a mystery. You show a man, a complete stranger that you've never clapped eyes on before, a patient who is unaccountably given to flying around the room like Peter Pan, and, wonder of wonders, he thinks to himself, what luck, a nice big glittering, gold-encrusted Nobel Prize for me! Gravett, you're a simpleton."

"Stop it, both of you!" Liz snapped at them. She marched over to the office door to check that it was closed. "This isn't getting us anywhere."

Gravett turned to her in desperation. "Did you actually phone any of the numbers he gave you?"

"Of course I did. I wouldn't take his word for it if he said the sky was blue."

"And?"

"And I got straight through to the man himself. Like he was sitting there with nothing else to do but wait for my call. He said – and I wrote it down, word for word – I request and require you to afford Dr Harding any and all possible assistance in his – let me repeat that, *his* – investigation of this unique scientific phenomenon."

"He said that?" Shallcross interrupted her. "He called it a unique phenomenon?"

"His words, I told you."

"Then he knows all about it. Harding has blabbed the whole thing to him."

154

"Of course he has. But wait, there's more to come. He is to have exclusive access to the subject – note that, if you please, Leonard Blake suddenly becomes a subject instead of a patient – with the exception of any essential medical and nursing staff, and the next of kin. Other than that, he and only he will decide if and when anyone else should be consulted in this matter."

"Carte blanche," Gravett said, aghast. "He can do what he wants."

"He can," Liz agreed. "And he will. And the rest of us can whistle." She slapped her pad down on the table in disgust.

"So," Shallcross said, "your little puppy dog has grown a pair of fangs and bitten right through his lead. Now what are you going to do, buy him a muzzle?"

Gravett was still reeling. "Do they have that kind of authority?" he asked vaguely.

"Of course they do. Push them hard enough and you'll find they can do what they like. It's called absolute power. It does exactly what it says on the label. Open up that can of worms and human rights go straight out the window."

"So where does all this leave us?" Shallcross asked.

"It leaves us not knowing who knows what, anymore. We're not in control."

Liz smiled wryly. "We never were. You're worried about everyone else knowing what's going on? I've been in on it from the beginning – and I know nothing!"

Both men fell silent, and chose instead to study the pattern of the carpet.

A new day dawned, bright, blue and unlived in, but with a sharp chill breeze that gathered pace as it crossed the beaches and the promenade and then whistled up the streets from the seafront. Gulls cried out with sad, plaintive voices in the sky above the hospital, and Don pinned back the front door and prepared for business.

There were crates of milk and trays of bread to load onto the trolley in the porch, and the breakfast tins were already clattering in the basement. Nurses arrived, slowly, leaving life and liberty behind them as they walked through the door.

Then a huge, black shadow plunged the switchboard into darkness, and an articulated lorry drew up at the kerb and belched exhaust fumes through the open window. Don slammed his novel shut and went to investigate.

A man jumped down from the cab and pushed his sunglasses back up his nose. He was only slight in build, and below average height, but he was dressed from head to toe in black, and he clearly chose to see himself as some kind of action man. He strutted towards the hospital steps as though he was musclebound and then held out a clipboard to Don with a peremptory nod of the head. "Sign here," he demanded in a voice much deeper than the one fate had given him.

Don pushed his hands into his pockets. For once his smile lacked real warmth. "Are you shooting a film around here, somewhere?" he asked. "You're a long way from Hollywood, if you've stopped for directions."

"Sign here," the man said again, thrusting the clipboard towards the porter.

"I'm not signing anything," Don advised him cordially.

"You've got to."

"No, I haven't."

"Yes, you have. It's a consignment."

"What are you delivering in a lorry that size? Bournemouth?"

The man blinked slowly a few times with his mouth open. "Can't tell you."

"Please yourself."

"Sign."

"Won't."

"Why?"

"Can't tell you." And Don leaned up against the doorpost to take in the morning air.

The man in black considered the stand-off for a moment. "I can't take it all back, you know."

"I dare say you can't."

"So you have got to sign."

Don shook his head this time. "I don't sign for anything unless I first know what it is and check it for myself."

"Can't do that. It's not allowed," the man in black informed him.

"You do surprise me."

The man in black finally withdrew the clipboard, then looked at the lorry, the sky, and finally the porter at the door again. "Is there someone else I can speak to?" he asked. "Someone in charge?"

Don pointed over the driver's shoulder. The driver turned round to find Liz Manners standing behind him, carrying a swollen briefcase and an armful of files.

"Grab them, they're falling!"

The driver caught the cascade of files and dropped his clipboard in the gutter.

"This way!" the Hospital Manager commanded, and led him up the steps and into the hospital, leaving Don to pick up the clipboard and follow them.

"On the counter. Just there. Stack them neatly." Then Liz took the clipboard from Don and scrutinized it closely. "What's all this about? A delivery? You're far too early. Isn't he far too early, Don! Why don't you go away and then come back again?"

"Can't do that, lady," the man in black said, missing the wink Liz aimed at Don.

"What is it: medical supplies, food, dead bodies? None of the departments are open yet, and the porters don't come in for another hour, do they, Don?"

"At least."

"I haven't got an hour. Sign here," the driver said, tapping the consignment document with a grubby biro.

"No, thanks. How do I know what I'm signing for? It might be dangerous."

"Where are you from?" Don finally thought to ask him.

"Base."

"Where's that?"

"The depot."

"This is like extracting teeth." Liz brushed the pen away and looked over the clipboard again. "Who is this consignment actually addressed to?" she asked.

The man in black fussed around her and peered over her shoulder. "There. There, look. Doctor Harding."

The Hospital Manager's mood changed in an instant. She shoved the clipboard into the driver's chest and headed back towards the door. "You're going to open that lorry and show me its contents now. And if you say 'can't' one more time…"

The man in black wisely obeyed. The interior of the huge lorry was filled with dozens of identical silver storage cases.

"What's in them?" Liz asked.

"Really no idea," the man in black said honestly, holding his hands up in case she wanted to hit him. "We don't get to see, us drivers. We just get given an address, a date and a time. That's all."

"Open one."

"Can't. Sorry. Really, I can't. They're sealed units. That means they're all locked. Only the key-holder gets to open them, and the key comes by special courier."

Liz suddenly gave up and turned to the night porter. "I'm bored now. Don, you must afford this man any and all possible assistance. That means show him the way to Ward 5."

"Do I help him unload?" Don asked.

Liz inspected the interior of the lorry, then the clipboard, and finally the man in black. She screwed her nose up disdainfully. "No."

––––––––

At 10.30 the brat interrupted Liz's daydream. She put down her half-finished mug of coffee and picked up the phone. When the telephonist came onto the line she simply said, "They're here." Liz thanked her, replaced the receiver, and left the office.

She walked along the passageway to Ward 4 and then she began to creep as quietly as she could up the stairs to the landing outside Ward 5, next to the lift. The lift and ward doors both stood open, and Liz could hear voices coming from somewhere inside the ward itself. She stepped onto the landing and tiptoed towards the ward, and then a harsh, loud voice accosted her from the back of the lift.

"You're not allowed in there!"

Liz spun round and found Angela Harris glaring at her like a guard dog. "I beg your pardon!" she said loftily, with all the hauteur she could muster.

"You heard me; you're not allowed in there. Authorized personnel only."

Liz gave her enemy a long, hard look and had her age, weight and dress size pegged in a moment. "Young lady," she said, icily calm, "I am the Hospital Manager. I will tell you who is and who is not authorized to be here." And with that she turned her back on her and marched into the ward.

Angela hurried after her. "Doctor Harding," she boomed like a fog horn, "there's someone out here!"

But Harding had already spied the new arrival. He came out to greet her, and he was delighted when Liz was stopped in her tracks by the sight of the sheer chaos that he had inflicted upon her precious little ward. He and Chris had pushed all the beds into one vast huddle against the back wall of the ward, along with a jumble of lockers and trolleys and a pile of cot sides, to make room for the silver packing cases that now littered the rest of the floor space. Some of the boxes had been opened already, and now there were stacks of machines and coils of cables strewn everywhere all around the room.

Harding took in the whole chaotic scene with a vast sweep of his arms. "Behold, the triumph of science!" he declared, with a smile so smug it made Liz want to tear his flesh from his body.

"Got everything you need?" she asked acidly, as soon as she got her voice back. "Playpen, toys, fellow kiddy-winks?"

But nothing that she could say would hurt Harding. He was in his element, and this particular victory was the sweetest of them all. To take a chunk out of this hysterical woman's territory and call it his own was deeply satisfying, but to be actually looking her in the eye at the moment he did it was sheer bliss. How typical of her type to treat this shabby little hovel like a brood of children. It would give him unimaginable pleasure to abduct the rest of her malnourished offspring from her, one by one. A study in pain. A study in anguish. He could take it all, if he wanted to. What fun!

"I have all I need, thank you. Once I have emptied all these boxes of their contents. So many lovely new experiments to play with. Plenty to keep us busy here for a very long time to come."

Liz gazed around the room. She really was horrified by the mess. Just a few hours ago there had been ten old women living in this room, receiving treatment and nursing and a little tender loving care. Now the place looked like a rubbish dump. On the raised lid of one of the storage boxes she could plainly see the letters M.O.D. Harding followed her eyes everywhere making no attempt to hide the extent of his influence and his pleasure.

"And you think all this equipment is going to help you solve the mystery of how one old man in a coma is defying the law of gravity?"

"Oh, I do hope so!" Harding replied with a huge, boyish grin.

"That's a pity," Liz said, beginning to turn away. "Because the real mystery that needs to be solved here is not *how* he's doing it but *why*." And she had the satisfaction of seeing the grin fade from his face.

The side room was even worse than the main ward. Leonard Blake wasn't wasting any time. He was already five feet from the floor and rising, even though he himself was as inert, as lifeless, as ever; but now he was enmeshed in a vast cat's cradle of machines and wires and probes, and long, tendril-like callipers, and bright red laser beams, and surrounded by enough instrumentation to launch a sizeable rocket to the Moon. And still, and never more incongruously than now, there sat Iris on her plastic chair, surrounded by the mayhem of Harding's technocracy.

"Are you alright?" Liz asked her, moved by the sight of the old woman's haggard face. "Do you really want to put up with all this?"

But before Iris could say a word, Harding appeared in the doorway, having followed Liz to the room expressly to hear what she might say. "You didn't read the small print in my letter, did you, Queen Elizabeth? I have already explained to Mrs Blake that I am happy for her to remain here, for sentimental reasons, but my primary concern is now with the purely scientific thrust of this investigation."

For a fleeting moment it looked as though Liz Manners might strike the man down if she could. Certainly Harding thought so, deciding to remain where he was in the doorway, out of range of anything she might try against him.

"You contemptible man!" she spat at him. She clicked her fingers in his face. "I don't give *that* for your scientific investigation. All the time this man and woman remain in this room, in this hospital, they are my responsibility. D'you hear that? *My* responsibility! They are in my care! And the first time you or any of your toys does anything – *anything at all* – to compromise that care, I will personally boot you and all your techno junk into the street. Do I make myself clear?"

Harding threw caution to the winds and stood toe to toe with her. All the mock charm had vanished from his face in a heartbeat. "Bottom line? He's not your patient anymore. It's as simple as that." He scoffed at her. "You can't even prove that he's still alive. I, however, have all the authority I need to examine this man – if indeed he still *is* a living man – by whatever means I see fit, and there is not a thing that you can do about it. Because you, dear lady, do not count any more. In fact, I don't even think you should be in this room or this ward. I require you to leave. Now."

Angela had crept up to the door and stood just behind Harding, listening to him speak with her mouth open. She would have been a material witness if Liz's attack had struck home on the man, but before that could happen, she herself was barged aside by Kim Maskell who rushed into the room and just managed to snatch Liz by both her wrists and hold her rooted to the spot. He looked over his shoulder at the scientist.

"I'm here to examine my patient," he said in a cold, hard voice. "I don't expect to be disturbed, so the two of you can get out now. Go off and wire yourselves up to something and keep out of my way."

When he was certain he could safely let go of Liz's wrists, he turned to face Harding. It was one thing to bully a woman, but Harding had no taste for standing his ground with a man half his age and twice his weight. He stepped backwards and stepped on Angela's toe this time, and when he turned towards her, Kim reached out and pushed them both through the door. Then he closed the door in their faces.

Liz was sobbing and it was Iris who held her. "Did you hear what he said? He's not a patient anymore. Because we can't prove that he's alive! What sort of a monster is that man?"

Kim frowned and shook his head. "He's a real piece of work, I'll give you that, but the man has some very influential friends." He walked over to the window and looked down into the street – as everyone did in that room sooner or later – while he sorted out what he needed to say. "Iris won't mind me saying this, but Harding's not so far from the mark, as it happens."

Liz gave Iris a hug and then stepped back from her and allowed her to sit down again. "What on earth do you mean by that?"

"You can see for yourself: he has no pulse, no respiratory function that I can detect. All the vital signs are missing except for the fact that he's warm to the touch and his eyes respond to the light. In a court of law you would indeed struggle, on that basis, to prove that this man is clinically alive."

"But you surely don't believe that."

"Of course I don't." But then he hesitated. "That is to say, I would argue that Leonard is not clinically dead. Whether or not that is the same thing as still being alive, I'm happy to leave others to decide. You see, this simply is not life as we know it. This is not life as life is currently defined by medical science." He waved his arm at the jumble of machines and wires and cables. "And none of that even begins to help us with our original problem, which is how this man, alive or dead, continues to just float there. If floating is the right term to use," he added, illustrating his point by pushing the patient's hip as hard as he could with the flat of his hand, but to no avail.

Liz turned to Iris Blake. "Mrs Blake," she began.

"Iris."

"Iris. What is going on here? He's your husband and yet you sit there and say nothing. You must know something. Surely. What is this? What's it all about?"

Iris shrank back into her chair, desperately tired. She, too, looked longingly at the window and the bright sunlight. From where she sat she could just glimpse the top of the church across the road from the hospital. Above its rooftop Iris could see a patch of blue sky and some tattered clouds drifting by in the breeze. She ached with weariness. She longed to be gone from here. Nevertheless, she folded her hands and sighed.

"I'm sure, if we wait," she said, "everything will be explained. In the fullness of time."

13

Poole studied it for some time before finally giving his opinion. He moved it under a halogen lamp to see it better, and when that didn't work he took it to the window to study it in natural daylight. He still didn't think he could do it justice. Finally he said he wanted a second opinion and proposed to carry out an immediate biopsy, and that was where Shallcross decided that enough was enough.

He knew there was going to be trouble – and plenty of it – right from the moment the bee stung him slap bang on the tip of his nose. It had his whole body to choose from. It could have crawled up a sleeve or a trouser leg and stung an ankle, a knee, a wrist. It could have nose-dived into a nostril or an earlobe. But, no, it had to sting his nose, the bee equivalent of a neon sign that proclaimed: "I got George Shallcross right on the hooter, and now it glows in the dark."

Trouble aplenty and plenty there was, beginning with his wife who insisted on daubing the wound with a blob of a white glue-like substance which she found in a caked-dry tube at the back of the medicine cabinet. It burned like sulphur.

He stopped at a traffic light on the way to work and a pensioner saw him and roared with laughter, using his walking stick to point out the vast, throbbing sting crater to his wife.

Then he finally reached the hospital. The walk from the car to the front door was easy enough; he simply blew his nose into a large, white handkerchief and went on blowing it all the way into the reception hall. There, just a few feet from the safety of his office, his luck ran out. The Senior Radiographer sat perched on a stool beside the telephonist and hailed him from afar with a wave of her hand and a warm Irish greeting. Then she took off her glasses, huffed on them, wiped them clean, returned them to the bridge of her nose, and considered his nose with a slow, sucking intake of breath. "That will hurt!" she declared. It was his cue to retreat from the world.

Word soon got round the building that the Stinger had been stung. Within minutes people hurried to his office to buttonhole him on an amazing variety of issues, all of them commenting on the mysterious sound of marauding bees coming from the reception area just beyond his door. Thankfully, Shallcross was due in Theatre for much of the morning and his mask would conceal his stigmata from the world, but the grapevine had climbed to the top of the building long before him, and the theatre staff was ready and waiting. At the first sound of approaching bees he fled straight into the changing room.

Poole, the Anaesthetist, found him hiding there, his mask already tightly laced into place. "Oh, come now, Stinger," he said in his broad Scottish brogue, "let me at least have a look at it, man. Pull the mask down and we'll get some light on the situation." And, when Shallcross did, Poole stroked his chin slowly and then said, "My! Oh my! That is a whopper! Would you like me to pump a local into that for you, George? Shall I jab it for you with a whopping great needle? Or would you prefer a quick whiff of entonox?" He led Shallcross around the room by his chin in search of the perfect light, and then he dragged him protesting through the swing doors into the much brighter light of the staff room, where he finally declared, "You've got yourself a real, old-fashioned retro wound there, George. It looks like a fruit pastille, old man. Strawberry, I'm thinking."

The morning dragged on and on, becoming a test of Shallcross's legendary patience and nerve. Every single operation was punctuated at some point by a gathering of bees, never seen but never far away. Whenever Shallcross looked in his direction he found Poole smiling at him benignly from his stool by the patient's head; but whenever Shallcross turned back to the task in hand, Poole would raise an eyebrow, and an ODA, busy in a corner with a tray of instruments, would obligingly buzz beneath his mask.

"George. Is it true that a bee dies immediately after stinging its victim?"

Shallcross muttered something beneath his mask.

"Will you speak up, George? Don't be shy, man."

"True. Yes. True."

"Ah. Then I trust the poor wee mite didn't feel its noble sacrifice was in vain." Then the Anaesthetist added, with a broad smile, "And is it true, George, that you can see your nose from the French coast?"

––––––––––––

At 11.00 a.m. the theatre phone rang and the ODA slipped out of the room to answer it. When he returned he asked Shallcross if he could spare Mrs Manners five minutes between cases.

"Where? Here or in her office?" Shallcross asked, glaring at him over the top of his mask.

"Her office. She said she'll be quick, as she knows what a busy little..."

"Don't!" Shallcross's eyes burrowed into the young man. "Make no mistake, if this is another feeble attempt at humour, your death will be agonizingly slow!"

"No wind-up, I promise! It's true! I swear on the life of my pet..." But his courage failed him.

"Then," said the consultant, with the last vestige of dignity remaining to him, "Doctor Poole, Sister, if you will both excuse me, I shall be no more than five minutes." And, with that, he left the theatre, pursued by a droning swarm of phantoms.

By the time he reached the Hospital Manager's office he was past caring and his mask dangled beneath his chin. But he needn't have worried. When he walked into the room he could have cut the atmosphere in two with a blunt scalpel. The hostility crackled all about him like lightning.

Paul Gravett and Kim Maskell sat on one side of the room, and facing them across the coffee table were Harding, Chris and Angela. That left Liz Manners to stand guard over the centre ground, the demilitarized zone, like a referee. Shallcross got the distinct impression when he walked in that they had all been sitting there in stony silence waiting for him. He noted the fact that the two students had left an empty chair between themselves and their tutor, but Shallcross preferred to take the one other empty chair, on the side of the righteous, even though it placed him next to Gravett.

Liz leaned back against her desk, folded her arms, and then addressed Harding in a voice dripping with contempt. "Well. You summoned us here, O Mighty One. Speak."

Harding smiled. He sat up in his chair and planted his thumbs in his waistcoat pockets. "The ward above Blake's room."

"Ward 6. What about it?"

"I need it moved. Today," Harding said with a kind of breathless glee.

Shallcross scoffed. "Do you indeed! Well, you can just go on wishing until your…"

"Why?" Liz asked loudly. She had heard the end of that sentence in the Porter's Lodge.

"I should have thought that was obvious, dear lady, even to someone like you. Blake is intent upon ascending through your precious building, floor by floor. We are monitoring him as he does so. Crucially, we will need to focus very closely upon the moment that he reaches the ceiling, something we were prevented from doing before. We will also need to focus upon the moment – and the manner – of his arrival in the next room on his route. That will require preparation, and a degree of duplication of equipment, but that was anticipated by our… oh, what shall I call them? By our 'supporting agencies'. He touched his fingertips together and looked straight at the Hospital Manager. "So you will clear that room. Today."

Liz turned to the Chief Executive, who had been watching Harding from under knitted brows. "That puts the ball in – oh, what shall I call it? – your court."

Gravett grunted, still staring at Harding. "We can move the ward. That's not a problem."

It wasn't quite the anguish he had wanted, but Harding smiled and nodded.

"That's it?" Shallcross asked, a long morning's anger beginning to well up inside him. "Is that what you called me down here for? He wants to move a mountain and you just sit there and meekly give in to him. Do you have a backbone to speak of?"

"George, I would remind you that Ward 6 contains precisely five patients. Moving it was anticipated – by our supporting agencies. It won't be a problem."

"Maybe not," Shallcross said. "But I do resent saying so in the presence of this pariah," he added, vaguely gesturing in Harding's direction.

"Ward 6 may only have five patients, but they all need to be kept in isolation," Liz reminded them. "They need separate rooms, and they have very particular medical and nursing needs."

"We know that," Shallcross snapped at her.

"*He* doesn't," Liz said, pointing at Harding.

"He doesn't care!"

For the first time in the meeting Harding registered disquiet. The barb had slipped under his defences. It came from Angela. She blushed deeply, but she stubbornly refused to return his furious glare.

"We can provide everything they need elsewhere," Gravett said quietly.

"Good!" Harding stood up abruptly and rubbed his hands. "That will be all for now."

"Sure there's nothing else you want while you're here?" Shallcross asked. "Crown jewels? Life peerage? Fillings from our teeth?"

Harding looked down on Shallcross and smirked at him. "I very much doubt whether you have anything further to bring to this investigation, Mr Shallcross," he said acidly. "But if anything should crop up in your area of expertize, I'll be sure to let you know." Then he walked towards the door, beckoning to the two students to follow him.

"Before you go..." Kim Maskell suddenly called out, the first time he had spoken at the meeting.

"Yes, Doctor?"

"What have you learned so far?"

"I beg your pardon?"

"It's a simple question. What have you learned so far?"

Harding's smile vanished. It was a simple question, but not one that he thought he would be called upon to answer in this company. For a moment he seemed quite lost. Then, very slowly, he said, "I think we have achieved a great deal."

"Such as?"

"I hardly think this is the time or place..."

"I do! Share some of your findings with us. After all, whether we like it or not, we are all trapped in this claustrophobic little drama with you. We are your inner circle, God help us! Speak. Confide in us. Wow us with your expertize."

"What do you wish to know?" Harding rashly enquired.

"How's he doing it?" Shallcross demanded, sitting forward in his chair eagerly.

"Doing what?" Harding asked, one hand straying to his bow tie to pluck at the knot.

"Balancing an egg on his toe! What do you think we want to know! Tell us how a comatose man like that is managing to turn the world upside down. Come on, you're the scientist, you're the great expert. You're the one with all the dazzling technology and the friends in low places. You explain to us, in words of few syllables, the whys and wherefores of the greatest mystery of our time."

A near perfect silence filled the room. Everyone looked at Harding, and Harding looked at the window, half-listening to the traffic in the street outside. A faint smile played upon his lips. He pouted a little. It had simply never occurred to him to compare notes with the intellectual half-wits inhabiting the margins of his great enterprise. It was Chris who finally broke the silence for him.

"We've investigated both the room and the building for any obvious anomalies," he said, sounding like a recording. He paused for a moment when Angela snatched at his sleeve and shook her head at him. "We've studied the light spectrum, magnetic fields, that kind of thing. Listened for inaudible sound waves." His voice trailed away.

But now Harding had regained his composure. "We can detect and record anything of note in the infrared and ultraviolet spectrum," he began. "We can detect the minutest pulses of seismic activity, sensations far beyond the capability of the human sensory system…"

"That's kid's stuff, that's all methodology," Kim said impatiently, tapping the arm of his chair. "I want a flavour of your results! Your findings! I want to know what you have discovered!"

"Experimentation cannot be rushed," Harding said demurely. "One always has to embark upon an exhausting as well as an exhaustive process of information-gathering before any substantive conclusions can be drawn."

"I thought so," Kim said with a scowl. "Nothing! You haven't found out a single thing, have you?"

Harding snatched at the door handle and then ordered his acolytes out of the room. He hovered in the doorway and looked down at Gravett. "If I can leave you to expedite matters, my colleagues and I will get on with more important work." He couldn't resist one final salvo in the Hospital Manager's direction. "And I'll be sure to let you know if there's anything else I want from you…" He waited an age before he finally added, "…dear lady," then he quietly closed the door.

"Sooner or later I will need to kill that man with my bare hands," Shallcross announced.

"What you need is a blob of anti-sting cream," Liz reminded him.

"He doesn't know a thing," Kim said again, still staring at the door, long after Harding had disappeared through it, leaving the pungent scent of his aftershave behind him.

"Of course he doesn't," Liz said, walking to the window to open it. "Does that surprise you?" She grabbed a handful of papers from the desk and began to waft the smell out of the room, hoping to take the memory of the man with it.

"Remember, this is still all your fault," Shallcross reminded Gravett, wagging a finger in his face.

"Mea culpa," Gravett said thoughtfully.

"I was going to say I'd like to know who all his so-called friends are, pulling these very expensive strings for him, but I find it hard to believe he has friends of any kind. He is loathsome enough to be in a league of his own."

Gravett shuddered as though someone had just walked over his grave. He sat up in the chair and cleared his throat. "You would not believe the phone calls I've had in the last twenty-four hours. Do you know, they've even invoked the Emergency Powers Act for him?"

Shallcross looked quite startled. "I didn't know there was still such a thing."

"Do they think we're at war?" Kim asked contemptuously.

"You may be closer to the truth than you know," Gravett said seriously.

"What on earth do you mean by that?" Liz demanded.

"Go and take a look at all his new toys. They belong to the M.O.D."

"We know that! It's printed on the blasted boxes. 'If you find this ballistic missile lying around in the street, please return to sender.'"

"And have you asked yourselves why the M.O.D. wants to be so helpful to such an odious little oik like Harding in these cash-strapped times? Why isn't this a matter for the Department of Health?"

"I must admit I've been asking myself that question," Liz confessed.

Gravett looked to Kim who just shrugged. "Pass."

"Ceilings and floors!" Gravett said, chanting the words like a mantra. "Ceilings and floors. Harding isn't their man, he's not their choice. They're stuck with him, like we are. But they'll cut him a lot of slack as long as he delivers on Leonard Blake, specifically how flesh and blood manages to pass through solid matter. They want in on the secret!"

Liz sank her head into her hands. "Oh my God," she muttered.

The Chief Executive was right, of course; transferring a unit as small as Ward 6 out of the building required no great feat of administrative dexterity. If time had not been an issue the whole process might have been carried out with little, if any, fuss. But time did matter. Time was now very much of the essence, because Leonard Blake had begun to accelerate his odyssey through Ward 5.

As soon as this fact was confirmed, Harding became like a man possessed. He left Chris and Angela to continue unpacking the equipment while he concentrated on hounding Gravett to get the job done as quickly as possible. Wherever Gravett went, there was sure to be someone waiting for him, phone in hand, with the news that Harding was at the other end of the line. He found out his office and bombarded his secretary, and he even contrived to phone Gravett at home, just as he was sitting down to a weary, warmed-over dinner. The man was a Mephistophelean shade.

Finally it took just three ambulances to move Ward 6 in one fell swoop, and another floor of the hospital stood empty and bare. Liz felt compelled to wander through all the empty rooms after they had gone, beginning to feel that the whole hospital was starting to slip through her fingers.

As she left the ward she bumped into Chris and Angela, arriving with a stack of silver boxes to take possession of it. They stopped on the landing and looked at each other awkwardly.

"Got everything you need?" Liz asked, whether bitterly or not they couldn't be sure.

"We borrowed a sack trolley from the porters," Chris explained quietly. "We'll try not to hog the lift too much."

"Got a flag with your tutor's face on it?" Liz asked without a smile.

"We're sorry," Angela began, very softly. "Well, *I'm* sorry. I heard what he said about the patient. That's not us, not me. We're not like that."

"Then what in God's name are you doing running around after him like a pair of lap dogs?" Liz exclaimed.

Chris shifted uncomfortably from foot to foot. "You've already worked out that he has influence. He can certainly make life difficult for the two of us if he wants to."

"But we still want to stay," Angela added. She gestured towards the pile of boxes. "I don't know if we'll ever get anywhere with all of this stuff, but we want to be here. To see for ourselves."

Liz nodded, and after a moment or two of uneasy silence she wandered away and left them to their work, with a changed opinion of them and a curious, nagging feeling that the young girl had just said something profoundly important.

Eventually all the rest of the boxes were brought up to the next floor, and then emptied of their contents. The tiny side room began to fill up like Pandora's Box with still more stacks of equipment, duplicating the technology currently surrounding Blake in the room below, until only a tiny space remained. And that was where the old man would finally appear – if all went to plan and if all the measurements and calculations were correct – right in the centre of all the hardware that would crack his secret and give him immortality.

But when everything was ready a sudden change came over Harding. He went into his shell. He no longer needed to hassle Gravett. There were no more explosive bursts of speed, up and down stairs, back and forth along corridors. There was no more impatience, no more frustration, no more of those oddly unnerving laughs when his eyes bulged from his head and he suddenly clapped his hands like a lunatic. He became introverted, withdrawn, and reclusive by his standards, leaving the two students to get on with the experiments while he sat apart from them, hunched in a corner of the ward, chewing the top of a pencil, and intermittently scribbling furiously on a thick pad of paper. Chris and Angela were happy to keep away from him and they worked on tiptoe and in whispers.

When the time came to leave, at the end of a long, hot, busy day, Harding looked up from the pad and curtly informed them that he had set up an account for them with the local taxi firm. They could now come and go as they pleased, and he didn't have to be their unpaid chauffeur anymore. They would not distract him from more pressing concerns.

"How do we call them?" Chris asked.

"Switchboard," Harding said, then put them both from his mind.

So the two students packed up and made their way to the switchboard, and there they waited a little self-consciously for the taxi to arrive. Tiny Adams was on hand to lean on the counter and lap up the view of the Himalayas. Then Chris remembered just in time that he had left his laptop on one of the boxes in Ward 6.

"Leave it there," Angela said, not wanting to be left alone with the Head Porter.

"I'll only be a moment," Chris insisted. "It's got all my research material on it. I can't risk losing that."

So he ran back up the stairs as quickly as he could, hoping to slip in and out of the ward without Harding noticing him. But Harding had already left Ward 6 and closed and locked the door. Chris retraced his steps and paused for a moment outside Ward 5. He could hear sounds coming from Blake's room, and occasional flashes of bright light lit up the edges of the door. Chris held his breath and peered through the crack in the door. He saw Harding alone with the patient. Iris was nowhere to be seen. The scientist had erected two bright arc lights either side of Blake's body, and he had removed the bed cover, leaving Blake fully exposed to view. Harding was standing alongside Blake, facing towards a camera he had mounted on a tripod between the two lights.

Chris backed away and tiptoed out of the ward, down the stairs, along the corridor past the Hospital Manager's office, and down one more flight of stairs to the switchboard.

"Well, what was he doing?" Angela asked, with a disdainful twist of her nose.

"Preparing to feather his nest," Chris answered her.

Much later that night, after even Harding had finally packed up and gone home, Iris returned to the room and sat quietly at her husband's side. She had sat at the kitchen table in the bungalow for much of the afternoon and evening, making up her mind what she should do. Nobody needed to tell her, she knew that Leonard would soon be out of reach again, as he drifted away from her towards the ceiling; but this time something told her that it would be different, that this time he really would be gone, at least from her. And so would what little privacy they had left in this crowded, humid, unbearable little room. She had what she wanted most: the memories. They were safe. She could take them with her. And she could take Leonard's spirit with her, too, because that had already gone from here, she was sure of that. The body remained, but the body seemed to belong to others now. Not to her.

So this was the time, she decided. Time to go. She stood up and took his hand and held it for a moment. Then she touched it against her cheek and kissed it, before she let it go one last time. It was warm. Her Leonard. Be at peace, she thought.

Then she picked up her handbag and let herself out of the room, and then out of the hospital, without anyone seeing her go.

Soon afterwards Kim Maskell came into the building through the side door, using his night key. He waved to Don and then made his way upstairs. Most of the landing lights had been switched off as usual, and the darkness seemed to intensify the emptiness and the silence left behind by the departure of so many people. Now there was nothing left above Ward 4 except one solitary old man, presumed but not proven to be alive, and surrounded by mechanical guardians. Little wonder that Kim felt the weight of spectral eyes on him as he stood in the doorway and looked at Leonard Blake. Harding had packed away all traces of his lights and camera, although a smell of hot metal remained, but Kim was surprised to find Iris's chair empty and the patient completely alone. He was getting closer and closer to the ceiling all the time. He had risen by more than a foot in just a couple of hours. Harding clearly thought he would reach the ceiling sometime in the morning, otherwise he would not have left him, but something seemed to be driving this old man on to finish whatever this strange journey might eventually turn out to be.

Unaware that he was doing so, he too reached up and took hold of Leonard's hand, just as Iris had done a short while before him. This time he wasn't trying to find a pulse; he simply wanted to hold the old man for a moment, to touch him, to be close to him, in case it should be for the last time.

The room was peaceful for now, very quiet, very still, in spite of all the humming machines. Kim doubted that it was a peace that would last very much longer.

14

A new day, a thin, pale sun rising through the veil of an early morning sea mist, and then the clink and clatter of the milk float. Soon, and suddenly, the squealing brakes and skidding tyres of Harding's Volvo, colliding with the kerb just outside the door. Harding hurried into the building, rubbing his hands briskly. He waved at Don, much as he might brush him from his sleeve, then he took the stairs two at a time, skipped along the corridor, and finally stomped his way up the stairs to Ward 5, whistling as loudly as he could.

This was the day, perhaps the hour, even the moment he had waited for. He had play-acted his own fame to himself enough times, anticipating its arrival in a hundred different ways. He had even briefly flirted with God in order to demand that fame from Him in a strident form of prayer. And now the moment was almost upon him. Every atom of his being thrilled and pulsated with life.

By now Blake would either be pinned to the ceiling in Ward 5, or already lying on the floor in Ward 6. Harding didn't much care which. He had no time for the patient, the old man; he was just a means to an end. Neither was Harding terribly much concerned with seeing the moment of transition for himself. There was plenty of technology piled around the subject of the experiment that would record that seminal event for history. What Harding wanted – so badly that he could taste it, like bile – was the beginnings of adulation. Ceiling or floor. Whichever. It really didn't matter. It was what they called a win-win scenario, all those people, all those dullards who didn't find the language of Shakespeare expressive enough.

He pushed open the door, half expecting to find the phantasmal wife still haunting the place, but when he found the room empty, he simply smiled and clicked his fingers, and ran up the stairs to Ward 6. Not once had he bothered to check on this last room in Blake's ascent. He had left all the boring preparations to Chris and Angela, but when he found the room crowded with machines, all switched off, and Leonard Blake nowhere to be seen, he stood perfectly still, and then he began to breathe very deeply.

"What have you done with my patient?"

Kim sat up in bed and stared at the phone in his hand. "Who is this?" he demanded angrily.

"Harding! Harding! Harding, Harding, Harding!" a voice screamed at him. "Where is Leonard Blake?"

The question jolted Kim fully awake in a moment. "What do you mean, where is he? Where I left him, I shouldn't wonder."

"He's not there! I looked! I checked! He's gone! You're hiding him somewhere. I'm not stupid. I know what you're doing! I demand to know where he is! I demand it!"

Kim waited until he could get a word in. Harding didn't seem to be stopping to breathe. "I thought the whole point of the exercise was that we couldn't move him, even if we wanted to. That's why we've been moving great big chunks of the hospital out of his way, isn't it? Does somebody pay you to be this stupid?"

The phone fell silent and Kim wondered if the scientist was still there at the other end of the line. "But he's gone," a faint voice whispered tearfully.

"He was there at midnight," Kim said more quietly.

"Gone," Harding said, almost inaudibly.

"I'm coming over," Kim said, slamming the phone down.

Harding was waiting at the switchboard, his eyes rheumy and bloodshot, as though he had already been crying. Without saying a word he turned on his heels and led the way back upstairs to the two deserted wards at the top of the building. Once there, the two men wandered aimlessly around the empty rooms and corridors, but it was obvious to Kim that they were wasting their time. Leonard Blake had gone.

Finally they faced one another across the dirty red linoleum of the landing on Ward 6.

Kim ran his fingers through his hair, just beginning to wonder how he felt. "So, this time he's *really* gone." He glanced up at the skylight above his head and blinked at the sunlight. A little voice told him that he might sleep well tonight. "I'm rather glad, in a way."

"Glad!" Harding spat the word out with disgust. "You're glad! You lying bastard! He's gone somewhere. He's flesh and blood, and he must be somewhere!"

Kim couldn't help himself. He burst out laughing. "Why? Because you say so?"

"People don't just disappear. I'm not stupid!"

"People don't pass through solid matter, either. Get with the script, Harding. We never did understand what all this was about. It's hardly the right time to be standing there, stamping your foot in rage, telling Leonard Blake what he should or should not be doing. Since when did we start following your agenda?"

The whole of Harding's face changed very suddenly. He stared at the young doctor with a look of pure malevolence. He pointed a finger at him as though it was a knife aimed at his throat. And then he scowled. "I'll finish you."

"Fine. You do that."

"I'll roll up your career before it even begins. You've lost a patient. You are to blame. You're incompetent."

He would never let Harding know it, but Kim's blood ran cold, standing there on that landing. Not at the suggestion that his career might suffer in any way, but because he suddenly realized, beyond a shadow of doubt, that the man standing before him, a very few inches away from him, was quite mad. But he was twice his size, and he would not budge.

"*My* patient? I thought he was yours. I thought he was your subject. Do you know what I think? I think you're the one who will have some explaining to do, especially to all your mysterious chums who give you all their expensive toys to play with. Bet they'll be happy." Kim's features hardened. "Or will they chew you up and spit you out?"

All this time somebody was noisily running up the stairs, and Liz Manners arrived on the landing just as Harding's eyes began to glaze over.

"Is it true?" she asked. When neither man spoke, choosing instead to go on staring at each other, she pushed them apart and then stood between them. "Is it true?"

"Seems to be," Kim said, still with his eyes riveted to the scientist. "He's not on 5, he's not here. Conclusion: he's gone."

Then perhaps I can begin to have my life back, Liz thought to herself. She stopped to think for a moment. "No sign of his wife?"

The question broke the spell. Kim blinked awake and turned to look at the Hospital Manager. "I hadn't even given her a thought!"

"Then I'll try phoning her," Liz said. "See if she's at home. I hope she's alright." She looked at the two of them. "Are you both going to stand there all day? There are things to do, procedures to follow, even if you have mislaid the body."

She started to move away slowly. After a moment, Kim began to follow her. Harding remained on the landing, alone, staring at the space where Kim had been.

———————

Kim left Liz at her office door and wandered back to the switchboard. It dawned on him, when the shock had begun to sink in, that now the great question – or questions – would remain unanswered; but it also began to dawn on him, as he stretched and twisted his aching body, that a great weight had suddenly and wonderfully been lifted from his shoulders, leaving him free, like Liz, to get on with his own life again. When he reached the switchboard he found Don still on duty, but with his book and his coat at the ready, waiting to be relieved.

"No luck?" Don asked diplomatically, keeping his voice down.

"No luck." Kim glanced at Shallcross's door. "He in yet?"

Don shook his head. "Too soon."

Kim nodded and then scratched his head thoughtfully, uncertain for the first time in days what to do with himself. Nothing was open, nobody else was around. There was nothing to do except wait for the rest of the day to catch up with him.

He felt a sudden great urge to wander out into the street, just to feel the warm spring sun full on his face. To breathe the air. Touch the earth. Have time to be. He smiled: he could celebrate idleness by being idle. He could be free, even if it was only for an hour or two. He could try to remember what it was like to live in a normal world again.

It would take a while to shake the tiredness out of his bones. He could do with a long run, a pounding, perspiring, chest-heaving blast of speed from one end of the promenade to the other, stacking up the endorphins and sucking down great drafts of pure, clean air, and feeling the exhaustion and the confinement of these last long days falling away from him like layers of hardened skin. Then he would like to sleep on a riverbank or somewhere high on a windswept hilltop. Somewhere far away from buildings and other people. Somewhere where he could be himself again, and find peace.

And so he stood in the middle of the street, just beyond the building's morning shadow, his eyes closed, feeling the sunlight warming his face. Then he opened his eyes and suddenly felt sad. Not for himself. He hadn't been here long enough to put down the sort of roots that people like Liz Manners had. He was only a journeyman quack, passing through this way, en route to a bigger and better salary. It was people like Liz he felt sad for. This place was their life. They gave it everything they had, and it seemed to give them very little back in return, from what he could make out, except for this odd, obscure sense of loving a scruffy great pile of old bricks and flaking mortar. Perhaps it was the memories, all the faces, the characters, the shared experiences. Perhaps it was just the way that some people were: needing a rock, an immovable core to their lives. Either way, the Liz Manners and the Dons and the Audreys of this world deserved more than this, a half empty hospital, teetering on the brink of the abyss.

Out of habit he counted the storeys of the building and the windows of each floor as he made his way from basement to rooftop. Physiotherapy was tucked away down there, in a subterranean world all on its own, among the steaming pipes and the smell of stale cabbage. Then came the Outpatients Department on the ground floor, to the right of the switchboard from where he stood. X-ray was still farther to the right, facing inwards, towards the courtyard. Then came Ward 4, up one storey, still just about intact for now. Then Ward 5 on the second floor, and finally Ward 6, tucked in right up there at the top of the building, squeezed in under the parapets of the rooftop like an afterthought.

Would the powers-that-be bring those wards home again, Kim wondered? It was a question hardly worth the asking. Of course they wouldn't. What sense would it make? Quite the reverse; they would grab at the heaven-sent opportunity to finish the place off altogether. Empty it. Close it down. Bury the dead. Move on. Even to Kim it made sense.

The two empty wards, 5 and 6, could be shuffled into a corner of any of the new wards in the modern, purpose-built, high-rise hospitals over on the other side of the city. The staff of Ward 6 would actually be able to stand up again, like normal human beings, instead of minding their heads on the sloping ceilings of a converted attic. The dormer windows looked even smaller from street level, like a doll's house, with grubby little panes of glass. No one in their right mind would want to go back up there again, once they had escaped into the real world and made good their getaway.

Kim was no builder, no architect, but even he couldn't work out how the building was put together in the first place. Nothing seemed to be in alignment with anything else. Even the drainpipes seemed to have a life of their own, zigzagging their way down the walls like outsize varicose veins...

Then everything stopped for Kim. The tension returned to his head like a clamp, and his bowels went into spasm at the first shock of adrenalin. He held his breath as a fierce muscular convulsion warped and twisted his whole body.

For a moment nothing happened. He couldn't move. Nothing would respond to him. Then he could breathe again, and his legs began to move – slowly, drunkenly, as though they were made of rubber. He needed his knees to work, to stop his legs sagging and wobbling. Then he stiffened, turned, and charged at the door of the building like a bull. He tore through the reception, along the corridor, up the stairs, filling the building with the thunder of his pounding feet.

Liz heard him tearing past her office door while she was still trying to find Iris Blake's number, and she instinctively threw down the phone and followed him. She caught up with him on Ward 6, where he was standing in the middle of the landing again, doubled up, with his hands on his knees, trying to suck down bigger and bigger gasps of air so that he could speak. Harding had vanished.

"Whatever is the matter?" Liz cried. "What's happened? What's gone wrong?"

Kim stabbed a finger in the air, prodding it repeatedly at the skylight until he could finally utter coherent sounds. "Wrong room!" he gasped painfully. "Wrong room." He grabbed her by the hand and dragged her into the side room that Chris and Angela had filled with Harding's junk. "Think! In your mind's eye, think, retrace your steps. The side room on Ward 5 is directly above the annex on Ward 4, exact to the inch. But these stairs leading up to Ward 6, and the whole layout of the ward, they're different. They're completely different. There is no alignment. They're different. They're wrong."

"So, what are you saying?"

"I'm saying this room is not above the room on Ward 5. It's nowhere near it. We're way off to the left of it."

"Meaning?" Liz asked, looking around in bewilderment.

"Meaning..." Kim said slowly, his voice tapering off as he wandered back out of the room to the landing. He found himself looking at the one last remaining flight of stairs leading up to a disused loft in the roof of the building. "Oh, dear God! Where's the nearest phone?"

Don was in the act of standing up to greet the telephonist when Kim's call came through. He answered the calling standing up, smiling at Jenny as she sighed and took her coat off. Kim's voice nearly deafened him.

"Don? Kim! Who's in? Who's in the building? Anyone yet? Engineers?"

"Ted's in, I've just given him his key. He'll be in the workshop by now, rolling a fag, knowing him."

"Get him for me! Now! Quickly! Get him up to Ward 6 with a socking great pickaxe or the next best thing he's got! And, Don, quickly. This could just be a matter of life and death!"

The phone went dead.

Liz was still waiting for an explanation, but before Kim had a chance to begin, they could both hear loud voices shouting at each other deep down in the basement of the building at the bottom of the lift shaft. Then they heard the commotion of another man in headlong flight through the building, closing in on them floor by floor, until Ted arrived on the landing at such speed that he skidded into a cupboard door before he could stop himself. Then he proudly brandished a shovel in the air.

"Any good?"

Kim snatched it from him and ran to the foot of the loft steps. He counted out loud the first three steps and then he pushed the blade of the shovel under the lip of the fourth step and pushed down on the handle as hard as he could.

The smouldering fag-end fell from Ted's lips as he screeched with horror. "What on earth are you doing?" He tried to snatch the shovel back from him, but Kim brushed him off and pushed down on the shovel again. This time the shovel sprang from his grasp and cartwheeled across the landing like a propeller, just missing Liz's face by a whisker.

"What the hell are you trying to do?" Liz exclaimed.

"He's off his rocker!" Ted said, wary of approaching him again.

"I'm trying to get in there!" Kim shouted, stamping his foot down on the fourth step of the staircase in a frustrated rage.

"Out of my way!" Ted suddenly ordered him, producing a screwdriver from the pocket of his overalls. He knelt down and began to scrape at the edges of the step. When he found what he was looking for he gouged the blade of the screwdriver deep down into the congealed varnish, and then he began to twist the screwdriver with short sharp turns, grunting loudly each time the screw yielded to the pressure.

"We need to get into places like this," he muttered. "Water pipes, gas, cables, that sort of thing." As each screw emerged from the wood he stuck it in his mouth. "Don said life or death. If this is because you've lost your blankety-blank lottery..."

He removed all the screws and tugged at the step with his fingertips, but nothing happened. The step was still glued into place by the varnish, so Kim marched across the landing, retrieved the shovel, jammed it back under the step, and this time pushed down on it hard with his foot. There was a long, loud, juddering groan of wood, like a ship's timber, and then suddenly a crack like a pistol shot. The step flew into the air, closely followed by the engineer who screamed in anguish.

The broken step had revealed a cavity – a dusty, cobwebbed void – and deep inside it, right down in the heart of the staircase, was the wraith-like face of Leonard Blake.

15

When Tiny Adams sauntered into the cafeteria he was more than a little surprised to find a stone-cold teapot, and the Cook, Edna, standing guard over Ted, her favourite engineer. Ted, for reasons best known to himself, was slumped over one of the dining tables with a face the colour of pea soup.

"Take deep breaths, my love," Edna was saying loudly. "You really should put your head between your knees. I can't because of my back, but I'm sure I read it somewhere. It's supposed to do something. I can't remember what. I'll make some tea in a minute."

Tiny slammed the teapot down with a thud and then wandered over to the table to inspect the afflicted engineer. "What's the matter with you?" he asked with a growl.

"He's only gone an' fainted!" Edna exclaimed, eyes wide with the thrill of it all. "'E keeled over, right 'ere, just now. Bang! Wallop! Clean out, like a light!"

Tiny grunted. "Why? Someone give him a job to do?"

"Don't you be 'orrible to 'im. You leave 'im alone," Edna retorted, patting the engineer on his head with a huge, floury hand. "'E's my little pet, 'e is. 'E's 'ad a nasty shock, 'n't yer? I'm going to nurse you back to 'ealth, Ted. Didn't I say I'd nurse yer back to 'ealth?"

Tiny grunted again. "Be kinder to put him out of his misery." He started to turn away when Edna stopped him in his tracks.

"'E's seen a body! Ain't yer, Ted?" she said proudly, jutting out her chin at Tiny defiantly in case he wanted to dispute the claim with her.

"In a hospital, Edna? Who would think it?"

"A dead body, I'm saying!" she added with a knowing nod of her head.

"You come along to the mortuary with me, Edna, and I'll show you plenty of dead bodies. Very likely you put half of 'em there with your cooking! You can take your pick."

"You can mock, Tiny Adams. You're an evil git when you put your mind to it!" She tossed her head with proud disdain, exactly as she had seen Katherine Hepburn do to Spencer Tracy, but her glasses flew off into a tray of cutlery. "This body was under a load of stairs, wasn't it, Ted? So there!" Once her glasses were back in place, she was gratified to see that the Head Porter was finally paying attention to her.

"I'm not sure he was dead," Ted's voice said from down between his knees.

"You told me 'e was dead!" Edna insisted, rounding on her patient with her floury hands on her hips.

"I said he looked dead. He did look dead. He scared the living daylights out of me. But he might have been alive. The doctor seemed to think he was."

"Where did all this happen?" Tiny asked quietly, leaning over the engineer to catch his reply.

"Just outside Ward 6. You know those stairs that go up to the loft? There. Just there. Foot of the stairs. Can't miss it now!"

Without saying another word, the Head Porter walked slowly over to the telephone on the wall and picked up the receiver.

This was going to be another one of Shallcross's really bad days. Like almost every other day it started with a visit to the hives. He walked down the garden and through the trees, breathing in the beautiful spring air, wanting nothing more than to share his good spirits with his swarming soul mates. But the bees had other ideas, and as soon as he got close enough, they pounced, stinging him with gay abandon. He reeled out of the trees and began to make his way back up the garden, and an alarm bell began to ring in his head when he saw great swathes of the lawn rising up to meet him like the swell of a deep green sea. His wife heard him crying out in the distance, and when she saw him staggering drunkenly towards her, she steered him straight to the little garden table by the chicken run and sat him there while she ran to his car for a phial of adrenalin. Tight-lipped with concentration, she administered the drug like a hammer blow, straight through his shirt sleeve. Then she stood back to admire her work, and to smile with deep satisfaction.

When he recovered his senses a little, his wife announced that she was going to drive him to work. Not for his sake, she added, but for the sake of the other road-users who might want to reach the end of the day still alive. He got ready for work, moving slowly and stiffly, like an automaton, and while he pulled his jacket on in slow motion, his wife treated him to a short lecture on the efficacy of keeping chickens instead of bees. Eggs equalled omelettes, was her concluding dictum, along with a reminder that as a general rule chickens didn't sting people to death.

And so, when they arrived at the hospital and Shallcross had to squeeze out of the passenger door of his own car because it was hard up against Harding's Volvo, he made it his first business of the day to phone the Police and have the unsightly wreck towed away.

After that little chore was completed he splashed his face with water at the washbasin and then studied his face in the mirror. He was covered with red blotches. He looked like an advertisement for chicken pox. Image, dear boy, he thought, looking long and hard into his own eyes. Hang on to that.

He emerged from his office to find the Hospital Manager approaching his door, looking very flustered. She whispered in his ear and he silently followed her through the building until they reached the Ward 6 landing.

The place was a shambles. Every square inch of the floor was covered with huge splinters of wood, and he couldn't help noticing a shovel propped up against a cupboard door with what looked like Kim Maskell's white coat jammed through its handle. He followed the devastation to the foot of the loft stairs and there found Kim squatting over a vast hole in the floor, sipping from a mug of tea. Kim himself was covered with scratches and dust and fragments of wood. He looked as though he had stood in a heavy shower of tiny white wood shavings. He was crouching on the first three steps of the staircase, and they were all that had survived his onslaught. All the rest of the steps had gone – destroyed, torn up, ripped out, and flung across the landing. Where once there had been a solid and secure flight of stairs, there was now a huge, gaping, jagged crater, with Leonard Blake in the middle of it, draped in a splinter-strewn blue coverlet, but otherwise quite unharmed.

Shallcross smiled at his young colleague sadly. "You're a lousy carpenter!"

Kim blushed and then smiled a little sheepishly. "Sorry," he said, "I got a bit carried away."

"You think?" Shallcross picked his way through the wreckage and looked closely at Blake's ashen white face. "How is he, apart from rather dusty?"

Kim shrugged and then stood up slowly, easing his aching back. "Much the same as before. But he's moved again already, even in the time since we found him. In the last half an hour."

"Who else knows about this?" Shallcross asked, turning to Liz and indicating all the debris all over the landing.

"You mean, who doesn't," she said with a dry chuckle.

"I see." A thought suddenly occurred to the consultant. "Does Harding know?"

"Haven't seen him since we found Blake," Kim said coldly. "But I'm ready for him when I do," he added, brandishing a piece of broken bannister rail about the size and weight of a cricket bat.

Shallcross turned back to Liz. "Usual question. Where does this leave us now?"

"Well and truly out of the bag," the lady said wearily.

"I want a phone!"

Harding's face filled the tiny reception hatch next to the switchboard, and the telephonist didn't much like the look of it.

The man had changed somehow. He was always unpleasant, but now there seemed to be something really hostile in the man's black, hawk-like stare. If she had been able to reach the door she would have gladly turned the key in the lock, but she was still midway through a call and she waved him away in the hope that he might alight elsewhere like a bothersome fly.

But Harding took the gesture to mean that he might use the phone in the room behind him. He turned and marched into Shallcross's office, sat down at the desk, picked up the phone, and drew a piece of paper from his pocket and flattened it on the blotter. On it was written a London number.

Whether or not the hospital was now half-full or half-empty, according to one's point of view, the outpatient clinics were still operating at optimum capacity and the ground floor of the building was packed with queues of people toing and froing between the reception area and the waiting rooms. There was a constant babble of voices, and squealing and banging doors, and clanking lifts, and over all a pervasive cloud of boredom.

People, listening despondently for their own names to be called, looked without seeing, and no one paid any attention to the two men who wandered into the building and studied the signs above the two corridors. Whether they were patients or staff did not matter to anyone else, and they soon disappeared anyway, met by a huge man who shook each of them by the hand and then ushered them out of sight.

"Go and get yourself cleaned up," Shallcross said, not unkindly. "Remind me, are you in clinic this morning?"

Kim had to think for a moment. "Yes. Yours."

"Then we'll have to manage without you, at least to begin with. Take it from me; you need a shower and a change of clothes before you even think of doing anything else. Meanwhile, we need to think about what we do next." He nudged some of the broken staircase with his foot. "To begin with, let's lock the stable door. We need to stop other people coming up here. It looks like a war zone. It's dangerous."

Liz agreed. "We can do that, but it won't change anything. The horse has bolted. One of the engineers was here when Blake was uncovered, and that means that by now the whole hospital knows. Or soon will."

"Not if but when?"

"I'm certain of that."

Shallcross considered for a moment while he scratched at one of the tender blotches on his face. Then he seemed to make his mind up. "Okay. Kim, you get off and change. I'll show my face in clinic and get the ball rolling there. Liz, can you spare someone to sit with Mr Blake for a while? I don't think we can afford to leave him alone now."

"I'll think of something," Liz said, at which point, predictably, the brat interrupted their conversation and caused all three of them to instantly forget Shallcross's words and leave the landing together.

As the sound of their footsteps drifted away down the stairs, the lift reached the landing of Ward 6 and stopped. The gate opened very slowly and then Tiny Adams stepped out with a ludicrously cat-like tread for a man of his size, looked about quickly, and then turned and put his finger to his lips. The two men followed him out of the lift and quickly stepped over to the foot of the loft stairs where they stopped and stared in astonishment at Leonard Blake. But there was no time to waste. Geoff Hallows took out a notebook and began to scribble furiously in shorthand, and his colleague took a small camcorder from his pocket and began to film the scene from every possible angle.

In two minutes they had gone. In three minutes Liz Manners returned to an empty landing to stand guard.

In another five minutes two quite different men had begun a noisy fight in the middle of the entrance hall, surrounded by bemused outpatients. Harding had only managed to grab one of Shallcross's lapels, but to make up for it he was waving his fist in the man's face, snarling at him so convincingly that spittle dribbled down his chin. Shallcross, meanwhile, as the shorter man, had a firm grip on both of Harding's lapels and was concentrating on trying to kick his slavering adversary in the shins.

"You dare to walk into my office, you verminous little cad?"

"You told them they could tow my car away!" Harding screamed at him in a high, piercing falsetto voice.

It was a simple enough matter for the two reporters to leave the lift and quietly slip past the battle, without anyone noticing them for a second time. There was even time for Hallows' colleague to slip the camcorder from his pocket again and hold it cupped in his hand while he filmed a few moments of the fight, before they left the building.

The end could not be delayed for very much longer. Until now the drama had mostly filled two small rooms with a meagre handful of characters. But soon the scale of the drama would change, and others would begin to crowd onto the stage in ever growing numbers.

A storm was coming. A maelstrom. It would break right over the top of the hospital. Soon.

The latter stages of the morning clinics were spilling over into lunchtime as they always did. Some of the staff ploughed on while others stopped to eat, and Liz Manners was just wondering if she might chance an early salad when Sister Corin tumbled into her office and tried to speak to her while her mouth was still stuffed with a turkey and mayonnaise sandwich. For a moment Liz thought she was choking, but when she leapt up and dashed round the desk to help her, Sister Corin grabbed her by the wrist and yanked her into the staff room next door. All the other occupants of the room – nurses, secretaries, housekeepers – were hanging out of the two windows, but Sister Corin pointed mutely at the large screen television in the centre of the room which was filled with a picture of the whole east frontage of the hospital. When it dawned on Liz that she was watching live television, she recognised the faces of the people waving to the camera from the windows of the room she was standing in.

With the volume turned up as loud as it would go, Greg Hallows' voice filled the room like a Hollywood god: "Earlier this morning doctors at the hospital ripped up an entire staircase in an attempt to locate and recover the body of one of their patients, a seventy-nine-year-old retired postman by the name of Leonard Blake. Mr Blake had been admitted to the hospital suffering from terminal cancer some weeks ago. How Mr Blake's body came to be hidden under the stairs in the first place remains shrouded in mystery. However, staff at the hospital have alleged that this same patient has featured prominently in an even more bizarre sequence of events that have occurred during the course of the last few days. Eyewitnesses claim to have seen Mr Blake's body rising into the air without any visible means of support. It has even been suggested that Mr Blake somehow managed to move between the floors of the building in this way. Members of the hospital's management team were not available for comment, but when I visited the hospital earlier this morning I was allowed to see Mr Blake and to discover for myself that at least some of these extraordinary claims are indeed true. As you will see, Mr Blake was neither conscious, nor in direct physical contact with any of his surroundings. I must warn you that there is some flash photography in this report."

A wobbling, flickering image of Leonard Blake's head and shoulders appeared, framed by the shattered edges of the staircase. Liz stood rooted to the spot, too horrified to speak, but the television held her attention just long enough for her to witness the moment when the camera jerked to the left and settled for the merest fraction of a second on the blurred shoulder and side profile of Tiny Adams. Without saying a single word, she turned and left the room.

When she took off down the corridor and then down the stairs, people wisely got out of her way and flattened themselves against the wall as she flew by. Tiny heard her coming long before he could see her and he fled through the door and into the street with surprising speed for a man of his size. But Liz's destination was the switchboard. Bursting into the kiosk she stood over the startled telephonist and pressed her hand against the mouthpiece.

"You're going to be receiving calls any minute now – lots of calls – all of them about a particular patient and an incident, or incidents, alleged to have taken place in this building. You will put those calls through to my office without comment. Is that clear?" But the telephonist wasn't listening to her. The whole switchboard had just lit up like a Christmas tree. Liz shook the telephonist's shoulder roughly. "I haven't got time for this! Did you understand what I just said to you?" This time the telephonist nodded her head slowly, visibly shell-shocked.

Next Liz launched herself at Shallcross's office door, catching the man himself as he came out and propelling him backwards into the room with a stunning blow to the chest.

"What have I done?" he exclaimed, wondering where he might hide from that murderous look.

"It's out!"

The consultant looked dismayed. "Already? How? Was it me? Was it the fight?"

"No, it wasn't your stupid fight," Liz snapped fiercely. "It's all over the lunchtime news like a rash, including footage of Leonard Blake himself!"

Shallcross's mouth had drooped open like Marley's ghost, but now it snapped shut again like a spring. "How on earth did they get hold of that?"

"I'm pretty sure I know the answer to that question. In the meantime, get hold of Gravett. If he doesn't know it already, tell him the shock waves are heading our way."

She tore out of Shallcross's office again at the perfect moment to take the Head Porter in the rear, just as he was returning to the switchboard with a relieved swagger. She was delighted to see the colour drain from his face when she confronted him.

"Are you in a union?"

"A what?" he stammered.

"It's a simple question. Are you in a union?"

"I'm the steward."

"Good. Then you can accompany yourself to my office in exactly ten minutes from now. Don't bother to knock. I'll be ready and waiting."

She started to walk away when he called out, "What's it about?"

She paused for a moment, incredulous, enraged. "What's it about? It's about high time!" she said, and left him standing there.

After the whirling dervish left his office, Shallcross picked up the phone to call Paul Gravett. Then a woman's piercing scream, followed by a sudden explosion of laughter, drew his attention to the window. A crowd had gathered on the other side of the street to watch Greg Hallows address his report to camera, but now the camera was pointing at the sky and two men were wrestling on the pavement. It was obviously the day for grown men to brawl among themselves. Shallcross had never clapped eyes on Hallows, but he knew the other man very well, having torn a lapel off that self-same jacket just a short while ago.

When the telephonist came on line and apologized for the delay, she found the consultant in a very forgiving mood. "Whenever you're ready, my dear. No rush. No rush at all. I would like to speak to the Police, please. What's that? Yes, yes, that's right. Again."

Gravett had no need of a phone call from Shallcross, or anyone else for that matter. He had watched the lunchtime news in his office, and he had even watched the footage of Shallcross's absurd fight with Harding. They would be sure to beat a path to his door about that one, he thought. The Chief Executive listened to Hallows spilling out their secrets like a sieve, and he didn't turn a hair. Not even when a very familiar figure emerged from the hospital in the background and raced across the road and jumped on the reporter's back, uttering some kind of hideous banshee wail. He could make out the words 'story' and 'bastard', but little else, and then he watched, enthralled, along with the rest of a television audience that would rise into tens of millions with the teatime re-runs, until the camera was head-butted and the live transmission suddenly ended.

Gravett picked up the phone and was answered at once. "Director of Facilities," he murmured to his secretary. Then, after a moment or two, "Clive? Paul. Are your painters still working in the old Fletching block? They are? How long before they finish and pack up? Two weeks? Change of plan. You've got twenty-four hours."

He quietly put the phone down, cutting off the stream of abuse. No, he didn't need anyone to tell him that the deluge, the maelstrom, was coming and would break right over their heads. A screaming, rampaging squall of sound and fury. This time he would be ready.

And, finally, ten minutes was more than enough time for Liz to type and then sign a short, succinct letter and then place it in the centre of her desk, along with a thick buff envelope stuffed with photocopied information sheets. Adams would be presented with the one, and then have urgent need of the other.

The Head Porter tapped at the open door and stepped into the room, an abject, beaten man.

"Don't bother to sit down. I can't spare another chair, and this won't take long anyway." She herself remained standing. She cleared her throat. She had prepared a very precise little speech for him. When she spoke her voice was calm and firm and clear. No hesitation, just a measured, well-paced, confident delivery. She relaxed into the speech, certain that he would not dare to interrupt her. "Suspension from duty is deemed to be a neutral act," she began.

In the far distance, they could both hear a siren.

16

Terry's journey to work took twenty minutes by bike, and the best part of an hour on foot. Either way, he considered that journey to be about half of his daily quota of exercise, and the journey home the balance owing. That way, he told himself, he would stay young, fit and healthy long past his sell-by date. Today he had delayed his departure from home so that he could try to make sense of what all the television stations were saying about the hospital he was heading to, so now it was the bike or nothing.

He usually began by free-wheeling all the way down the hill to the edge of the estate, and then he crossed the busy main road by cycling over the pedestrian crossing. Next he cycled through the middle of a cemetery, and finally he peddled along a dense labyrinth of narrow terraced streets, hardly ever changing out of low gear with all the twists and turns, until at last he arrived at the back gate of the hospital, let himself in with a key, and chained his bike to the gate of the oxygen shed.

He would usually arrive a little before 2.00 p.m., giving himself time to cool off, change his clothes, and make himself ready for the start of the late duty. As far as he was aware, he would then spend the rest of the afternoon helping the other porters to clear rubbish from the building, perhaps take a turn in theatre, ferry some patients backwards and forwards between the wards and the X-ray Department and, of course, shift his share of the endless convoys of cylinders that trundled in and out of the chest wards. There would be plenty to do, even with two wards closed, whether or not there were television cameras buzzing about the place. At the end of the afternoon the rest of the department would go home and he would have the Lodge to himself. He would work on through the evening, shifting still more rubbish, trundling the meal trolleys along to the remaining wards and, of course, topping up all the racks of cylinders outside each ward, and then the night porter, usually Don, would arrive on duty bang on time to let Terry go home, ticking off the second half of his exercise quotient as he went. There were worse ways of earning an honest wage.

But today wasn't going to be a normal day, and when Terry took the last tight left turn, leaning over as far as he dared on the old Raleigh Equipe, barely more than fifty yards from the hospital, he realized at once that his neat and tidy life had started to come apart at the seams. The road was choked with traffic, most of it double and treble parked in a hopeless muddle, and all of it, every last vehicle, bearing a television company logo of some kind. He hopped the bike up onto the pavement and tried to weave his way through the little knots of reporters and camera crews, but finally he gave up and dismounted and pushed the bike along the gutter between milling crowds of people, holding it by the saddle.

When he reached the main entrance he noticed a police car parked on the pavement on the other side of the main road. Its blue light was still flashing but its driver was nowhere to be seen. Terry thought it very likely he was lost inside that large crowd of people somewhere. Certainly that was where all the shouting was coming from, and when Terry looked more closely he was sure he could see two men writhing around on the ground between the legs of the onlookers.

"Fisticuffs!" a voice behind him announced. "They've been at it since I came back from lunch."

The telephonist had abandoned her flashing switchboard so that she could catch up on the progress of the fight. Seeing Terry's troubled face reminded her of the message she had been keeping for him. She narrowed her eyes and poked a finger at him accusingly.

"Mrs Manners wants to see you. Soon as you get here, so don't hang about!"

Terry looked horrified. "Me? Seriously?"

"Very."

"What about? Do you know?" He could feel his young, fit and healthy heart beginning to thud on the inside of his chest like a steam hammer.

"Yes."

"So tell me! Put me out of my misery!"

The telephonist chuckled. "I wouldn't know where to begin."

"Where's Tiny?" Terry asked, starting to look around, presumably for the neat and orderly life he had just mislaid.

"On second thoughts, that's where I would begin."

"What do you mean?"

The telephonist pressed her lips together and then zipped them up.

"Is Mrs Manners in her office?"

"Nope. Ward 5."

"Ward 5's empty."

"Not now it's not! Full of all sorts: police, heads of department, big-wigs galore. They're having a toffs' tea party. Go and join them!"

"You must be joking," Terry said with real feeling.

But the telephonist just smiled and shook her head.

———————

Terry pushed his bike through the building in a trance and quickly parked it by the mortuary door. Then he hurried to Ward 5 and stopped at the entrance to listen to the voices he could hear coming from inside the ward. His mouth was dry, and he could feel streams of sweat trickling down his back inside his shirt. He tried to dry his hands on the backs of his trousers, but he couldn't stop them shaking. Suddenly somebody shouted into a loud hailer in the street outside, and Terry nearly jumped out of his skin. There was a roar of noise and then a burst of applause. At least somebody was having fun, Terry thought. He took a deep breath and tried to creep into the ward unseen.

Liz Manners was on the lookout for him, and she jumped up to welcome him as soon as she caught sight of him. The meeting paused, allowing everyone to study the look of sheer terror on his peaky white face. Liz grabbed his elbow and marched him towards the one remaining empty seat, quietly wondering to herself if she had made the right decision after all. Still, she was lumbered with it now. Terry sat on the chair, and then he sat on his hands and cringed with fright. The telephonist had been right about all the heads of department. They were all there. But she hadn't mentioned Kim Maskell, and Shallcross, and somebody whom he thought might just be the Chief Executive, the one they all called the Butcher behind his back. And that was definitely the Chief Constable. Terry had seen him on the front page of the Evening Herald, just a few days ago, moaning about the amount of dog poo on the city's pavements. And the two students were there, too, although not the freaky guy they usually hung out with. He was a serious head case in Terry's book.

"Come in, Terry. Everyone, this is Terry. Terry, this is everyone. Terry, no time to dress this up; I want to put you in temporary charge of Portering Services, and I want you to sit in on this meeting."

Terry looked just about ready to faint. He leaned towards the Hospital Manager and whispered "Where's Tiny?" He could feel his bowels beginning to move.

"That's for later. For now I want you to take part in the meeting. Speak up. Don't be afraid. You're here to contribute."

"What are we talking about?" he asked, shifting to the edge of his seat.

Liz hesitated, and then she looked all around the circle of faces, some of them still registering shock like Terry. "What are we talking about?" She needed to take a deep breath before she went on. "How to decommission a hospital, that's what we're talking about." She gave Terry a sad smile.

"In less than a day," somebody added sourly in the background.

"Yes. That's right," Liz said quietly. "In less than a day."

Derek Harding was sitting on the pavement, covered in dust, staring at the large round hole in the knees of his trousers. He was also mystified by the wires of the Taser gun that had just short-circuited his central nervous system and dumped him on the ground like a felled ox. An ambulance driver was standing over him and asking him a stream of very silly questions. He appeared to think that Harding had an amazingly low I.Q., but Harding couldn't find a voice to answer him with.

Only one thought preoccupied his mind now. His face would soon be splashed all over the news bulletins. He would be famous for five minutes, and his career would be over. Dead. Completely and utterly. His contract would be over, too; all over the Principal's desk in tiny little pieces. The vindictive swine would enjoy that. He had been living for that moment ever since Harding caught him debriefing his secretary.

Amazingly, Greg Hallows was still standing, albeit unsteadily. He was very much the worse for wear, and he was keeping most of his weight off his left leg, which was swollen at the knee joint just where Harding had tried to kick it into touch. The reporter was enjoying himself. He was speaking to camera again, but this time it wasn't his camera, and he was the one being interviewed. They were queuing up to stick microphones under his nose, and all Harding could do was look on mutely, while Hallows gleefully tipped the last dregs of his life, his career, his reason for living, into the dust at his feet.

"... at which point, as many of you will have seen for yourselves, I became the victim of an unprovoked and savage attack by the man you see here before you."

"But what did you see in the hospital?" several voices tried to ask him at once.

Hallows took a deep breath. "I saw the patient we have since identified as Leonard Blake lying – as I thought – in the debris of a demolished staircase. So far we haven't been able to determine how or why he came to be there, and the hospital has still not confirmed whether Mr Blake is actually dead or alive. The hospital authorities have stubbornly refused to comment on any of the claims actually being made by their own members of staff that Mr

Blake has somehow managed to move from floor to floor of the hospital whilst remaining in what they describe as a catatonic state. My own impression of the man, when I saw him this morning, is that he is quite literally defying the laws of gravity. He's unconscious, he is not able to support himself in any way, and he is not in physical contact with anything around him. If you were to ask me to explain what I saw... I can't. It's as simple as that. I don't understand it. I don't understand how a human being can do that. But I've seen it with my own eyes. I know it to be true."

A chorus of voices bombarded Hallows with more questions the moment he stopped speaking, and in the confusion that followed no one heard Harding's long, lamenting groan, although one camera turned around just in time to see him slump to the ground.

"What level of security can you give us?" Liz Manners asked.

The Chief Constable was listening to his radio, receiving a report on the arrest following the fight in the street outside. Returning his attention to the meeting, he consulted his clipboard while he tried to remember what they had been discussing. He frowned officiously, which was always a good place to start.

"If you intend to evacuate the whole building – which, under the circumstances, I would strongly urge you to do – then we'll impose a total lockdown on the site and place officers at the front and back entrances."

"Inside or out?"

"Outside. There'd be no point in having men inside the building. Access will be strictly limited to those looking after Mr... Thingummy."

"Blake."

"Blake. That's him. Our main duty will be crowd control outside the premises. Now, who are your people on the inside going to be?" And he poised his pen in readiness to take dictation.

Liz pointed to Kim. "Doctor Maskell has agreed to be responsible for Mr Blake's ongoing medical care, such as it is. He's going to move his gear into the Common Room on the ground floor and work from there. That way he won't have to run the gauntlet every time he needs a pee and a shave. Also, Chris and Angela have asked if they can stay on and continue to…"

"Let me just stop you there!" the Chief Constable interrupted her, holding up his hand as though he was directing traffic. "Do you have any idea just how big this media circus is going to be? I do. I've been there; I've seen it, done it, and I've got the T-shirt and the scars to prove it. Even by the time I got here – and I didn't hang around – you already had BBC, ITV and Sky setting up. Give it another hour and you'll have the likes of CNN et al. camped all over your doorstep. After that it's not a question of if but when all the others follow suit. First the coverage will go national, then it will extend to most major European countries, and then Uncle Tom Cobley and all will jump on the bandwagon, quicker than you can wince.

"I've been sitting here sketching out a contingency plan for dealing with the Press while I've listened to you all talking. At the very least, I'm going to need to close off all the streets in the immediate vicinity of the building itself. No traffic, no pedestrians, local residents excepted, and we'll have them on a tight leash, too. The Press will still try to do it their way – they always do – but very soon you can expect the world and his dog to turn up here, and that means everyone from the bored and the curious, right the way through to the certifiably insane. There's not a lot we can do about that except put up barriers and hope that it rains."

Shallcross stood up and stretched his legs and then wandered over to the window to look at the scene outside. As he watched all the chaos unfolding below him, he poked his thumbs into the pockets of his waistcoat thoughtfully. Once upon a time this had seemed a great deal to him, this little street corner hospital. It was his turf, his patch. It was his to command. It was the place where he practiced his trade, where he tried to help people suffering from life-threatening diseases and conditions that were rooted in the chest, in his area of expertize. He was proud of the unit, proud of what it had achieved. And, secretly, he loved it; the place, the people. But now it was all just a tiny part of Gravett's far flung

Empire, and it was about to pass out of his hands for ever. He watched the CNN unit arriving, just as the Chief Constable had predicted it would, and he watched it pin an ambulance to the kerb, preventing it from pulling away, and then he watched the two drivers waving their fists at each other. The decision had already been made. Of course it had. He turned back into the room with a sigh.

"How quickly can we get everyone out of here before we really are besieged?" he asked quietly.

The Chief Constable tapped his clipboard with his pen. "That was going to be my next question."

The Senior Radiographer decided that it was high time to say what she had been thinking. She folded her arms, sat back in her chair and gave everyone a deeply reassuring smile. "Come on, now, folks! Let's not start wetting ourselves. We've done this sort of thing before, it's nothing new. Let's not make it any more difficult than it is already. Departments like mine, we just get on with it. We transfer all our patients by phone, and then we cancel the papers, put the cat out, switch off the machinery, and lock the door. When all is said and done, it's just a building, and not a very big building at that. What we do here, we can do elsewhere easily enough."

The Senior Physiotherapist was seated at her side. "True. Ditto. Same with us, but without the machines. We need a gym and we need equipment. We can find both elsewhere. Nothing that any of us do is wholly dependent on this one building, is it?"

"My job is," the Catering Manager muttered sourly.

The Senior Radiographer swung round in her chair to face him. "Phil, if you can bake a pie here, you can bake a pie somewhere else. All you need is an oven."

"Not if 'somewhere else' already has a Catering Manager," Phil replied caustically.

"And an engineer!" Ted added.

The Medical Records Officer was next in line after Physiotherapy. She shifted in her chair uneasily. "It's not that straightforward for me either, I'm afraid," she said timidly. "I come with considerable clutter! As a department we've still got thousands of current and archived patient record files, both here and in our overflow facility, a terraced house the hospital owns just along the road. All of it's confidential, of course, and most of it's recorded on paper and/or film, the old-fashioned way. It's all due to be recorded electronically soon, but until then there's tons of the stuff, and it all needs to be packed up and taken with us, wherever we end up going."

Gravett nodded but said nothing. Shallcross looked at Liz and raised his eyebrows.

"How about you, Mother Goose?"

Liz was heartbroken, but she would not let anyone see her cry this day. She was listening to her family preparing to separate and go their different ways. "My job does depend upon this place," she said, staring at the floor, "but that's another matter. I still have three wards that do not, and they will all be in need of a new home; whether as individual wards or as one body of displaced patients, others will decide." She looked as far as Gravett's shoes without lifting her head, but no farther. "We also need to cancel all operations and to re-route our theatre staff. All nursing staff, pretty much without exception, will go with their respective wards or disciplines, as some have done already. We all have – what is the phrase I'm looking for? – transferable skills. Most of us," she added. "We can ply our trade elsewhere, once all the wards are decanted into…"

"Fletching," Gravett prompted her quietly.

"Really? Fletching?" Shallcross looked at Gravett quizzically. "I thought that old ward block was still upside down. Is the refurbishment finished?"

"No!" Gravett said in a crisp, business-like voice, sitting up to address everyone. "Not even close. Some of it's going to stink of new paint; some of it's going to have bare walls, and some of it we haven't even touched yet. But none of that need worry you, because beggars can't be choosers, and Fletching will be a heck of a lot better than staying here and trying to weather the storm," he concluded bluntly.

"We've got no choice," Liz said shortly. "Now tell us something we don't know." She waited for a moment but there was no response forthcoming. "In some ways, choosing where to put the wards is the easiest part of the problem facing us. As long as Fletching has enough serviceable beds, all we need is a fleet of ambulances, unhindered parking for half a day, and the job's done." Then she turned to face Terry and the Catering Manager sitting alongside him. "But then, you're right, Phil, it does get harder, a lot harder. And, Terry, this is going to be quite a baptism of fire for you in your first day in charge. You and your team are going to be kept very busy helping to empty this place. And, Phil, you have to go on feeding the troops and the patients, right up to the moment they go. But then we're going to have to find new homes for all of you, and I'm afraid that's unlikely to be the same home for everyone in the same team. And that applies to Housekeeping, Engineering, Administration, and the Switchboard," she said, glancing around at all the solemn faces. "I hate to put it this way, but you'll just have to go where we send you, for now."

"If you study the small print in your contracts of employment," Gravett announced magisterially, "you will see that as a Trust we always have the option to redeploy you. The Trust employs you, not the individual hospital."

The Catering Manager glowered at Gravett and jabbed his finger towards Liz Manners. "I prefer it the way she puts it!"

"How long are we likely to be away?" Terry asked, not sure how he was going to break the news to the others in the Lodge, or double the distance of his cycle ride each day. But that was a question that no one tried to answer.

Then a thought suddenly occurred to Liz Manners. "Terry, how many tenants do you have in Rose Cottage at the moment?"

The Chief Executive's head shot up. "Rose Cottage?"

"The mortuary," Liz answered him, still without looking in his direction.

Terry bit his thumbnail and tried to remember the names on the guest list in the Lodge. "Four. I think. One's been cleared and is waiting for collection. The other three we haven't heard about. If they're burials, they can go any time, now, if you like. If they're cremations, they need forms to be signed."

Gravett didn't seem unduly concerned. He scribbled a brief note on his pad. "Not a problem. We'll get them moved today, as soon as we can get suitable transport. We can process them equally well from the County or the Borough Mortuary." Then he shifted in his seat to bring the Hospital Manager into his direct line of fire. "And what about you, Liz? Will you stay here after everyone else has gone and hold the fort for us?"

Liz was surprised to be asked so publically. "Does that mean I have a choice?"

"No."

"I thought not."

People waited a few moments to be sure that the silence meant the meeting was over, and then they stood up and began to tidy their chairs away and pick up their jackets and files and notebooks. Gravett quickly spirited the Chief Constable away, and after they had both left the ward a low murmur of conversation began, very subdued, as though they were all leaving a funeral.

Kim hadn't uttered a single word during the whole meeting. Now he suddenly clapped his hands and made everyone jump. "Come on; don't just leave it like this. Don't just walk away with all those po-faces. Somebody tell me some good news, please!"

Shallcross laughed and slapped him on the back. "I hear the Landlord of the Queen's Head is cock-a-hoop, if that counts as good news. He gets to be the sole purveyor of sustenance – some solid, but mostly liquid – to Doctor Kim Alexander Maskell, Doctor in Residence. Otherwise known as 'him wot copped the shortest straw'!"

17

Somewhere in among all the carnage and the mayhem of this rapidly disintegrating day, it was possible to chart the beginning of the end of many things. The neat and tidy, carefully planned, carefully regimented life of a hospital that people like Terry so gratefully tied the rest of their lives to, had entirely vanished. When five o'clock came and went, all the departments stayed open, frantically leafing through their appointment books so that they could deflect a human tide of outpatients onto other more distant shores. And while the phone lines were kept busy, the ambulances began to arrive, signalling the final exodus of patients from the three remaining wards. Finally, at dusk, a lorry backed up to the rear gates of the hospital, and Terry and his team emptied every last cylinder from the oxygen shed into it, thereby handing over the keys of the kingdom. Without oxygen, without quite literally the breath of life to give them, the hospital could no longer care for its people. And when the lorry drove away, the Chief Constable's barriers began to spring up all round the building, signalling the start of the siege of an almost completely deserted citadel.

Nobody remembered seeing Shallcross leave. As he had no material part to play in the mass exodus of the wards and departments, he felt redundant, so he waited for a gap in the convoys of ambulances and then telephoned his wife and asked her to collect him from the front door. When she arrived he filled the boot of the car with files and papers from his office, then he closed the door and left without saying a word to anyone.

At home Shallcross didn't even bother to walk down to the hives among the trees. Instead he sat at the little green garden table and quietly watched the chickens picking at their feed until late into the evening. At dusk the chickens slowly wandered back into their egloo, but the consultant remained where he was, staring into the gathering darkness. His wife called out to him several times from the sitting room as the light faded, sometimes trying to interest him in the news coverage on the television, but he ignored her.

And Harding sat in a prison cell, waiting for the solicitor that someone had promised him hours ago. He complained bitterly about the pain in his chest where the darts from the Taser gun had hit him. He insisted that he needed a doctor, so they promised him a doctor too. Later. If he behaved. In fact, they had already decided to call one, in case the prisoner needed to be sectioned. After a while he stopped shouting and then fell silent. Instead of ranting and raving he concentrated on the walls of the cell and mechanically worked his way through all the spidery hieroglyphics left behind by other inmates. On his way into the holding cell he had glimpsed a television behind the reception counter and he had seen crowds of people beginning to assemble outside the hospital. That one brief glimpse of the outside world took the wind from his sails, and after that he had nothing more to say to anyone. The moment had come – and then it had gone. His moment. He knew that. And he knew that it would not come his way again.

He looked down at his shoes and smiled to himself. He had wisely chosen to wear the shiny brown brogues, the ones with the sturdy extra-long laces.

Kim turned his back on everyone and everything and headed back to the landing on Ward 6, and when he got there he needed a moment or two to collect his thoughts. Had he really done all this, he wondered? That morning seemed a long, long time ago, but had he really done this much damage to a two-hundred-year-old staircase? How? With the shovel? With his bare hands? Where had that strength come from?

Angela and Chris were there already. They had tidied up some of the mess and now they were setting up a very modest selection of Harding's abandoned spyware for the night vigil. They waited for Kim to snap out of his daydream and notice them, and when he did the three of them stood close together and listened to the silence. All the rest of the world was going mad, but here, just here in this one place it seemed to them, a sense of deep peace surrounded them, so real, so powerful that each of them wanted to hold out a hand to touch it.

While the sunlight still poured in through the skylight above their heads they could see tiny motes of dust, hardly moving at all, hanging motionless in the hot, still air.

And Leonard Blake floated there, too, his eyes closed, his face serene, his arms folded across his chest like a Viking King awaiting burial at sea. He was halfway between the stairs and the sloping ceiling, detached from everything, from all the consequences of his simply being there.

He was a sign of wonder.

Kim found it hard to tear his eyes away from him. He was utterly compelling, mesmerizing. If they could see him now – whoever they were – if they could just stand here where Kim was now, not to touch him, not to pry or probe or disturb him in any way, but just to stand very near him and witness the stillness and the beautiful quietude that flowed from him, what would they all have to say then, Kim wondered? All the children who wandered through the world asking so many questions?

Kim was sure by now of one thing. It had a meaning. All of this had a meaning. It had to. He was standing on the top floor of a building which had suffered a complete apocalypse in a matter of days, and yet he was sure it had a meaning. Not a solution, necessarily; not a neat, precise scientific summation, not the sort of stuff Harding worshipped when he wasn't worshipping himself. None of that seemed to matter much anymore. That was, after all, the methodology, not the miracle. Leonard Blake, Everyman, was reaching for the stars, and Kim knew beyond any measure of doubt that his gentle unhurried ascension had a meaning for them all.

No one was quite sure where the first one came from. There were cameras just about everywhere and yet no one caught the exact moment and enshrined it for posterity, no one scooped it up for prime time television, for the people watching all agog all around the world. Someone suggested afterwards that it might have been the vicar of the church just across the road from the hospital, that it was just the sort of thing that either he or someone in his congregation might do. A little ostentatious, if he did; a rather unsubtle piece of attention-seeking ministry and outreach, if true, but no one could be sure. Whoever it was, and however they did it, quite suddenly there was a solitary candle perched on the iron railings of the hospital, just by the front door, as twilight fell. One tiny, wavering, flickering pin-point of light. But as the evening progressed and as the shadows slowly deepened all around the empty building, that one little light grew in intensity and, for want of anything else to focus upon in the gathering darkness, all the television cameras watched the candle until it had become a living symbol of a time of waiting.

Then, inevitably, long before nightfall, people began to gather at the barriers carrying other candles, other gifts, other tributes for the hospital railings. Candles large and small – some as thin as pencils, some as thick as rolling pins – tea-lights, even lanterns began to appear from all directions. At first people were content to hand them over to the policemen on duty, but when their numbers grew they were accompanied through the barriers in ones and twos and allowed to approach the railings and position the candles for themselves. When the BBC's main evening news bulletin began there were more than a hundred points of flickering light on its opening sequence; an hour after the bulletin had ended, there were thousands. And by midnight the whole building stood in the midst of a metrical sea of fire.

At dawn, impossibly early, long before any of the local florists had opened, but perfectly timed to coincide with peak viewing times on breakfast television, the first bunch of flowers appeared. It was nothing much to speak of. It was just a simple bunch of tulips and carnations, still wrapped up in cellophane, and still bearing a price tag. Someone had hastily picked it up at a petrol station – yesterday's leftovers – so that it could be laid with all due reverence on the pavement in front of the east face of the hospital, like a votive offering at a shrine.

By mid-morning flowers had begun to appear on each of the pavements on all three accessible sides of the building. And now they were elaborate, expensive bouquets, or even wreaths, and alongside them people stood wilting plants in gaudy gold and silver pots. Soon anything would do, anything that came to hand, as long as it was distinct and different, as long as it stood out and caught the eye.

Once the pavements were filled, still more flowers were left on the raised terrace on the east front of the hospital until that, too, was swamped and inundated, layers deep, and then the offerings began to spill onto the road and sweep towards the barriers like a creeping tide. Here the flowers and the plant pots were punctuated by teddy bears, helium-filled balloons, children's pictures, football scarves, anything and everything that people could think of, or lay their hands on, or just slavishly imitate, until only the cameras high up on hydraulic platforms far above the sea of faces could embrace the full scale of the vast jumble of flotsam.

In the middle of the morning a small white van inched its way towards the back of the hospital, eventually parking behind the Pharmacy, close to the barred and bolted wooden gates. Before it could get there, however, a great many people had to be persuaded to move so that two of the steel barriers could be lifted out of the way, followed by a host of flowers and gifts and spent candles.

Once the vehicle had reached the kerb all the medication remaining in the Pharmacy was quickly packed and loaded, then the van slowly crept away again, and when it had gone, all the flowers and gifts and candles – and the barriers – settled back into place again, like the tide silently reclaiming a sandbank.

Now everyone had gone who was going, and Liz Manners, with nothing else to do, wandered the empty corridors and wards and offices in search of ghosts. But they had all gone, too. Sometimes she lingered by a window to study the crowds continuing to grow all around the building, but the throng of upturned faces only deepened the emptiness within the hospital. Without people, without even the mix of rank and subtle smells, with only the dust, and tired paintwork, and empty chairs and desks, with only scraps of paper scattered on the floors, and nothing else, Liz found it hard to believe that the building would ever be a hospital again. Why would anyone choose to come back here, once the shock of separation had passed and people found themselves in modern buildings, with room to move and all the resources of a purpose-built healthcare unit to hand? No-one. Not out of loyalty to a pile of bricks and mortar and a scrapbook full of memories. After all, it was just a building, when all was said and done. Most people knew that. But, then, most people were not Liz Manners, and she would come back tomorrow – today – to the building she loved.

It was the end of her career, that much was obvious. The end of its upward curve, anyway. When all this was over they would probably hide her away somewhere, like a mad aunt. They'd find her an office and give her an obscure job to do, but that was all. They would try to keep her out of sight and out of mind, and she could spend the rest of her days watching other people through a glass ceiling as they passed her by without even waving. She could never manage a hospital again. Who would ever trust her? She would always be the jinxed manager, the one who had a freak show tucked away out of sight in a tiny little side room someone called an annexe.

She began to make her way back to Ward 6. Kim heard her coming and met her at the top of the stairs. Perhaps because he guessed a little of what she was going through, he gave her a brief hug.

Angela and Chris were brewing tea in the kitchen. They had spent the night in the ward in sleeping bags. Liz accepted a mug of tea from Angela, waved away the offer of a huge bowl of sugar, and then sipped her drink, quietly surveying the scene before them.

"Odd," Kim said thoughtfully. "It never occurred to me to fill in the hole again or cover it up. What if he falls?"

"Or turns around and heads the other way?" Liz suggested.

"Or hangs a right and heads for the kitchen?" Chris joined in with a smile.

Angela looked shocked. "What do we do if he does?" she asked, in deadly earnest.

Liz went on sipping her tea. The tension had gone, she suddenly realized; that tightness between her eyes, the ache in her shoulders and at the base of her spine. For the first time in days she actually felt relaxed. "Fill it in when he's finished with it," she said with a chuckle. "Or leave it ready for the next one!"

Kim pretended to shudder. "Will there be a next time?" he asked.

Liz shook her head. "No. Not here. And not with me." She peered into the hole and then shook her head again. "It's served its purpose. This place. End of story. Time to move on."

Chris meanwhile was inspecting the ceiling just above Leonard Blake's head.

"What do you think?" Kim asked, reading his thoughts. "A few hours?"

Chris nodded. "Sounds about right, unless he accelerates again. Sometime today."

"I wonder if he's following a timetable," Liz said. The thought intrigued them and they all looked at Blake for a moment in case he should choose to answer her.

214

"That's for him to know and us to wonder," Kim said. "What matters now is that he's got one more ceiling to go, and this time he's got the whole world waiting for him on the other side." The thought seemed to trouble Chris, and Kim caught the look that flashed across his face. "Okay, Einstein. Spit it out."

Chris looked at all three of their faces one by one. "Probably just me being silly, but do any of you feel frightened?"

Liz blinked with surprize. "Frightened? Why should we feel frightened? Do you know something we don't?" she added with a nervous laugh.

Chris wandered over to the kitchen door and sat down heavily on the bottom step, slopping some of his tea. "No, it's just me. And this place. Gives me the creeps, to be honest. It's alright for you two; you work in places like this all the time. I don't. And I don't like hospitals, not one little bit. I hate them, and I don't go anywhere near them unless I have to. I don't like their smell; I don't like the sound they make. It's just somewhere I don't ever want to be. Me, I live in a college. It's got clean buildings, clean classrooms, and clean people most of the time, believe it or not. So to me this place is terra incognita. It's full of old, sick people, and the sounds and smells they make. In my world most of us are young. Fit, healthy. No one falls ill, no one dies. My world is all about facts and theories. Learning. Learning how you get to the facts and the theories by experimentation, by checking and rechecking empirical observation. My world is about increasing certainty. The law of science, the law of nature. I like – I *need* – fixed, immutable points in my life. Facts are my rock. I depend on them. They don't move or change, and I can build on them. They're what I have, or what I thought I had until now. Until him." And he abruptly jabbed an accusing finger at Leonard Blake. "He's turned my world upside down for me."

"Why does that frighten you?" Angela asked with some concern, staring right into the heart of the man who had scaled the mountaintops.

"It scares me. At that meeting, yesterday, we all talked about emptying the hospital as though this was the most natural thing in the world to be doing. Let's all pat ourselves on the back, we said, and tell each other how clever we all are in the face of a crisis. But no one said a word about this. About all our facts and our theories, about everything we've ever known and believed in, going up in smoke!"

"Did it not occur to you," Liz asked, "that maybe we all just needed to be kept busy yesterday, so that we didn't have time to think about what this means?"

Kim began to scuff his foot across the floor, clearing a patch of the linoleum of dust and splinters. "For the last few days I've been too busy and too tired to care about anything much, other than getting through the day in one piece and reaching my very damp and uncomfortable bed each night in time to sleep in it. And, believe me, that is life for a lot of people. Then they wake up, one day, and they've grown old just getting through the days in one piece. Surviving. But now the pressure's off me, and I haven't really got anything much to do now except think about what this means." He raised his head and looked Chris straight in the eye. "And it leaves me feeling excited, uplifted, in a way I've never felt excited or uplifted before."

"Excited?" Chris said, bewildered.

"Sure! You said it yourself: we've all been running around this place like blue-arsed flies, keeping very busy, and carefully avoiding the fact that we are in at the start of something that no one else has ever seen before, as far as we know. According to your book of rules this is impossible, it can't be happening. But it *is* happening. It's here. Right in front of our noses. And it's undeniable." He, too, pointed to Leonard Blake's motionless body. "I don't know who this man is. I'm not even sure that matters much. But he's got my undivided attention now. I don't want to take my eyes off him. I don't want to miss a thing, not even a moment of what this is. While it's here, and while it lasts, there is nowhere else I could even imagine wanting to be. And if I have to sum all that up in one word then, yes, I'm excited."

No one spoke for a while, and Kim's words seemed to hang there in the air, much like the man who had inspired them. Then Liz suddenly heard herself saying, "Ditto. I want to be here, too."

And she shuddered from head to foot as someone walked right over her grave.

Angela nodded her head firmly. "I'm very sure I want to be here. This is…"

They all waited for her to end the sentence, but, after frowning intently for a few moments, she let it drift away from her unfinished. Being lost for words seemed about right, anyway.

After another lengthy silence Kim took hold of Chris's shoulder and shook it powerfully, breaking the spell. "So, what about it, Einstein? Are you staying?"

Chris blinked awake to what the doctor was saying. "Of course. Yes. Yes!"

18

Now there was nothing to do but wait. From time to time Liz wandered back to her office and busied herself at her desk, but her heart wasn't in it. The phones were still connected so she called her husband at home and he flicked through the television channels for her, bringing her up to date with 'who was saying what'. She knew better than anyone that there was nothing new to report, but there were plenty of people willing to stand in front of television cameras and talk about that nothing, over and over again. There were endless re-runs of the grainy images of Leonard Blake, there was even an artist's impression of what he might look like now, and there were experts galore ready to give judgement: the pictures were faked; they were doctored; they were a deliberate hoax; Blake was a fake; and he was an alien, a dummy, an angel, and a conman. Sometimes there were glimpses of the bungalow with the cherry tree in the front garden. It stood out from the other bungalows in the street because it had a dozen lights aimed at it, as though it was the scene of a siege on a film set, awaiting the final shoot-out.

But there was no sign of Iris Blake. She had gone.

And when all else failed, the news channels puzzled over the footage of Shallcross and Harding pulling each other's jackets to pieces, but no one seemed remotely able to grasp the significance of this strange ritual.

It also became clear to Liz, from her husband's reports, that Paul Gravett was now making his own bid for stardom. He gave regular Press briefings from the front steps of the County Hospital, on the other side of the city, but she had no idea where all his up-to-the-minute information was coming from, because he refused all her calls.

"When is all this going to be over, wife of mine?" her husband asked her in a patient voice, but for the twentieth time.

"God knows. Soon."

"Why soon?"

"He's running out of building. One more ceiling and he's out!"

Her husband pondered what she had just said. "Will you still love me when you're rich and famous?" he asked with a chuckle that warmed her heart.

"Will you still love me when I'm out of a job?" she asked him half-seriously in return.

"It won't come to that."

"Why not? They won't be coming back here, not now, not after all this. And Gravett will want me well out of the way when he gets his sainthood. He won't want me telling people what I know. I've seen too much of his dirty linen!"

Her husband choked down the phone, not much wanting that particular image in his head. "You can write a book. Do a lecture tour. Leave the Health Service and have your own chat show. Fame and fortune await you."

"I'd settle for a good night's sleep."

"Come home soon, then. Soon as you can. I want your autograph while it's still cheap."

"I will," she said, and then she waited for him to put the phone down first.

The evening stole up on her while they were talking. She sat on the edge of her desk, phone in hand, deep in shadows, but she had no inclination to turn the light on. A new wave of candles had appeared on the pavement outside, and their wavering, spectral light sent shadows leaping and dancing across the ceiling above her head. She watched entranced as hundreds of people queued patiently at the barriers, waiting for their turn to step forward and place their candles among the tributes. When they finally did, Liz noticed that many of them knelt on the ground and closed their eyes.

"Mrs Manners."

She leapt off the table and spun round, clutching her chest with shock. A tall man was standing in the doorway, featureless; a black shape with a soft and courteous voice. He made no move to enter the room. There was nothing to fear, but he was a stranger, she was sure of that. A stranger who could walk into a locked and guarded building with the world looking on.

"Who the hell are you?" she demanded when she got her voice back.

"Would you come with me, please?" the black shape asked her politely.

"Who are you? How did you get in here? And what do you want?"

Without answering any of her questions her unknown visitor ran his fingers up and down the wall until he found the light switch. Without warning the room was suddenly filled with an intense bright light, and Liz was completely blinded for a moment. She rubbed her eyes and waited. When she opened them again her late-night caller was still standing in the doorway, watching her, but now she could see him, too. Young, slim, with short, neat hair, dressed in a black suit. A tie, neatly, carefully knotted, and a face that was devoid of expression. He stood with his feet placed squarely but slightly apart. His hands were loosely coupled together. He gave her the odd impression that he was trying not to stand to attention, but that he could move in a moment, like lightning, in any direction he chose. And his eyes. She noted his eyes. They were a hawk's eyes, pitch black and cold. She was quite certain that he had noted the entire contents of the room, all in a moment, all without moving his head or his eyes. She had no idea why he was standing on the threshold of her office, but she knew for sure that he scared the living daylights out of her.

"Police?" she asked, aware that her throat was dry with fear.

"Would you come with me, please?" he asked again, still not moving, but this time with a slightly keener edge to his voice.

"I've asked you once who you are," Liz reminded him. "I'm not going to ask you again."

She had no idea what she meant by that. She had dropped the phone when she leapt off the desk. It was hanging down to the floor, spinning backwards and forwards on the carpet. Always assuming that he would even let her pick it up, who would she call, what would she say that would make a man like him turn and run?

The man reached into his pocket; a quick, neat, precise movement. Then he took three steps forward, reached down, picked up the receiver, replaced it carefully on the cradle, stood up straight, offered her a momentary glimpse of a warrant card he held cupped in his hand, then he stepped back to the exact spot he had occupied before.

"What did that say? Show me it again." And she held out her hand.

"It says Military Intelligence, Section 5, Mrs Manners. It says that I now have full responsibility for the security of the building. It says that I can ask you one more time – and very politely – to come with me. Please."

She would go, of course she would go. She would do exactly as she was told. She knew that and so did he. All that was left to do in the meantime was to play out a little charade for the sake of her wounded pride. If his patience allowed.

"Where are we going to?" she asked.

"To the police barriers. I'm going to escort you from the building. Please bring your personal effects with you."

Liz was taken aback. "You're making me leave!" she exclaimed.

"Of course I am. You have no further function here. I'm taking you to the barriers and it will not be possible – or necessary – for you to return during the period of this emergency."

"What emergency might that be?"

"That's not for me to define, Mrs Manners," the young man said, glancing for the first time towards the window and the scene in the street outside. "Will you come with me now, please?"

"You do realize I'm the manager of this hospital?"

"Yes. I also know that the hospital has been decommissioned, and it is time for you to realize that my authority wholly supersedes yours."

This time he stood to one side and pointed to the passageway behind him. It was time to leave. She picked up her coat and handbag and walked quickly past him, and then she waited for him to switch off the light and close the door. With perfect timing they were joined by Kim, Chris and Angela, walking ahead of another man with equally short hair and a matching black suit. Kim's face was set and stern, but when he saw Liz he grinned with a kind of savage elation.

"I must be really stupid," he said, with a loud, angry laugh, shaking his head despondently. "Really stupid!" He reached Liz's visitor and stood toe to toe with him, staring him in the face. "Because it never entered my thick skull that they would put out the call for James Bond!" He looked him up and down and then glanced back at the man who had evicted them from Ward 6. "And I see they've mastered the art of cloning."

Liz gently pushed Kim with her fingertips until he consented to take a step back, then she herself turned to face her visitor. "You cannot make Dr Maskell leave the building, even if you shoo the rest of us out. That would be ridiculous – and don't quote your orders to me. Dr Maskell is solely responsible for Mr Blake's ongoing medical care. He stays. That's non-negotiable." And she knew before she reached the end of the sentence that she was wasting her breath.

"Mr Blake is in our care, now. You may rest assured that he will be well looked after."

This time Kim took Liz by the elbow and gently pulled her away. Side by side they walked along the passageway and down the stairs, followed by Chris and Angela, the two matching men in black bringing up the rear. When they reached the ground floor another man stood outside the common room, holding Kim's holdall at the ready.

"Do you want to check that it's all there?" the Bond man asked him, but Kim merely snatched the bag out of the man's hand and walked on past him without breaking step.

"What about all our equipment?" Chris asked, as they approached the door.

A fourth man was standing at the door, waiting to open it for them. When the door stood ajar, the Bond man turned to answer Chris, taking in his shambolic appearance with one swift movement of his eyes. His face registered no emotion. "You may recall that we own the equipment. We've decided to call in the loan."

"But the notes and all the recordings are ours," Angela insisted furiously. "You can't take them. They're the results of all our experiments, and they certainly don't belong to you. They belong to us!"

"We'll take care of everything," the Bond man replied, with a thin smile and a long, lingering look into her eyes that made Angela shiver from head to toe.

They stepped through the door and it was instantly closed behind them. They listened to the huge old Victorian key being turned in the lock, and then the security chain rattling into place. They were out. They were gone. They were history. Blake and the building had been taken away from them.

A policeman stood on the pavement and pointed to a narrow pathway that had been cleared through all the wilting flowers and guttering candles. They followed him in single file until he handed them through a narrow gap in the barrier just outside the newsagent's shop where Harding had assaulted the journalist what seemed like a distant lifetime ago. There the four of them stood on the pavement among the milling crowds of people and looked back at the hospital on the other side of the road. From the outside the building itself appeared to be in darkness. There was no sign of its new owners. Candles trembled in the occasional evening breeze, and from time to time television lights played across the front of the building, causing gigantic shadowy figures to rise and fall as they passed.

They stood there for a long time before they went their separate ways. Not one of them could think of a thing to say as they parted.

19

That was the last night Kim spent in the basement flat across the road from the hospital. When he remembered that night in later years, as everyone did, his skin always prickled at the thought of those sticky, humid hours spent in that prison cell of a bedroom. What Kim hadn't realized was that his decision to move into the common room would signal an immediate raid on the flat by the housekeeping department. When he stumbled down the steps and barged the door open on that memorable night he found that all the bedding had gone, along with the kettle, three loo rolls and, remarkably, all the accumulated mould in the fridge. There was just a bare mattress to lie on, but he was too tired to care, so he pulled a towel from his holdall and laid that on the mattress for protection. The bedroom smelt like a locker room at a rugby club and he tried not to think about the tattooed stains he was lying on, but soon he could feel beads of sweat running down his chest and dripping onto the towel.

He got up again, wide awake, and opened all the doors and windows, but it was still hard to breathe in that fetid atmosphere. The night had become unbelievably hot and still, and hour after hour all Kim could hear was the shuffling feet and muttering voices of milling crowds of people walking up and down the road outside the flat, awake and restless, stewing in the heat, but refusing to go home.

He sat in a chair for a while and tried to read, but the pages of the book stuck to his sweaty hand, just like in his dream. He switched on the portable T.V. his sister didn't know she had loaned him, and every channel treated him to the self-same live feed of the now-famous empty building across the road. He stood at the kitchen sink and splashed his face with cold water, feeling hot, grubby and tired. He was bored, he was restless. Like everyone else, he was impatient for the night to end.

As soon as there was enough light to see by, he showered in cold water, then pulled on another rugby shirt, a pair of running shorts, and some old flip-flop sandals, and then went out to explore the streets. At the top of the basement steps he nearly tripped over a sleeping bag. There were people everywhere, literally everywhere, as though everyone had decided to sleep out of doors because of the heat. There were people sprawled across the pavements; there were people propped up against garden walls. There were people sitting in the gutter, or huddled together in little groups, cross-legged on the road. Some were still dozing; some had brought rugs and pillows with them. Some talked; some still nursed candles that they had held on to throughout the night. Some just sat and stared. There were men, women and children, newborn, young, careworn and old; there were dogs, prams, wheelchairs, deckchairs, picnic blankets. Everyone was there. No one wanted to be left out.

From time to time everyone glanced up just for a moment, checking, making sure that the building was still there. The building that magnetized them, mesmerized them, held them close, held them in thrall. Sometimes, as Kim looked on, people would stand up and then carefully step between their sleeping neighbours until they could find another spot on the road or the pavement that was just a little closer, a few precious feet nearer to the hospital. It was spellbinding, but it didn't feel odd or wrong. Kim knew for a certainty that he was no more capable of leaving this place than anyone else among the thousands who shared this night with him.

Amazingly, Kim found the newsagent's shop on the street corner open, and he suddenly felt ravenously hungry. Anything would do, as long as it was quick and simple, and required no effort on his part. One of Mo's cold, stale, congealed meat pies would do, or a past-its-sell-by-date sandwich with curling edges and solidified filling that looked a little like a mouldy fossil. But when Kim walked into the shop he found that nearly all the shelves were empty. All the food had gone; all the drinks had vanished from the cooling cabinet, and nearly all the sweets had gone, too. There wasn't a newspaper to be had in the place.

"Mo!" Kim cried, thrusting his arms out towards the empty shelves. "Mo, where's my breakfast?"

The newsagent was leaning on the counter flicking through a magazine he had reached down from the top shelf. "You're too late, my son! Look at the place! I've been ravaged, I should be so lucky. I've been picked clean. They're like locusts out there. I've been feeding them all night long. They're like you, they eat any old crap. I've emptied the place, stock room, too. I might retire. Great night."

"Are you rich?" Kim asked.

"Must be! Don't tell the wife, she'll go on a spree. She'll be off to Ikea with her bloody mother, like as not!"

"My heart bleeds for you. But I need my breakfast, Mo! I'm a growing lad. I'm a starving, desperate man who will turn violent if he is not soon fed." Then Kim had a sudden inspiration. "Mo, what are you having for breakfast? Don't lie to me; I can see it in your eyes. You've got a bowl of cornflakes tucked away somewhere. Give me your cornflakes, Mo!"

"You want my breakfast, you mean man?" Mo plunged his hand under the counter and pulled out a large box of Mars bars.

"That's it?" Kim said incredulously. "I ask you for breakfast and you give me something from under the counter?"

Mo held up two bars. "You want lunch?"

———

When Kim finally turned to leave the shop he almost collided with the Himalayas. Chris and Angela had spotted him and followed him into the shop.

"What's the matter with you two?" Kim asked. "Can't you keep away?"

"We think we slept outside your flat," Chris said. "You stepped over us just now when you decided to go walkabout in your summer wear." Chris, of course, was still wearing his anorak.

"You were better off on the pavement," Kim said ruefully.

"No big deal," Angela said, yawning and stretching the sleep out of her limbs in a way that fully occupied Kim and Mo until she was finished. "A bit like queuing for the Proms, but stickier."

"Don't you two have a home to go to?" Kim asked.

"What's the point?" Chris said, thrusting his hands deep into his coat pockets. "Everyone's here. The whole campus is empty, like it's Christmas Day!"

"We went down to the beach for a while," Angela said. "Studied here for nearly five years and I finally make it to the beach at three o'clock in the morning when the world's gone mad." She jabbed her thumb over her shoulder at the road outside which led straight down to the seafront. "We sat there on the pebbles, watching the tide come in. Paddled our feet, just like when we were kids on holiday. You could see for miles. A sky full of stars. People everywhere. On the beach, on the groynes, on the promenade. Hundreds of them everywhere. Everyone waiting."

"For what?" Kim asked. "What do they expect? What do they want to see?"

Chris peered through the shop window at the hospital. "One guess. The amazing flying postman. Personal appearance. One night only."

"So watch a television!" Kim said abruptly. "It's all they're showing anyway. You don't have to sleep rough to get a ticket."

Chris shrugged. "They need to be here," he said simply.

"And you need to be here?" Kim asked quietly.

"Of course. Same as you. Won't go, can't go, so don't make me."

"But what do you want? What are you expecting?" Kim asked, mostly because he needed to know himself.

"God knows," Chris muttered.

Angela suddenly crushed his head into the Himalayas and then hugged him. "So we'll wait along with everyone else until we find out!" she said with a maternal smile.

Kim spotted a man outside the shop window who was wearing a gaudy waistcoat that looked like a Union Jack. "That reminds me. What happened to the Mad Scientist?"

Chris pulled a face. "I don't want to know," he said disdainfully. "They carted him off in handcuffs, to the Funny Farm with any luck."

"Slime ball," Angela added succinctly.

"You won't be standing bail for him, then?" Kim asked. The look on Angela's face left him in no doubt. "Hey, if you two want breakfast, ask Mo to show you what he keeps under the counter. And if he refuses, just say, 'Ikea.'"

———————————

Kim walked back into the street and stared at the hospital. The sun had risen and he was standing in a welcome patch of shade, but the windows of the empty building were already blazing with a fierce golden light that made him flinch his eyes away quickly. It was impossible to make out any signs of life from within. After a few moments Chris and Angela joined him and the three of them chewed their breakfast together thoughtfully.

Then Chris moved to one side to change the angle at which the sun was reflecting from the windows, and pulled a tiny pair of binoculars from his pocket. He aimed them at the roof.

"Officer thinking," Kim said, "but you won't see anything from here."

"Wrong angle," Chris said, giving up and offering the binoculars to Kim.

"Wrong side of the building," Angela added. "You'd need to be up high somewhere, too."

Chris stubbed the toe of his trainers on the edge of the kerb moodily. "Too late, anyway. Whatever happened in there happened last night. It could all be over. Done and dusted."

"And we weren't there to see it," Angela said, suddenly very full of resentment, pouting. Tears welled into her eyes.

"Well, there weren't any fanfares or peals of thunder," Kim said wryly. "I can vouch for that in my sleepless state." Then he looked long and hard at the roof again. "But if he's where I think he is now, they're not going to be able to keep it to themselves much longer."

"Why should they?" Angela snapped, instantly angry and squeezing her hands into tight fists. "There's never a shortage of people who think they're in charge, is there, at times like this? Worse than that, they actually think they should be in charge. Nobody else. Just them. Because they can control the chaos. All the chaos." Chris looked quite startled, but Angela was getting into her stride. "Because that's what you get with people, isn't it? Chaos. It's the thing they do best. Look at other people long enough and you end up thinking that chaos is all there is. You look for chaos everywhere. Everything under the sun, all of creation, must be chaos. But, you know, it's not. Not at all. Look at creation and look for chaos, and what you find instead is order. That's what science is about in a nutshell. Looking at chaos and finding order, an order you can identify and codify. And where you find order you always find intelligence. Always. Intelligence, design, intention. You said it yourself! This isn't just for them, whoever they might be." And she stabbed an accusing finger at the dazzling, sun-drenched building. "This is for everyone. This is for us!" Then she reached up and closed Chris's gaping mouth.

And that, curiously enough, was the moment that Kim always remembered most clearly about that day, standing there on the edge of the pavement with the two young students. The paradigm moment. The moment when he knew beyond any shadow of doubt that nothing would ever be quite the same again.

———————————

Liz had a leisurely breakfast at home with her husband. He studied her as she sat there on a stool at the kitchen table, and he asked her aloud if she could remember the last time they had eaten breakfast together. But she didn't answer him, so he made the coffee, poured in into a mug for her, placed the mug in her hand, and then raised it to her lips. She drank it without noticing, taking short sips while she stared into the distance. He dolloped a pile of jam onto her toast for her, spread it evenly, sliced it in two, and then he held it up for her to bite. She chewed the toast slowly, absently; quite unaware that he was there.

"Oh dear," he said, "my leg just fell off." He waited a few moments and then he added, "I think I'll have some breast implants." When still nothing happened he moved closer to her ear. "Sex reassignment surgery." She was just possibly in a trance, so he went for broke. "I'm gay!" he shouted in her ear.

At last she tore her eyes away from the television screen and stared at him with a frown as though he was a perfect stranger. She had the remote in her hand and she'd been channel-hopping for the last half-an-hour, moving from one breakfast news bulletin to another, finding on each and every one of them the self-same picture of the hospital – *her* hospital – sizzling in the early morning sunlight. Yesterday she'd been able to walk around that building. Even when everyone else had gone, it had still been hers. Now she was in exile, forbidden even to cross the threshold of her own little kingdom. They had staged a bloodless coup. They had won without a shot being fired.

Strangely, she felt rested after a good night's sleep, and she hadn't been able to say that in a very long time. She remembered climbing into bed feeling exhausted, and she remembered listening to the fan humming and watching the corner of the bedroom curtain lifting each time the rush of air turned towards it. For once she felt able to relax, to let go, to give in. She almost imagined a voice actually telling her to rest, to sleep. There's nothing to worry about, the voice said. Sleep. So she slept.

"And what are you going to do today?" her husband asked, finding her face much more fun than the television. "Shopping? Gardening? Knitting! Swapping yarns with the ladies-wot-lunch!"

Liz prized her eyes away from the screen again just long enough to confront him. "What are you wittering on about?" she demanded.

He chuckled, and then he gave way to a full-blooded, booming laugh, once the penny had dropped. "You're going in to work, aren't you?"

"Of course I'm going in to work! What a stupid question! Why shouldn't I go in to work? I'm not my day off! It's not my holiday!" This time she reached for her coffee without his help and was rather puzzled to find she had already drunk it. "What do you expect me to do? Phone in sick?"

"Who would you phone?"

"Whom. Exactly."

"And," her husband said slowly, giving his words time to sink in, "neither do you have a place of work to go to."

"What!" she exclaimed indignantly. "'Course I have! It's there!" She picked his mug up and waved it at the screen, slopping hot coffee everywhere. "It's just that I can't get in!"

———————————

The doorbell rang just as Father Geoffrey was raising his own piece of toast to his lips. The morsel of charred bread stopped in mid-air, and he closed his eyes and slowly counted to ten. A piece of home-spun therapy. It worked sometimes. Deep breath, count to ten, and you might not kick the cat or shoot the postman. Perils of the job.

Everyone had rung that doorbell in the last twenty-four hours: television crews who wanted to erect vast gantries on the top of the church roof; policemen who wanted to confirm his identity and make sure that his kettle worked; and all the great unwashed who were milling up and down outside his front door wondering where the nearest loo was and deciding that it must be his. The mistake was to say yes even once. Thereafter the precedent was set and the queue formed. He welcomed them all in with the same set, cheerful smile, and over and over again, like a mantra, he heard the same words of grudging thanks. "We thought you'd say yes. Being a church." I am a church, he thought, and bought Mo's last two packs of toilet paper.

But why answer it now, he thought, at breakfast time? Why not just sit there and do nothing? "Cock a deaf'n" as the dustman would say each tip-less Christmastide. No one would know. No one could see him. Bother the lot of them, my toast's getting cold, he thought, even as he got up to answer it. Knowing his luck, if he ignored it just this once, it would be the Bishop, all cassock, crozier and mitre, enrobed in splendour and spitting hell-fire and damnation. Not worth the risk, so he balanced the piece of toast right on the lip of his plate, wagged a chubby finger at it and warned it not to go away. Then he pushed himself up from the table, took a deep breath, looked into the mirror, attached the disposable smile, and opened the door.

A woman stood on the doorstep with her own polite, slightly uncertain smile. Mid-fifties, smart, fairish hair, definitely not an all-night sleeper, and with an unmistakably commanding presence. When this woman spoke, men jumped, no doubt of that. And she knew him, and he knew her. But what was her name?

"Father Geoffrey!"

She was ahead on points. "Indeed. Good morning," he said sweetly, hoping the syrupy smile would hide his amnesia.

"Liz Manners!"

"Of course you are!"

She jerked her thumb at the building behind her without looking round. He stared at the hospital, then at her face, and then at the hospital again. Eventually his memory chip connected with the mainframe.

"Liz! Oh, my goodness, I'm so sorry; what must you think of me? I'm afraid my brain just isn't switched on at this time of day. Not enough sleep! Or tea! Clearly! How are you? Come in, come in!"

So she did, and suddenly there was a woman standing on his doormat. They had never done this before. He had crossed the road to enter her world a dozen times and more in his five years at St Andrew's. He'd even had tea with her once, in her quaint little office on the first floor. Hardy-esque, he seemed to recall. And plain biscuits, of course. NHS; no chocolate. He blushed with embarrassment and then he blushed again when she stepped past him and stood in the hall, surrounded by his cast off coats and shoes.

"Role reversal," Liz said pleasantly. "This time it's my turn to come calling on you." She even managed to go on smiling when he closed the front door and all the musty charm and accumulated cooking smells of a Victorian vicarage were hers to admire.

"Do make yourself at home," the priest encouraged her, following her eyes wherever they went. "My turn to offer you tea."

"Coffee?"

"Coffee. Yes, coffee. Do-able. If you don't mind instant."

"Instant is fine," Liz assured him, noting all the dusty, half-dead potted plants around the place in need of a good watering.

He led her into the breakfast room and suddenly saw it himself for the first time. It was like every other room on the ground floor of the house, a variation on his study, full of books, bibles, papers, cast-off vestments, dirty cups and ashtrays. It was a bachelor's home, vast, unpolished and cavernous.

Liz saw the piece of toast teetering on the edge of the plate. "Sorry, I'm disturbing your breakfast." They both looked at the clock.

"More like elevenses, I'm afraid," Father Geoffrey admitted solemnly, presenting her with a mug of what looked like warm sump oil. "Slow off the mark, today."

The breakfast room was an offshoot of the kitchen, and it overlooked a heavily overgrown garden which was separated from the road by a high brick-and-flint wall and the densely interweaved foliage of a long line of elm trees. Liz craned her neck and peered through the thick, nicotine-stained curtains in search of the hospital. The room was quiet, like a chapel. The heavy, dusty air had absorbed all traces of the world beyond the garden wall.

Father Geoffrey guessed a little of what she was thinking. "I was wondering if I should install a coin box on the lavatory door. What do you think? The whole world seems to be queuing up to use my facilities."

"I feel I should apologize for bothering you," Liz said, gingerly tidying the curtains back into place. "Especially as I've come here today to ask a really cheeky favour of you."

Here it comes, he thought. The woman speaks, men jump. "I'm all ears. Fire away."

Liz took a deep breath and smiled. "Do you have a room I could use? Briefly. What you might call a temporary base of operations. In fact it might only be for a day," she added quickly.

"You've probably guessed by now that I've been evicted from over the road."

The vicar looked terribly flustered and his smile was fading fast. How could he refuse? The vicarage was vast, but which room had she set her heart on?

This time she read his thoughts. "A room that overlooks the hospital. Doesn't matter how small, or what's in it, as long as it has a clear view of the hospital from roughly this direction, preferably from a high vantage point."

"High." Luckily for them both, his bachelor bedroom was on the other side of the vicarage, overlooking a rather hideous railway bridge. "How about a tower?" he asked nervously while he tried to think on his feet.

Liz's face lit up. "You have a tower! Great! Show me! Can we get into it?"

"I've no idea," the priest said, looking shocked. "I was joking."

"I'm not."

After which it didn't even occur to him to argue.

It took them a while. To begin with they had to find a bunch of well-hidden keys, and then they had to make their way from the vicarage to the church itself through a succession of small doors and low narrow corridors. Then they had to climb up a narrow concrete staircase that rose in a tight spiral all the way up into the roof of the sanctuary, high above the nave. Eventually they arrived at a small, creaking, damp-smelling wooden landing where they had to squat down to avoid banging their heads against a low, plasterboard ceiling. Bent double, shuffling along almost with their hands on the floor, they reached a padlocked trapdoor. Father Geoffrey took forever to find the right key on the bunch and then fit it into the padlock, but when he did, and when the door dropped down with a crash, the sudden rush of sunlight, dead leaves and pigeon droppings took them both by surprise.

"People don't come up here very often, as you can see," Father Geoffrey told his visitor.

Liz peered up through the narrow hatchway at the underside of the turreted roof of the tower. "You have no bell."

"I have no bell," Father Geoffrey confessed sadly. "And nothing to hang it from, and no mechanism to ring it with, either."

"So why have a bell tower? – if that's not a silly question."

"To tell you the truth, Liz, I have absolutely no idea. You may want to ask the Victorian designers that very question, should you ever encounter them in the afterlife."

"Is it safe?"

"The afterlife?"

"The tower."

"I have no reason to think otherwise. And it should be big enough to hold the two of us, if we go carefully, and take it in turns to breathe. Let me go first, I'm expendable."

But not athletic. It soon became clear that the vicar was not built with noble gestures in mind. His bottom all but blotted out the daylight before he could hoist himself up into the tower and then reach down a rather moist and grubby hand to his visitor. Liz squeezed into the tower alongside him and tested the strength of the railing before she trusted her weight to it. Then she turned her attention to the panoramic view of the city spread out all around them.

"Toy town," Father Geoffrey said.

Some parts of the vicarage were as high as the hospital on the other side of the road. Both buildings were an odd mix of storeys, and neither of them seemed to be the brainchild of any one architect, but by far the highest point of either building was the funny little redundant bell tower, sat right up on the apex of the sanctuary roof like a pagoda and consisting of a tiny oval platform and a railing, topped by a miniature minaret, clad in half-size roof tiles. From this windy vantage point they could see the sea half a mile away, and above the sea there was a cloudless, pure cobalt blue sky that stretched away to the ends of the earth. And there, far below them, partly hidden by the steep slope of the church roof, was the road on the other side of that brick-and-flint wall, filled with flowers and candles and tributes, fluttering in the warm spring air.

Then Liz's eyes became riveted to the hospital's rooftop, directly across the road from the bell tower. Here, on the flat asphalted roof just above the dormer windows of Ward 6, she could see what looked like a bright blue plastic tent, surrounded by and tied to a framework of metal pipes that had been erected all around it to anchor it firmly in place.

The vicar was fascinated by her face. Then he studied the strange new structure for himself. "I take it it's true, then," he said simply.

Liz found it hard to tear her eyes away from the awning, but when she did, and when she thought about what he had just asked her, their two faces just inches apart in that tiny, windy bell tower, she suddenly felt heartily sick and tired of lying. "Yes," she said softly. "Yes, it's quite true."

The vicar puffed his cheeks out, leaned for a moment against the railing, and then crossed himself. It was a simple enough thing to do, a gesture, a reflex action on his part, not made for her benefit, but when Liz saw it, and when she saw the tears beginning to form in the corners of his eyes, she was filled with a sense of burning shame. Now, at last, it was as clear as day to her. A fog had lifted to show her the world as it really was, as she had never seen it before. "Oh my God," she said in a whisper. "Oh my God. I should have told you. Of course. I should have told you."

Father Geoffrey blushed very deeply and then he smiled, feeling very confused, but conscious, too, that his visitor had just penetrated to the heart of the matter. He would pray for her.

"Shall I lead the way down?" he suggested.

20

Throughout the rest of that long spring day the crowds continued to grow in number until they began to push against the barriers in ceaseless, surging waves, like a great press of water probing at the fabric of a crumbling dam. The police patrolled the edges of the crowds nervously, trying to push, urge, entreat, and cajole the people back from the barriers whenever they threatened to knock them over and spill into the road. Beyond the church, to the north, where the road dipped under the railway bridge, a neverending surge of sightseers poured down the hill towards the hospital, adding to the seething, swaying mass of humanity that surrounded the building on every side. And still they came with flowers – hundreds, thousands of flowers – and when the police could no longer risk moving the barriers to let them through, they threw them instead, until volleys of them struck the walls and windows of the building and covered the window ledges and the pavements and the road with heaps of broken stems and petals.

And the people came with still more candles, too, so that when night fell thousands of pinpoints of light rose and fell among the darkened faces as though they were adrift on a restless sea. And at dusk they began to sing – songs, choruses, chants – that they repeated over and over again, urgently, passionately, their numbers growing all the time.

The time of waiting was coming to an end. Soon, very soon now, something was going to happen. Everyone felt that. No. Everyone *knew* that. Something would happen. Something wonderful. Something that would change the world. At long last.

No one went home. No one slept. Everyone sang and talked, and laughed, and everyone faced towards the hospital, utterly spellbound.

A police siren rent the air, harsh and loud and ugly, painfully ill-timed. Everyone looked in the direction of the sound and saw two bright yellow motorcycles weaving their way through the crowds of people and the barriers, slow, funereal, moving at walking pace until they reached the edge of the sea of flowers and there came to a dead stop.

A car stopped just behind them, a large black limousine, flanked by two lines of policemen struggling on foot to hold back the crowds of people. People began to shout. Cat-calls drifted up and down the upturned faces, people standing on tiptoe, straining to see. Then there was a huge, loud, lingering groan, full of disappointment, and then derision, when Chiltern stepped from the car and began to wave. People heckled him. A bunch of flowers just missed his head and landed on the roof of the car behind him, spraying him with pink petals. Then a roar of hard, cruel laughter when the crowd suddenly surged towards him and he was pinned to the car door. A scrum of policemen linked arms around him and rescued him, dragging him to his feet again and brushing him down. When he could, he began to walk among the flowers, picking his way carefully, tenderly, stopping every few steps so that he could reach down and pretend to read the words written on their cards. No one believed him. Insults rained down all around him, but he seemed impervious to them. Wary as he was, his face remained fixed and immovable, a study in concern and compassion, the kind of politician's look that would fool no one at all. But none of that mattered anymore. This was the new script. The new beginning, thought out so very carefully in advance. Subtle. Oblique. Daring. Dazzling. This was the march to power. This was the slow, unhurried moment of accession, at least in Chiltern's mind, as he sought the will of craven human gods.

238

Kim was in the Queen's Head. He had been there all day, leading a chorus of drunken revellers in an endless stream of raucous rugby songs. They were singing to each other, they were singing to the television, which stayed on all day, and they were singing at the crowds in the street outside. They waved their glasses and they showered the saloon bar floor with sticky pools of pungent ale.

Kim was drunk. He had been drunk for hours, trying to numb a pain he couldn't diagnose or treat any other way. He needed to addle his brains so that he couldn't think any more, or try to find a way back to that one place in the world where he longed to be. All the day long, ever since that moment outside the newsagents, he had fixed his whole mind unwaveringly on that rooftop. Because he needed to be there. Simple as that. He needed to be there because he had been a part of it, a part of the adventure, and a part of the journey. He had travelled a part of the way, and he needed to be there at the end. For the sake of his sanity. For himself. When the moment came. As it would. Revelation. And the feeling wouldn't go away, however much beer he swilled down his throat.

When he saw Chiltern's face on the screen, and when he saw him begin his cynical procession through the ocean of flowers, Kim bellowed with rage, with a thunderous baritone anger that could be heard from end to end of the street, even among the masses of people watching the event for themselves. And that anger travelled through the crowd like a charge of electricity until people all around the stranded car began to chant, seething with resentment.

Then the camera platforms began to lift up into the air over the heads of the people, aiming their beams of light at Chiltern, and then at the flowers, and at all the faces baying at him and heckling him on every side. News time. Live and unvarnished.

Then, with a sudden roar that left people giddy with shock, everyone turned to face one hydraulic platform that had risen right up into the sky so that it could aim its light and its camera down onto the flat roof of the hospital. At that seminal moment someone in the control room beneath the platform leaned across a console and flicked a switch, causing a gigantic image of the hidden rooftop to spring into life across the whole facade of the building. As though waiting for that moment, the blue awning parted like a membrane, like the petals of a fragile flower, to reveal Leonard Blake, rising slowly above the parapet of the building for all the world to see.

People screamed and sobbed and cheered. People clapped, people fell to their knees, and people began to sing hymns, to chant mantras. People stood quite still, shocked and speechless. In that moment everyone, everyone in the world, looked up at this irresistible man, this sign, this revelation.

No one gave the signal, no one shouted the word of command, but the crowd with one mind began to surge forward, sweeping the barriers away. Kim ran into the street and started to make his own way towards the hospital, beating and punching and pushing and clawing at everyone as he went. He was a man possessed. He jumped onto garden walls, onto the roofs of parked cars; he jumped onto the backs and shoulders of the people who blocked his way, but he would not stop and he would not be beaten. He struck out blindly, with his fists, with his feet. Some people struck back at him, some fended him off, some shied away, but he knew that nothing would stop him now.

He reached the hospital in time to see Chiltern and his escort swept away – people clambering over the car, knocking over the motorcycles – and he reached the wooden gates at the back of the hospital in time to kick and batter and hammer them with his fists until the lock and the bolts were ripped out of them and they were hurled back by a living torrent of people pouring into the courtyard. Sprinting ahead of them Kim charged up the fire escapes, floor by floor, until he was on the roof. A flawless circle of radiant white light picked him out of the darkness as a helicopter circled the building, capturing the moment of epiphany. Others joined him, some raced past him – Chris, Angela and Liz among them – until the whole of the rooftop and the fire escape and the courtyard, and every inch of ground all around the building was filled with joyous people, all turning their faces to the sky.

240

And the night sky was filled with stars and a crescent moon at the end of this perfect spring day. Beams of light probed the darkness until they came to rest, high in the air, far beyond the reach of the people, upon Leonard Blake, making him seem so white, like an angel.

Now all was ready.